UNTIL HELL
Freezes Over

UNTIL HELL Freezes Over

Ernie Moulton

Copyright © 2021 Ernie Moulton.

All rights reserved. No part of this book may be reproduced in any form or by any electronic or mechanical means, including information storage and retrieval systems, without permission in writing from the publisher, except by reviewers, who may quote brief passages in a review.

ISBN: 978-1-956074-22-2 (Paperback Edition)
ISBN: 978-1-956074-23-9 (Hardcover Edition)
ISBN: 978-1-956074-21-5 (E-book Edition)

Some characters and events in this book are fictitious. Any similarity to real persons, living or dead, is coincidental and not intended by the author.

Book Ordering Information

Phone Number: 315 288-7939 ext. 1000 or 347-901-4920
Email: info@globalsummithouse.com
Global Summit House
www.globalsummithouse.com

Printed in the United States of America

Prologue

It was a hot sunny day in southern Florida as 11-year-old Sheila Mictackic walked home from school. It was so hot that she had taken off her sandals and was walking barefoot in the sand.

She didn't go straight home when she got off the school bus, but walked up to the corner store to buy a teddy bear she had seen in the window. Yesterday was my birthday, and I finally have enough money to buy it. I cuddled it against my shoulder at first, but it was too hot, so then I carried it in the bag. I was carefully holding my school books against my side in the other hand.

A thought made me giggle. My brother, George, is such a worry wart. This morning, he told me not to go to the store by myself. He had said there were too many mean people in the world. Then he had said that if anything happened to me, he would look for me till Hell froze over. Good thing Daddy didn't hear him say that.

I looked down at my dress for the dozenth time that afternoon. It was a beautiful white dress with little holes in it here and there. My father had said it was organdy when he gave it to me yesterday. I thought that maybe one day I would be able to sew something like this, but with no one to teach me, mother's old sewing machine sits mostly idle. Anyway, I thought, whatever it was called it was just beautiful. My latest 'Daddy dress'.

She was so lost in her thoughts, that she did not hear the car glide up and stop beside her. She started when a man said, through the open window, "Hey, little girl would you like a ride home?"

She looked up and clutched her book to her. "No, thank you, sir. I'm not allowed to ride with strangers."

Gee, that was a huge car. She had seen limousines on TV, but did not know that anyone around here had one. It was shiny black and about a block long.

The man in the back looked like somebody's grandfather, but he was no one that she remembered ever seeing before. He did look kindly, though.

He said, "Don't you live down in that old camp site at Crystal Beach?"

"Yes." How did he know that? Did he know her after all?

"I'll be glad to drop you off. It's right on my way. And it looks like you could use some cool air."

Well, a limousine would be air conditioned. But still ... Daddy always said, never talk to strangers. But if he knows where I live, then maybe he isn't a stranger. Better not, though. "No, sir. Thank you, but I'll just walk. It's not far."

"Well, your daddy probably said not to talk to strangers. I kind of wanted to ask you some questions about his work, and thought if you rode with me, we could talk."

"Well ... Okay. You promise, you'll drop me off at home?"

"Yes, of course. I wouldn't lie to you." He opened the door and waited.

She hesitated a little longer, and then thought, *Well, he promised.* She got in, and the car started up.

The car had hardly started forward when the man sitting beside the old gentleman suddenly reached over and slid a black bag over her head. She screamed and struggled, but he was much too strong. He tied the bag tight around her knees and threw her down on the seat. There were holes in the bag, so she could breathe, but she could not see anything. Then she felt a prick on her leg, and everything passed into darkness.

Chapter 1

Twenty-three years later near Atlanta,. Georgia.
Sheila screamed and screamed. "Nooooo. Nooooo. Nooooo!"
Strong hands held her down and she screamed.

A voice said, "It's all right, baby sister, wake up now. Wake!"

Sheila Demalis came awake, slowly at first, and then looked around with eyes wide with fear. "What's happening?"

Mista said, "I think we hit a wall."

"Oh. You were getting my memories back. I think I was about to remember something terrible." She sat up and shuddered.

Jasmine laid her hand on Sheila's forehead and prayed for peace and healing. "You don't need to go there, dear. Our minds are able to hide really bad things from us, and that is good. Let it lie." Jasmine, an African American, was many things to this little group. She was a trained nurse-practitioner and also a licensed minister. She had been known as priestess in another time and place. Her hands had healing power.

Mista sank back into his chair and said, "We know who you are, and now you know who I am." Mista was 38 years old by the calendar, but his white hair made him look much older. Sheila had disappeared during the summer he was 15, and that summer his hair had turned white. All that they had known for years had been that she did not come home from school one day. They had just heard for the first time what had happened on that day.

Sheila looked at him and her eyes lighted in love. "Yes. I was born here, just as you were. No wonder so many of our memories were the same. But if I was born here, how did I get to that other world?"

Mista said, "We don't know that, yet, and I'm not willing to push into that dark place in your mind to find out. It doesn't really matter. I'm glad to know you really are my sister, and that I have you back."

They had recently returned from another world. No one knew how they had been transported there, or how they had been returned. It seemed like magic, but it could have been a technological artifact of an advanced civilization. The other world had been like Earth in many ways, but also unlike it. Mista thought that perhaps they had been on the island of Atlantis in a parallel world where the fabled island had indeed existed and had not been destroyed.

The man who had taken them there had blocked their memories of Earth and made them think that they had been born on that world. They had found people there who had doubles on this Earth, but had found no doubles of themselves. They had found his sister, Sheila, there, but had not known whether she was indeed his sister who had been transported to that world, or whether she had been native there.

Now they knew. They had put her into a deep sleep and removed the memory blocks in her mind, causing her to relive the last day in Mista's memory of her as a child.

She remembered it being a hot sunny day in southern Florida when she had walked home from school. It was so hot that she had taken off her sandals and was walking barefoot in the sand.

I didn't go straight home when I got off the school bus, but walked up to the corner store to buy a teddy bear I had seen in the window. Yesterday was my birthday, and I finally had enough money to buy it. I cuddled it against my shoulder at first, but it was too hot, so then I carried it in the bag. I was carefully holding my school books against my side in my other hand.

A thought made her giggle. My brother, Mista, is such a worry wart. This morning, he told me not to go to the store by myself. He had said there were too many mean people in the world. Then he had said that if anything happened to me, he would look for me till Hell froze over. Good thing Daddy didn't hear him say that.

I looked down at my dress for the dozenth time that afternoon. It was a beautiful white dress with little holes in it here and there. My father had said it was organdy when he gave it to me yesterday. I thought that maybe one day I would be able to sew something like this, but with no one to teach me, mother's old sewing machine sits mostly idle. Anyway, I thought, whatever it was called it was just beautiful. My latest 'Daddy dress'.

Daddy always liked to take me shopping and buy special dresses – had for as long as I could remember. I called them my Daddy Dress, and liked to priss around for him. George, used to get mad, but he had no reason to. Boys didn't wear dresses, and Daddy always did special things with George, too.

I put a finger in the rip just below the waist. Daddy told me not to wear it to school. Said it was too nice for school. Now, it's ruined. If I'd had jeans on, I could have beat up that old Sally good. She had no call to talk about Daddy and George like that. I'll wear jeans tomorrow and teach her a lesson. If I hold the book right, maybe Daddy won't notice. Can't hide the dirty spot and the rip at the same time, though. Maybe he won't care about the dirt. That washes out. Then I can sneak and sew it up. If I'm lucky, nobody'll ever know.

She knew that even if her daddy did notice, he wouldn't say anything. He never did. Something like, "Been fighting again, Sugar?"

Maybe he wouldn't ask what it was about. He didn't need to know what people said about him. Nobody had a better daddy. Nobody. Maybe George will help. He knows how to do everything. But, he is never mean to me, like other brothers are. Maybe because we don't have a mother. She couldn't remember her mother. George said she had died when she was born. She often wondered why God would let a mother die, but nobody ever had an answer for that. Daddy was always busy, so she and George had been left alone a lot, and had grown very close. George had tried to cook some when daddy was too busy, but he always made a mess of it. At least that was one thing that she could do better than he could. She already cooked most of their meals.

Her thoughts turned to her father again. *I wish he weren't always so busy.* He was pastor of a tiny little church in Crystal Beach, Florida. You wouldn't think that a dozen families would keep him so busy, but they did. Plus he had a boys club that met every afternoon after school for boys whose parents both worked. No one ever offered to pay him for keeping their boys, but he kept a lot of boys out of trouble. Not all of them, of course. That bully, Barnat Dithers probably only went because his father made him go.

Nights are good, though. We rarely watch TV. Daddy says there is enough meanness in the world without watching imaginary meanness. He would study or read while she and George did their homework, and then he would take her in his lap and read stories. George said he was too old for the stories she liked. He would read his own books. He liked to read about magic and dragons, and sword fighting. Like there was any such thing as magic.

Then Daddy would tuck her into bed and read by her bedside until she went to sleep, while George did something else. Probably like studying his Spanish. A lot of the kids at school were Cubans, and George had gotten pretty good at Spanish. One day he found their father's Greek New Testament and decided that he wanted to learn Greek. Had, too. He was smart that way.

She sighed. *I wish that I were as smart as George. At least he never teases me about it.* They did everything together, and he never made fun of her. They would often ride their bikes to Tarpon Springs to go swimming at the pool there. It was five miles, but it didn't seem like all that far. He would practice his Spanish on her – *like I even understood what he said. And he listens when I talk about my friends at school. Some day I will marry a man just like George.*

Not like Daddy. Daddy was wonderful, but I want a man who smiles more. Daddy had coal black hair, but hers was almost white. People often asked where I got my hair; like, hey, I was born with it. After all, where do people get hair? Some who had known our mother said I was the spitting image of mother. She had seen pictures, and her mother had white hair. Daddy said from time to time that she looked more like her mother every day.

I'm glad he never remarried, like so many men do. Although, it would have been nice to have had a mother, even a step mother. Well, you couldn't have everything. If I had a mother, she would have been waiting at home for me, and would surely be able to fix the dress. George will be waiting for me, but he can't sew a lick.

Sheila had screamed, and had kept screaming until Mista woke her.

Chapter 2

Sheila continued. "Some of the memories came back. There was a dark period that I remember only vaguely. I think terrible things must have happened. But I think I was about 19 or 20 when Gary was born. A little later a man took me and said he was going to take me to a man who would look after me like I should be cared for. His name was Bill Demallis. I just remembered. He had a nice house, and was kind to me. He said he had paid to set me free. I was not free to leave, however – not that I had anywhere to go. I was like a slave, but he was good to me, and eventually married me."

Sheila laughed, a short barking laugh. "He didn't ask me to marry him. I was a virtual slave, or maybe really a slave. He just told me that he was marrying me, and then he did. Then Mary Alice – Jania – was born five years later. I guess I came to love him. He was good to me, and kind, even though I think he actually did buy me."

She waited a beat. "I couldn't say I was happy in those years, but at least I had a home. Bill was a businessman, but he never told me what he did. He did not share his life with me. Then right after Jania was born, another man came to the house. He went into Bill's office and closed the door. They were there for a long time. When they finally came out, Bill said the man was Red Zanes. He told me to get the children, that something had come up. Mr. Zanes had something that looked like a globe. He touched it and suddenly we were somewhere else. That was Central Port in your other world. Bill went out every day on business for a few days, and then said we had to travel to another country. He said it was dangerous, but that we had to go.

"You know all the rest. We were traveling through the mountains and were attacked by bandits. He was killed, they made me a slave again, and left Mary Alice by the side of the road. I thought that they left her to die – and that's what they wanted me to think. They actually took her to that temple to sell." Sheila shuddered. "I had no idea."

Jania had come to Mista when she was 18. She came to his school, but it soon became apparent that she was no ordinary student. She was the very image of Mista, standing nearly as tall as his six feet, and with platinum blond hair close in color to his white. She was in medical school, at this time, but was home now for the Christmas holidays.

Only when Sheila finished her recital did she notice that Mista was sitting rigidly in his chair, looking out the window with a glassy stare. His jaw was rigid, and his hazel eyes had changed to steel blue. Sheila said, "George? George, it's all right. I survived and you found me again." She went over to him and sat on the arm of his chair, stroking his hair.

"Talk to me, George." George Mictackic was known to most people as Mista because they had trouble pronouncing his last name, even when told that it was pronounced 'Mistaskitch'. He had suggested Mista as a short cut, and it had stuck as a nickname. When Mista did not respond, she leaned on him and put her arms around his neck, crying silently, and said, "Please, George. It's all right.

Mista shook himself. Then he reached up and pulled Sheila into his lap. He pulled her tight against his chest and laid his head on hers. He began to cry. Sheila could feel his body shaking, not with sobs, but like he was violently controlling a rage within. He whispered, "I'm sorry, baby sister. I'm so sorry."

Sharra, Mista's wife, put her hand to her mouth. She had never seen Mista cry. Not when his children were killed, not when she was threatened, not when his friends were killed in battle, or wounded and near death. Not even when he himself had been near death. She realized that this was a Mista that she did not know. Not that he was cold – far from it. But he never showed his emotion in tears. He never showed emotion at all. He might have been a Greek Stoic, whose writings he admired so much. Sharra was petite and trim, scarcely five feet two, with coal black hair and obsidian eyes. They had been married about eight years. Sharra had the ability to read minds and to move things with the power of her mind. She had entered Sheila's mind to find and remove memory blocks so that they would know who she really was and where she came from.

Sheila laid her head against his neck and cried with him. After a while she said, "Don't cry for me, George. I survived. You found me and restored me to health. God was in it somewhere, and he brought us together when the time was right."

When Mista made no reply, she went on, "They must have had me on drugs all those years. I don't remember any of it until Bill took me in. I already had Gary, but I don't know who his father might have been." She looked up at her son Gary. "I'm sorry, Gary."

Gary said, "Don't apologize, Mother. It was a terrible life for you, and one not of your choosing."

"I'm still sorry. And I had Mary Alice by Bill, my beautiful Mary Alice --Jania. At least a lot of good came of it."

Mista finally began to speak. His voice was a growl, far from the usual gentle tones. "No man can do that to my sister and get away with it. No man should do that to any girl. But he will not get away with it if I have anything to say about it. I will find that man, if he is still alive and ... I'll cut him up in little pieces and feed him to the alligators. While he watches."

He relaxed enough that Sheila was able to sit up. She laid a finger on his mouth. "Brother, dear, don't let your desire for revenge burn your soul. God kept me safe, and he brought you to me in time. What if I had never been taken to your world? What if you had not stumbled on Mary Alice and followed her back trail to the corrupt temple system? God's hand was in it as surely as there is a God who cares what happens to us."

"God did not place you in that evil system!"

"No, but he delivered me from it. It was not chance that brought you into my world. God sent Mary Alice to you, and he guided you in your search for me."

Mista pulled her to him again, and held her, stroking her back. "I thank God for that. But I will find that man and utterly destroy him. And if he is part of a gang, I'll destroy the entire gang. I cannot allow that to continue any longer. All this time I've had you back and have done nothing about your abductor. I should be *whipped*." He held Sheila up and looked into her eyes. When he had found her, she was crippled by arthritis and looked like a woman of 60 years. Her hair was gray and her face wrinkled. With her health restored, she looked like a beautiful woman of 35, which was her true age. There was sadness in her eyes, and now he knew why.

"You've been busy. It is enough that you found me. I remember what you said that morning – till Hell freezes over."

"Well, I never stopped looking. Wasn't much hope left after 25 years, but I kept looking." Mista gave her a grim smile. "Well, it hasn't frozen over, yet. But when I find the man that took you, he's going to wish that it had."

His voice was now deadly calm. "I tell you true, Sis, I will find that man if he is alive and I will *destroy* him. He cannot do this to my sister."

Chapter 3

The next morning was Sunday. Sheila brought breakfast out from the kitchen as each person came down and joined the group. The house had originally been a research center with a main wing holding a large common room in the front, which they had divided into a dining area and a lounge area. The kitchen and two storage rooms occupied the space behind the common room, and then the rest of that section had been offices and labs. The house had two wings which housed private rooms and suites. They also had several separate houses in the woods behind the main building. The facility was designed and built to house up to 100 workers and researchers and their families.

After Sheila's third trip out, Mista said, "Sis, you aren't a servant any more. We can all get our own."

She smiled. "I know. I need to do something useful, though, and I've had practice at this. I don't mind."

Mischal said, "Jasmine, are you going to start a church for us, or do we go somewhere?"

"I could. Is that what you want?"

Mista said, "I believe you would be good. But we live with you. That is not a bad thing, and you always have words of wisdom for us. But, I think it would be good for all of us to hear from an outside source."

"I agree," Jasmine said. "I don't know how to preach, anyway."

Chandri said, "I thought you were going to start a church here and be our pastor." Chandri was barely five feet two and had blond hair and big, deep, blue eyes. She had training as a woods ranger and could make friends with almost any animal. She and Mischal had been married for several years and had two children.

"I would, Honey Child, but maybe we could have the best of both? It's always good to hear outside opinions. Maybe we could form a church and do our own thing, but go out whenever we want. After all, we are gone from here as much as we are at home."

"That's true," Mista said. "We went to Hillview Baptist before, and that seemed the most agreeable to everyone, I believe. Let's try that this morning."

They had just returned from a tour around the world that Mista had arranged with a tour company. The company usually provided pre-planned tours to different places, but had been willing to set up the tour for Mista and two other families who had expressed an interest in such a tour. The basic plan was to fly to major cities or cultural centers, spend two nights and one day in each chosen city, and fly to the next city on the list the next day.

Molly Greene said, "I'd join you, but I need to go to Atlanta." She was already dressed for church, and was carrying a small bag. "I'm going to stay a few days and renew my relationship with Karl."

"Staying with him?" Mista asked. "Not that it is any of my business."

"No, I'll take a room for the week."

As Molly closed the door, Mischal said, "I wonder if she will sleep in that room."

The door popped open. Molly said, "I heard that. Rest assured that I will sleep in that room, and alone. I hope that some day you come to believe that I really have changed. I want this man, but I want him the right way. Have a good week." She slammed the door.

Molly had a history. She had been a student in Mista's school when a teenager, but she had only stayed one year. She learned enough to begin her climb upward, but rejected ethics and morals. When they saw her again, she was part of a revolutionary group trying to overthrow the government. When that failed, she was sentenced to one year of menial servitude. Three years later, she came to Mista for help. Her husband had been murdered and an attempt made on her life. She had made an about face in her life, and she stayed with the group to help. Mischal still had trouble believing that she had actually changed.

Chandri said, "Shame, Misch. She helped rescue me and she helped rescue Sharra. If she still had dishonorable impulses, she could have just let us stay lost."

"We would have eventually found you, and then she would have been exposed. I never said she was not smart."

"You would never have found me without her help. And if you had found me, you would have been shot splashing across the swamp long before you came close enough to do anything."

"Maybe."

Mista said, "She opened her mind to Sharra, and she found nothing bad there. That's good enough for me."

"I think she still secretly loves you, Mista," Mischal said.

"Maybe so, but she is making no effort to steal me. Not that it would do her any good to try," Mista said, looking at Sharra.

Chapter 4

The next week was the week before Christmas. It was also their first week at home in several months. Everyone was busy. Mischal and Njondac went up the valley and cut a huge cedar tree, which they set up in the common room. Then they had to buy lights and decorations.

When it was finished, Mista stepped back to look it over. "Perfect. You know, we have never done this. As a group, I mean."

Jasmine said, "Well, Christianity was spreading in Mindeshara, where we spent so many years, but that world did not have the centuries of customs and heritage that we have. And it seemed like we were always on a quest around Christmastime."

Jania said, "Yes. Last year, I was having a birthday ball, sort of. It's not the way I would prefer to spend Christmas."

"Did you learn anything from it, Kitten?" asked Mista.

"You know I did, Daddy. But, I guess I didn't learn enough. I still fell for that Aram Bleaker. But you have to trust somebody. How do you know who to trust?"

"You just have to learn, Kitten. I misread people sometimes, too. But you have not had enough experience to know the difference. How does it go in college?"

"I never knew that there was so much to learn. Guys hit on me all the time, but I'm too busy, between school and study, and taking care of Don Miguel. I've heard talk about my getting the reputation of being an iceberg. Whatever that is."

"Well, that won't hurt you. When you are ready to get serious about a guy, it won't take long to warm them up. An iceberg is a mountain of ice. How is my old friend?" Don Miguel owned a coffee plantation in Puerto Rico and had befriended them when they found themselves in Puerto Rico on a previous assignment. He was well up in years, and Jania had volunteered to live in his home and care for him while she was in pre-med and medical school.

"He's doing fine. He is quite strong, actually, now that he js not suffering from the arthritis. His financial secretary is still a little stiff. I think he thinks I just want to get my hand on the old Don's money when he dies. He doesn't believe that I don't need it or want it."

"Well, I wish you had been able to leave school for our trip around the world. But that would have been too much time away. We could schedule some review classes this week and show you where all we went with Google Earth."

"What is Google Earth?"

"Pictures of the world taken from a satellite above Earth. In some places the detail is so fine that you can see cars on the streets. It could give you a pretty good idea of what this world looks like."

"Why would I care? You can see cars anywhere."

Mista smiled. "It's not the cars, Kitten. It is a way to learn where all the different countries are and what they look like."

"What if you decide that you want to go somewhere? Then you'd know where it was," Mista said, with a shake of his head.

She shrugged. "I'll just buy a ticket and let them worry about where it is."

Molly came back on the Thursday before Christmas, bringing Karl Spicewood with her. They had just finished the evening meal and were all sitting in the common room. Mista looked up and said, "Well, I thought you'd be busy this weekend."

"The troopers will have to work extra shifts. We'll be busy next week with investigations. So I took a day of vacation to make it a long weekend." Karl was commander of the Georgia State Police Special Investigations unit. He was retired from the Marine Corps, and had become friends with Mista when Mista was in the Navy. He sometimes hired Mista and his group to work undercover. Since they were not active duty police officers, and received no pay until after the investigation was over, they could often go places and talk to people who were not candid with police. Since there was no paper trail to the police – during the investigation – people who had access to public records did not find any link between them and the police. It had been especially useful during their last case, when someone in police headquarters was feeding information about under cover officers to the person they were trying to catch.

Molly made sure that everyone saw the diamond on her left hand as she entered behind Karl. Mista said, "Well, Molly, looks like you had one of your diamonds mounted. Oh, you didn't have diamonds, did you? Yours was gold. You buy that?"

Mischal picked up the teasing line on cue. "Yeah, Molly. We know you like flashy jewelry, but that seems a little much, even for you."

Charly said, "Why did you decide to start wearing rings? I see you don't have any other rings."

Molly put her hands on her hips. "Like you didn't know what an engagement ring means?"

Mista said, "Oh. Engaged? To whom? I wouldn't have thought that Karl would trust his super neat rooms to a woman."

Chandri said, "Yeah, and I wouldn't have thought you'd want Karl. I've seen your room."

Molly was not sure if the teasing was really just teasing, or if there were some buried barbs in it. She still felt like an outsider at times, and she was well aware that they all knew of the harm she had tried to bring to the group earlier in her life. "I told him we could hire a maid to keep it the way he likes it."

"You mean pick up after you?" asked Mista.

She colored slightly. "I'm not that messy. Is it so hard to believe? We've been dating for a long time."

"We're just having a little fun with you, dear," Sharra said. "Congratulations."

Mischal said, "Yeah, congratulations. You didn't need that room, after all?"

Something snapped inside Molly. It was none of their business what she did while away, or even if she went away. Mista had told her that in so many words the last time she went away for a weekend, and she was glad that at least he knew that. Besides, she really had changed her life style, but they seemed to slow to believe it. She had taken a room and had slept alone in it. She walked up to Mischal, hips working, and shook her finger in his face.

"Listen, you. I've had enough. A little teasing is okay, but you go too far. You're supposed to be a paladin. A paladin is kind, courteous, generous and forgiving. You have done none of that. You have been arrogant and hateful. I know what I used to be, but that is *past*. I came back to you a changed women, and I have done nothing out of line for the past year. I thought the motto of this group was that what was past was past, never to be remembered. What matters with a person is how they come out of the past and what they do with the future.

"You have anything in your past you don't want brought out and talked about? How about that, mister holy paladin? Do you think that when I tried to seduce you that I didn't have reason to think that I could? I did my research. Or how about, since I know more about the real history of all of you – I mean you that came from this world – what did you do in Iraq or Afghanistan or wherever you went as a Marine? You do anything there you wouldn't want us to know about? Tell me, are you so perfect that you cannot accept another imperfect person?"

Mischal's temper rose. "There were things I did, before my life changed –"

"My life changed, too, but you don't want to believe it."

Charly stood up and went to put an arm around Molly. "She's got you there, Misch. Those were some of the things you drilled into me when I was training. And I'll never forget how you all jumped on me when I asked Uncle Mista about his life story. 'Past is past. We do not ask' you said. Well let her past be past. She's one of us now."

Mischal said, "I –." He suddenly bowed his head, closed his eyes and prayed silently for forgiveness. Then he stood up, then knelt before Molly and said, "You are correct. I have not been true to my vows. I could make all sorts of excuses, but they don't really matter. I have failed in my duty. I humbly beg forgiveness, lady."

Molly's eyes went wide. She said, "I –" She looked over at Mista for guidance. He nodded. She laid a hand on Mischal's shoulder. "I forgive you. I just wanted to be accepted."

Mischal took her hand and kissed it. "Thank you, lady." He stood up and then sat back down in his chair.

Chandri came over and sat in his lap. She kissed his cheek and said, "That was sweet, Misch."

Njondac said, "Nice show, Bigun. I didna know ya could do thet."

"You stay out of it, Stubbs."

Molly said, "Yeah, Njondac, what do you know about it? I'm not so sure you've accepted me, either. But you aren't supposed to be a paladin, so I guess I'll just have to live with that. Or, maybe I should say what you said when Chandri was last in trouble. Would you like that?"

Chandri sat up. "What *did* you say? Should I know about that?"

"Shucks. We didna know whut had happened."

Chandri looked from Njondac to Molly and back again. "You thought I'd run away with that man, didn't you?" She jumped up and stomped over to Njondac. She was no longer the timid girl they had adopted so long ago. She could beat Njondac in a fair fight, now, and she was not afraid of him. Standing face to face with him she repeated, "Didn't you!"

"Well, it cud of happened."

"After 12 years of fighting and camping with you, you can say that? After saving your worthless hide more than once, you can believe I'd run off with another man?" She went back to Mischal and plopped down in his lap. "I don't want any man but my big barbarian warrior."

Then she leaned up and put her hands on his shoulders. "After all, I had to ask you twenty questions to trick you into saying yes to the right one. I'm not bailing after all that work."

Mischal squeezed her tightly. "I'd be lost without you. You have no idea how scared I was."

"I knew you'd come for me. Again. I wasn't sure you'd be able to find me, so I was going to escape anyway. But I'm glad you came."

Molly said, "Well, I didn't mean to cause such a stir. Anyway, it's official. We haven't set a date yet. Maybe next June? Hard to be definite, the way we pick up and go."

"You still going to let her travel with us, Karl?" asked Mista.

"*Let* her? Me? Tell Molly what she can and can't do? Yeah, right. Anyway, if I didn't say she could go, she'd die of boredom. I do want her to live with me after we're married, though, when she's home, and not with you."

Mista put on a mock serious expression. "Well, she's never lived with me, you know."

Karl laughed. "You know what I mean."

Chapter 5

They did not talk business during the weekend. The periods of relaxation between projects Were important to healing and bonding, and they all intuitively knew it. They went to a Christmas Eve service in Toccoa on Sunday night, and then shared presents the next morning.

After everyone had opened their gifts, Sheila went over and sat on the arm of Mista's chair. She turned so that she was facing him and ran a finger up and down his arm. "George – no, Mista. Tell me sometime how you got that name. But anyway, I just wanted to say thank you for doing what you are doing for me. You know I'm going with you when you go?"

"I assumed that you would. I could not do anything else, Sis. I see that something else happened. You're beautiful again."

She blushed. "Not really. But I feel like I'm alive again. All those years, I just existed. I survived somehow, but I felt dead inside."

She did look radiant. She had taken advantage of a ladies' day special at a local salon. 'The works' included a facial, some lessons in makeup, haircut and perm among other things. She was wearing a short light blue dress that made her hazel eyes look blue.

"Well, I for one, am glad to have you back. I mean, finding you was great. But it's even better to see you alive again."

Karl said, "Mista I think you have a couple new people. We've all been going different directions, and I never got around to asking you."

"Only one, Em. Her real name is Emaroud Evockovic. Can you spell it?'

Karl smiled. "Yes. I've worked with many men with Slavic names. Including you, Mista. Glad to meet you, Em. How did you happen to join, if I may ask? Notice, I am careful not to ask about your past."

"Oh, that's all right. I don't have anything to hide. I was the nurse at Mayo Clinic assigned to Sam when they brought her down. I fell in love with the little tyke, and, since I liked what they were doing, I asked to join." She had been a little puzzled at the drama played out on Thursday evening, since she had not been briefed on Molly's background, or any of the others.

"They told you what they did?"

"Not they. Sharra and I talked for a long time while we were captive on an island in the Okefenokee Swamp. Mostly I liked the idea of working with all these precious children. And the way they travel, I knew that caring for them and educating them could be a problem."

"Well, I'm sure you'll find your place. Now, Mista who is the young lady perched on the arm of your chair?"

"You've met her, Karl. This is my sister, Sheila."

"Oh. Sorry, Sheila, I didn't recognize you. You do look like a different person. I remember you as – well, drab. I only saw you in the kitchen or serving tables or something. And you didn't wear clothes like that. Molly take you shopping? Oh, no. Molly was with me."

Sheila laughed. "Sharra took me shopping. She has great taste. We did some talking about what had happened to me – I'm sure Mista will be talking to you about it later. I feel much better about myself."

"Well, it shows. Maybe I jumped too quick. Maybe I should have waited for you."

Molly said, "All right. None of that now. You can't be unfaithful until after we're married."

"Don't worry, dear. She is beautiful, though, don't you think?"

"Yes. Looks like she's come alive again."

Mista said, "All kidding aside, Karl, do you have anything in the wings?"

"Not at the moment. You never know when that might change, of course."

"Of course. I don't want to dwell on it this morning, but I have something I need to do. Can you stay over tomorrow?"

"Sure. Matter of fact, I already took tomorrow off. I had reason to stay awhile," he said, smiling at Molly.

Chapter 6

After breakfast the next morning, Mista asked Karl Spicewood to meet with him in his office as soon as it was convenient. Karl was commander of the special crimes unit of the Georgia State Police. He and Mista had served together in the Navy and Marine Corps. And now Mista and his team did special assignment for Karl. Mischal and Sheila were in the office with Mista when Karl knocked on the door later.

Karl looked them over and said, "Well, I didn't expect you here. Maybe I should have brought Molly for my own protection."

Mista smiled. "You aren't in danger. And Molly doesn't know anything about this. Not secret from her, but she just wasn't here when we talked about it. We have done a lot of talking this past week, and I have some ideas I want to kick around with you. I have a special project in mind, and I want to make sure that we stay legal, and I might need the loan of some equipment."

"Well, let's hear it," Karl said, taking a seat. "The equipment should be no problem, depending on what exactly you want. The legality should not be a problem, I hope. I'll tell you what I know, and if I'm not sure, then we can run it by the legal staff."

"Maybe. I want to keep this one close to the chest. People can't talk about what they don't know. You know that Jeremy is studying to be a lawyer? Just starting, so there is a lot he doesn't know. But he's smart. I think, rather than ask your legal department to get involved, I would rather that he go and pose a few hypothetical questions at his university. As a student, interested in the law enforcement activities. Which is all very true. They don't need to know what is about to happen."

"Lawyers are a close-mouthed lot. They are very careful of the client-privilege issue."

"But we would not be clients. A single word in the wrong ears could ruin everything."

"Okay. Let's hear it."

"First, Sheila, tell him your story."

Sheila recounted her story for Karl. She told him of her abduction and forced sexual career, her marriage and children, and her rescue by Mista and friends. Some of it Karl knew already, but he had never heard the gory details. His jaw set in a hard line.

"Sheila, you can't know how sorry I am that this happened to you. I know that it goes on – it happens every day. But it's extraordinarily hard to get a line on these people. Most girls, if they survive, are not willing to talk about it."

"I was not exactly eager. But we wanted to recover some of my memories. Specifically, Mista and I wanted to know if we were actually brother and sister, or if I was born on that other world and was just a duplicate of his real sister. Turns out I was born here."

Karl said, "When I think about an eleven-year-old girl taken like that … it makes me sick inside. I guess that's one reason I'm in law enforcement. I want to stop people like that."

"Don't do this to yourself, Karl. I survived."

"Survived, yes, and we can be glad. But it should never have happened. Well, let's hear your plan. I presume that you intend to do something about this."

"You got that right, Karl. I will see this man dead if he is not already dead. I want to try to find some 11-year-old girls to use as bait. You can call that entrapment if you want to, but if a man wants to engage in that kind of activity, he should be trapped. Like a rabid dog. I do not intend to see the men go through with any acts. I do expect them to come to me, come to the girls. We will send them away crippled. That's all you need to know about that. It will be legal and untraceable. They will know, but I guarantee you that they will not report it. I believe that it is illegal to offer sex to an eleven-year-old girl?"

"Hah! Yes, it is illegal."

"Then, if we turned them in, they would go to jail?"

"Presumably. Unfortunately, not every criminal goes to jail. You ran a dirty sheriff to ground, and he never did jail time. Just be sure that you remain legal. It is illegal to punish someone without due process of law."

"Illegal for courts or police. It isn't illegal for a parent or brother to hit back when someone attacks him is it?"

"No. But you can't kill them. This is not your barbarian world."

Mista sighed. "I know. Next question. What if I find a homeless girl, or boy. Can I take her in and give her a home?"

"You have to qualify for the foster parent program to get any support from the state."

"That's not what I asked you."

"I don't know anything to prevent your taking them in. The state takes an interest in homeless children, though."

"Is that why there are so many homeless living downtown Atlanta?"

Karl grimaced. "Yeah. Not a very practical interest. It could be risky, but as long as you don't mistreat them, and they truly have no other home …"

"All right. Here is my plan. I will advertise on the Internet. Or have the girls go into chat rooms or IM conversations. We'll probably get some respondents. I don't mean to invite them here. I might buy a vacant lot near Toccoa and set up a trailer there. I am not especially interested in these perverts but I'll take out any that appear. But I'm sure that there is one or more organization that promote pre-teen sex. I will find them. I am also sure that one of them took my sister. I hope to find that one."

"And then?" Karl said carefully.

"I'll put them out of business. If I can be sure that it is illegal, then I'll collect evidence and turn them over to authorities."

"It is illegal. But hard to prove. Besides, if you are not careful, you'll step on some toes in the local police departments, if you don't tell them what you are doing and get their cooperation."

"And, if I tell them, and it leaks to the perverts?"

"That is a risk you'll have to take."

"Okay. I'll keep that under advisement."

"You didn't say that you would contact them."

His jaw snapped. "I said exactly what I meant."

Karl rolled his eyes. "Well, I wish you luck. I presume that you intend to travel? And that you will want Molly with you?"

"I will surely travel, but I don't know where yet. I do intend to go to Clearwater, Florida to start. That's a few miles from Crystal Beach, where we lived when Sheila was taken. I could use Molly's talents, but that is up to her."

"I think she had other plans, but you talk to her. If she wants to go, I won't object."

"Thanks. I will need the phones we have been using, and would like some transmitter wires for the girls to wear."

"I can arrange that. Take care, friend."

Chapter 7

They put an ad in the Atlanta Journal and Constitution and in the local paper for 11-year-old girls willing to face danger in a bold experiment. They had to be willing to travel and they had to be free to travel.

Then while they waited for responses, Mista talked with Em about school. "You said you could set up home-schooling for our children. If I get some girls willing to take on this project, we will need to provide for their schooling."

"I'll register for home schooling and get the necessary materials. How many and how old?"

"Say five at eleven. You ought to start Brut and Cato, also."

Mista set up an 800 number for applicants to call in on. He also intended to use that for the Internet connection when he set out the bait. They got a flood of calls. They got a flood of calls. They had not anticipated that so many girls of that age would consider danger to be romantic. Most of them were weeded out on the first phone call. Most did not have a ghost of a chance of getting parental permission to travel with strangers for six months.

Mista bought a small farm outside of Toccoa and then bought a used travel trailer and parked it on the land, screened from the road by trees. He invited 15 girls to visit them there for further interviews. Nine showed up, some with parents, and some alone.

Sharra and Mista conducted the interviews in the newly acquired trailer on the Tuesday after New Years. They had a transcript of Sheila's account of her abduction, and started the interview by asking the girl to read the account. Then they told her that they intended to catch the men responsible for that crime. The first three that they talked to came in with one or two parents. They also read the account. When Mista told them that they intended to use the girls to help catch the perpetrators, the parents immediately said 'NO!' and left.

Shortly after the third girl had left, they got another call. Sharra answered. A girl asked, in an accent that clearly tagged her as black, "Yo' lookin' fo' guls?"

"Yes," Sharra said. "We have a project that girls can help us with."

"Where yo' at?"

Sharra gave her directions and the street number. "There is big sign out front that says, 'Project 909'. Take that dirt road to the trailer parked on the lot."

"How I knows I be safe?"

"We'll leave a door open, if you like, so you can run out any time you want to."

"I be there in ten minutes."

She showed up twenty minutes later, knocking timidly on the door. When Sharra opened the door, she said, "That doh' stay open?"

"No problem, except the cold."

Mista said, "How about we put a stick in the door and close it most of the way to keep out the cold. It would be open enough that you could snatch it open and run if you wanted to."

"Okay. What yo' want?"

Sharra handed her the transcript. The girl glanced at it and said, "Yo' read it. I don' read so good."

The girl said, "Yo want me to have sex with old men? My uncle already done it."

"No," Sharra said. "We want you to help us catch the man who did this. We'll string him up to the nearest tree."

"He black."

"I have no idea what color he is. It doesn't matter. If he did this, he's dead," Mista said.

"Okay. I'll help. What do I have to do?"

Sharra raised her eyebrow slightly. The accent was gone. "Can you use a computer and email?"

"Yes. I like to IM friends. I read good, too. I was faking to see what you'd say."

"Well, you did a good job of it. We would want you to send out your picture and some video pictures, and tell them that you are eleven. Then when you get their interest, they will want to come here." The girl stirred. Sharra held up her hand. "When they come here we intend to tag them so we can find them again, damage them mentally, and then send them away. You will greet them when they come, and then say you are going to change out of your clothes. That is the last they will see of you."

"I can do that. I'd like to do that."

"Good. What's your name?"

"Shawnah Kingsberry."

"Okay, Shawnah. We will have to travel to several states, and may be gone six months or more. Can you get permission to do that?"

"Don't need none. My mother is on – can't take care of me. She sent me to my uncle, and he did me the second night I was there. I'm leaving. If you take me, I'll go with you. I'm leaving anyhow."

Mista looked at Sharra. She sent, She is telling the truth. She will run away whether we take her or not.

Mista said, "There are about ten of us in this group. Men and women, children and nurses and teachers. We will ask you to sign a statement saying that you are coming voluntarily. That is for our protection, since we will be crossing state lines, and we don't want the FBI thinking that we kidnapped you. We will feed you, give you a good place to live, and buy you everything that you need. We cannot pay you, because of your age, but we will take good care of you. If you want to, you can stay with us and we will give you a good home as long as you want to stay, even send you to college if you want to go."

"You would do all that for me? And don't even know who I am?"

"Yes. We know that you need a home and that you have been hurt. That's all we need to know. You will not be a prisoner. You can leave anytime you want to."

She looked from Sharra to Mista, decided to trust them, and said, "When do I come back?"

"If you don't need to go home for anything, you don't have to leave. You would be living in this trailer."

"I can't go home. Everything I have is in a bag. I hid it out by the road."

Mista said, "Jasmine!"

Jasmine opened a door and entered. "Yes?"

"Would you show this young lady her new room?"

"Sure. You want me to go with you to get your things?"

"Sure."

Just before the door closed behind them, they heard the girl say, "Is he for real?"

"You better believe it, honey. He meant exactly what he said. Every word."

Chapter 8

Two days later two girls came in together. The older one was about 14, and drove to the location, even though she could not have had a license. She said, "This is Candy Applebee. She wants to do whatever you want."

"Why don't we ask her what she wants to do?" Sharra asked.

Candy said, "I'll do anything."

The older girl said, "Her parents were divorced a few years ago, and her father left. He never came back or wrote. We don't know where he is. Her mother doesn't like her, and so she spends all her time at our house. Two weeks ago, her mother went off with her boyfriend. We think they were killed in a car wreck."

"You don't know?" Mista asked.

"No. They put her picture in the paper, but she had no identification, so they don't know who she is."

"You could call and tell them."

"No," Candy said. "She don't like me. I crimp her style."

They explained the program to her and signed her up. Her friend said that she would bring her things over later. "I'll tell Mom that you ran away. She'll be glad to see you gone."

Janice Johnson came to them from the homeless shelters in Atlanta, glad to have a home, even if it was temporary.

The next day, a woman called and said she was bringing a girl over to give to them. She brought a sullen girl who would not talk to them. She showed identification that identified her as a social worker.

"Her name is Carol Jennings. Her parents are deceased. She has been in five foster homes in the last two years. No one will keep her. If you have use for her, I'll assign her to you, no strings attached."

"You will need to sign a statement authorizing her to travel with us," Mista said. "We will be gone for several months, and will probably cross several state lines. We don't want people thinking that we kidnapped her."

"No problem."

"I know that in your position, you cannot just give her to us. But you can assign her to us temporarily. If she wants to stay with us after six months, will you release her?"

"You can have her with my blessings."

Sharra said, "Carol, are you willing to go with us and help with our project?"

She shrugged.

"I take that as a yes. If we take you, it will be as a ward of the state. That makes us responsible for you. It means that we cannot allow you to run away. We assure you that we will not mistreat you, and that if you should desire to run away, it will be because of your own decision. But we cannot allow that. Do you understand?"

She shrugged again.

"She won't talk to you. You are authorized to take her, whether she wants to go or not."

"We do not have the facilities to imprison her, nor the time to deal with an unwilling child. If we cannot handle her, we will have to bring her back."

"You can do that, like the other five have done. But I'm telling you, you are her last chance."

Sharra touched the woman's mind briefly. She saw that her name was Shelly and that Carol was not hers to give. She sent to Mista, *Something wrong here. We need to take this girl. She's in danger at that house.*

"We'll give it a try," Sharra said.

The social worker stood up and handed Mista the small suitcase she was carrying. These are all of her clothes. Good luck."

Carol watched her leave, and then got up to follow. Sharra asked, "Do you want to go with her?"

She shook her head.

"You just want to leave. You can't do that."

Carol opened the door and started out. She stopped as if she had hit an invisible wall. In fact, Sharra had made a wall in front of her of nothing but air and her mental power. "I have several ways to keep you from running away."

The next day Mista recorded a message for his answering machine. "If you are calling about our ad in the paper, we have filled our quota."

Chapter 9

After the last girl had joined the group, Mista called them all into the front room. The travel trailer only had two rooms, the main living/dining room and the bedroom, which Mischal had converted into a bunkroom.

"Let me tell you what our immediate plans are. First thing that is going to happen is Jasmine needs to examine each one of you and make sure that you are healthy. If we find something wrong, we will know what to fix. Next, I need to get you all computers. If you don't know how to use one, some of us can show you. You can also learn from each other. I will set up an Internet account for each of you, and give you free rein. I will monitor traffic, the sites that you go to, and the chat rooms that you join. I will maintain a chat log of all conversations. This is not to spy on you, but to have a record of what people say to you. If we go to court – and I expect that we will – I will have a legal log of what they have said to you and what you said to them.

"Why would that matter?" asked Candy.

"Most things that you say won't matter. But if he says that you came on to him, for example, and you did not, then the logs will support that. If he offers you sex, which is illegal, then that will be in the log.

"You will have complete freedom of the Internet. You could easily abuse that. I don't want you on pornographic sites, but if you do what we need for you to do, you will need wide access. I want you to entice men to come here and have sex with you. Well, entice is not the right word. The men we want to catch and get off the street will just want to come. You don't have to do anything but be there. We will make some pictures and videos to post on the Internet for them. They will not be porno, but we need for them to think that you might provide them with some good pictures. Only the perverts will want them, but it is the perverts that we want to catch. This could be dangerous. If you want out, you are free to go. I certainly don't want to force this on anyone."

They all shook their heads. They saw this as an adventure, and his warning of danger did not sink in. Carol still was not talking, but she did shake her head, no.

"Okay. It seems to me that you don't have very many clothes, any of you. Is that a problem for you?"

Shawnah said, "I had more, but my mom wouldn't let me take them when I left home."

Janice said, "I had to leave my other shirt. I never had more than two. It would be nice to have a change of clothes."

Mista said, "It looks like a problem to me, and I'm not even a girl." They all laughed. Even Carol smiled.

"We are going to drive to our real home tonight, and have a big welcome supper. I promise you, you can have all you want. I want you to meet the girl who got abducted in that little script that you read. It really did happen. And I want you to meet the rest of the family.

"Then we'll set up real rooms for you at the house. I guess we should put two in each room, for company. Tomorrow we'll go to town – Atlanta – and buy your computers and some clothes."

Mista stopped and rubbed his chin. "I guess the best thing is for one of our women to pair up with one of you, and take you shopping. You will need shoes, dresses, jeans, shirts, underwear, and swimsuits. Be sure to get a dress or three that you can wear to church. You need something provocative, like short shorts and a halter-top. Any questions?"

Candy said, "You could spend a lot of money."

"I promised you whatever you need. You need clothes. Get whatever you want, within reason. At least four or five sets of clothes. You can keep your old ones or not, as you choose. Janice, you don't have anything else, do you?"

Janice said, "No. This is all I own."

Mista rubbed his chin. "Let's make a quick run into Toccoa and get you some jeans and a shirt."

"This is too good to be true. What's the catch?"

"No catch. We have a job to do. That's all. Since none of you have homes that you can call home, I would like you to think of this as home for as long as you like. If you want me to, I'll draw up formal adoption papers somewhere down the road. I understand that you might not want to stay after this little caper is over. That's all right, too. You are not slaves or prisoners."

"Me, too?" Carol asked.

Mista cradled his chin and thought. "I can't let you go away until after we have finished. You can go back to the social services lady, if you want to. But I can't turn you out with no place to go, even after we have finished. I really hope that you will want to stay, but if you don't then I guess I have to return you to the social services place. I'm not part of the foster parents program in any way. But, I could foster you or adopt you if that is what you decide that you want. No need to make a decision now, unless it's to return to Ms Shelly."

Carol's eyes narrowed. "How did you know her name?"

"She had an identification card."

"That wasn't her card."

"Oh? Well, now, that's interesting. Sharra?"

Sharra took a minute to read Carol's surface thoughts. The woman was named Shelly, but her card had read Johnson. *I guess* I gave you the name without thinking about it. She picked the girl up off the street and tried to force her to live with her. She was never in the foster program. Let me pick this one up.

"Hon, you were never part of the foster program, were you? You have been terribly hurt. I'd like to be a friend to you, but I'm not going to try to force you to talk."

Carol clenched her teeth and looked away, as if to signal that she was not going to talk.

Sharra said, "If we let you go, where would you go?"

A tear appeared in the corner of her eye, and she brushed it angrily away. Sharra could barely hear her as she whispered, "Nowhere."

"Ah, you have nowhere to go. Well, we are offering you a place to call home."

Carol refused to say anything else. *They're too smart. If I say anything, they'll know. Turn me out on my ear. They say I can stay here. Anything is better than ... but if they knew, they wouldn't let me stay. Can't say anything. Nothing at all. Seal your lips, Robin.*

Sharra turned to Mista and said, "We should ask Em to take her in the morning. She will love her."

Chapter 10

When the girls went to bed that night, they were all excited about the shopping trip scheduled for the next day. Only Carol remained sullen and silent. Janice went over to her and placed her hands on her shoulders. "Come on, Carol, cheer up. Have you ever had anything so nice happen to you?"

Carol shook her head, but did not say anything. Janice said, "Don't you want to be here? Are you being sent away for some reason? I can't remember my parents, so I don't know what it's like."

Carol blinked back tears, but still refused to talk.

Janice said, "I picked you for a roommate, but you have to talk to me. Maybe this is too good to be true, but if they really buy me clothes and a computer, I'll have to believe. I don't even know how to use a computer. Do you? Could you teach me?"

"I ..." You'll ruin it. She would be sure to let something slip, if she didn't just tell them. I used to have a computer. But not any more. I could show her, but she'd want to know how I knew. Maybe if I teach her real good, she won't tattle on me. "I'll show you." She climbed into the bed and turned her face to the wall, refusing to say anything else. Janice shrugged, turned off the light and climbed in bed beside her.

Suddenly, Carol realized that Janice had not changed into a nightgown. She was going to sleep in her clothes. Clothes she had worn for who knew how long. She got up, went to her suitcase and got her spare gown out. They had promised to buy her clothes – they would surely replace it. She tapped Janice on the shoulder and held out the gown.

"Oh. Thanks. I guess my clothes are kind of dirty. I didn't want to sleep in my new ones. You know, I don't know what it's like to be clean. I like it." They had all had baths, but she had nothing else to wear.

Carol bit her lip. When Janice had changed into her gown, she said, "You can wear something of mine when we go to town tomorrow." They were not the same size, but close enough. Carol was a little chubby, and Janice rail thin, but they were the same height.

"Mr. Mista bought me some jeans and a shirt, remember?"

Sharra asked Em to walk to Em's room with her. Em raised an eyebrow, but said, "Sure."

Sharra looked around the room. It was as neat as she expected a nurse to keep it. "You keep a real neat room. It's yours, you know – you don't have to impress anyone."

"This is the way I like it. I'm not trying to impress anyone at all."

"Okay. But you only have one chair in here?"

"Can't use but one at a time."

"I guess that's true. Let's get a couple more for now. You can take them out later if you want to."

They brought two easy chairs from the next room, which was vacant. Sharra sat in one and said, "What do you think of the girl we assigned to you? We can change that, if you don't like her."

"Oh, she's such a pretty little thing. But so sad. No, don't change it. I'd like the challenge of drawing her out."

"Sad? Yes, you're right. I was thinking sullen and angry at something. But you're right. Sad and also scared of something."

"What could it be? Afraid that you will send her back? Or that you'll mistreat her, and she has no way out?"

"Could be either," Sharra said. "I want to bring her in here and try to break into her shell. I can read her mind, and you can love her. I think that that is one of the keys to her. She desperately needs love."

"Okay. That's why you wanted two chairs. Okay. Bring her up."

Sharra knocked on the girls' door and opened it. "Carol would you come with me, please."

Carol stiffened, and then pretended to be asleep. Janice touched her shoulder. "They want you."

Carol sat up and looked at Sharra with wide frightened eyes. *This is it. They found out, somehow.* "I'll get my clothes on."

"No, you don't need to. We're just going upstairs."

Carol obediently followed Sharra, not willing to walk beside her.

She opened Em's door and beckoned Carol inside. *Oh, no! She doesn't want me. Oh well. Nothing new in that.*

Em said, "Sit down, hon." She scooted her own chair over next to Carol's. "Are you excited about the trip tomorrow? I am. We're going to have such fun buying you all the clothes you want. Mr. Mista said there was no limit."

Carol looked up at her, eyes wide. *Could it really be true? Don't ruin it. Don't say a word. Nothing, nothing, nothing.* She looked back down at the floor.

Em said, "Can I hold your hand, dear? Are you afraid of me?"

Carol shook her head without looking up. She did not withdraw her hand when Em took it.

Sharra said, "Carol, I see a pretty little girl, but one who is sad and lonely. Something else, though. I see fear."

Carol looked up sharply. *They know! How? I knew it couldn't be true.*

Sharra said, "Don't be surprised. I'm a teacher, and I love working with girls and boys. Em is, too. We just want to help. Would you tell me what you are so afraid of?"

"You'll thro…" *Nothing! Nothing, nothing, nothing.*

"I promise that we will not throw you out." She sent to Em, *Take over. I'll read and see what she is really thinking and pass it on to you. That way you can ask leading questions. Just be sure not to give her the impression that you are reading her mind. That would scare her worse.*

Okay. She squeezed Carol's hand. "Hon, we just want to be good to you. How can we help you?"

Carol thought, 'no way. They'll know.' She said nothing.

Sharra got a picture of a fire, Carol running into the night, screaming. She caught the thought, 'they won't believe that I didn't do it.'

She sent to Em, *Tell her that we called and verified that Ms Johnson never saw her. But that she lost her card. Maybe when she was visiting Ms Shelly. Ms Shelly is in the foster program, but did not tell Ms Johnson about Carol.*

Em said, "You can trust us, Carol. We called Mrs. Johnson. That was the name on the card that that woman had. She said that she lost the card, maybe while visiting Ms Shelly. But she didn't know anything about you. Did Ms Shelly steal you somewhere?"

She shook her head. "I was running. She caught …" *Nothing! You've already said too much.*

Sharra said, "You're completely safe here, Hon. Ms Shelly signed papers giving us permission to keep you and to travel with you. Ms Johnson – whoever she is – doesn't know about you." Sharra had an inspiration. She was afraid of the police, although Sharra did not know why, yet. "She can't tell the police, so they won't ever know you are here."

"You'll tell them."

"No. Promise."

Carol said, "You'll tell them and then they'll take me away." She suddenly burst into tears and put her head down.

Em said, "Come here, dear. Let me hold you." She took Carol in her arms and held her tight, rocking her and crooning softly. Carol put her arms around Em's neck and held on.

Sharra sent, Good. She's afraid of the police. We might be harboring a fugitive here, but I don't think so. We'll worry about it later, if we are.

After Carol had calmed some, Em said, "Tell Aunt Em all about it, hon. We aren't going to throw you out, or tell police that you are here, no matter what."

"They'll think I did it." She started crying harder.

Sharra sent, Fire. There was a fire and she thinks the police think she set it. But she did not. I read that. She really did not.

Em rocked her some more, and then said, "Tell me about it. I believe that you did not do anything wrong. Tell me what happened."

Carol leaned up and looked into Em's eyes. Her eyes were large and luminous, a bright green. "You promise?"

"Cross my heart and hope to die."

She looked over at Sharra. "What about her?"

Sharra suppressed a smile. Em had won. She did not ask Sharra directly. "I promise, I won't tell. Just between us. I'll have to tell my husband, but he will do whatever I say."

Carol took a deep breath. "Okay. Our house burned down. My mother was inside and she died. But I didn't do it, I swear to God. I tried to wake my mother up, but she was passed out, and I couldn't. I ran out, just in time. The police saw me, and tried to catch me, but I ran as hard as I could. I climbed a tree and hid, and they never found me."

"What happened to your mother, dear," Em asked.

"She was an alcoholic, and she passed out. Did it all the time. Must have been smoking. I stayed up in the tree all night, and when it got light, I ran away. Mrs. Shelly saw me and caught me. Made me go inside her house and tried to make me tell her why I was running and who I was. I wouldn't talk, so she locked me in a room to make me talk. Three or four days, I don't remember. Then she brought me to you."

Sharra said, "The police will still be looking for you, you know."

"I know. You said you wouldn't tell!"

"You have my promise. I won't tell them. We'll keep you safe. I know that you are telling me the truth, so don't worry. I always know."

"Can you read minds?"

"You could say that," Sharra said, with a smile. "I told you that I could prevent you from running away. I won't do that, now. But I think you will be much safer to stay here than to try to run."

"You promise I'll be safe?"

"Yes."

"But … I'll have to get naked in front of those men!"

Sharra smiled. "Oh, no, dear heart. You won't have to get naked at all. We never intended that. You would greet them when they came, and then leave the room, saying you were going to change. But, you won't have to change. We will take over from there. You won't see them again."

Carol relaxed visibly and clung tighter to Em. Em said, "You poor dear. You were afraid to run and afraid to stay, weren't you?"

She nodded. "But you said to buy skimpy clothes."

Sharra said, "Yes, skimpy, but not too much. You and Em decide what would attract a pervert, without being too revealing. You want to just tease them."

Then a thought struck Sharra. "If we put your picture on the Internet, someone will recognize you. Do they have pictures of you, or did they get a good look at you?"

"No. It was dark. I don't even know if they knew that I was in the house. It burned down, so there aren't any pictures. Oh. The landlady. She might remember me. We had rooms upstairs. With an outside door and stairs. We had only just moved in, and nobody knew us."

"Well, we better change the way you look, just in case. We could dye your hair red. It'd go with those big green eyes."

"Like Little Orphan Annie?"

"Yep. Yes, we could cut it short like that, and give you a perm with lots of curls. Are you satisfied, now?"

"Oh, yes. I can't wait to go shopping. I promised Janice I'd teach her how to use a computer. Can I sleep with you, Aunt Em?"

"Janice will be lonely."

"She'll be asleep."

Em smiled. "Yes, dear, you can sleep with me tonight."

"Oh," Carol said, "My name is not Jennings. I just told her that. It's Robin Smith."

Sharra told Mista later. "She's a sweet thing. She was just scared to death."

"The police will be looking for her."

"Yes. And they will think that she set the fire, probably. But I know that she did not. We'll never be able to prove it, though."

"No. But they might find evidence that it started with a cigarette when the woman passed out."

"Maybe later. Let's keep her. She has no place to go, and I don't want to see her put in the foster care program."

"They do a lot of good."

"Yes, that's true. But so do we."

Mista smiled. "A child we couldn't have? Fine with me."

"By the way, she is not eleven, yet," Sharra said.

"Oh? How old is she?"

"I didn't pick that up. Just that she was afraid that we would find out that she wasn't actually eleven, and then wouldn't take her. I'd guess she must be ten."

"Close enough. The exact age is not all that important. Eleven is just a target age. The same gang that took Sheila might not even be in operation any more, and even if they are, they might have different age requirements."

Chapter 11

Sharra took the girls into the clinic after breakfast. Jasmine said, "Basic exam, of course. What about blood work?"

"Mista said get a complete physical. All the basic blood tests. He wants to know everything about them medically. He mentioned allergy tests."

"Those are expensive. I think it's $150 or more."

"Yes, but what if one of them is allergic to peanuts or bee stings? We don't want to find out the hard way."

"There is that. Okay. You've got it."

Sharra left them, and Jasmine closed and locked the door. "Okay, girls. Lets have your clothes off. Nobody's coming in here, and I need to see everything."

They set the girls up in their trailer. Mista put their computers in the bunkroom and set up a server in the front room. If they got visitors, they would see only one computer. The girls were happier about their free access to the Internet than anything else. He arranged broadband telephone connections so that they could all access the net at the same time. Em moved in with them, and set up a regular class schedule.

Then Mista, Mischal and Njondac began plans for travel. Mista would pull his trailer with his Range Rover, and Charly and Mischal would drive their motor homes. The only vehicle that they had that could pull the old trailer was Njondac's truck.

"Sure. I'll pull her."

"What about your camper," Mista asked. "You can't load the camper and pull a trailer, too."

"Humph. We kin sleep on tha ground."

Mischal said, "Just for sleeping? Why don't you get a small trailer, like 22 feet. Charly's Range Rover could pull that. Sleep on the ground, if you want to, but you also have stuff to haul. Clothes, weapons, tools and all."

"Thet would work. We'd have an extra trailer, five instead of four."

"Yes, but we have five extra people," Mista said. "Em and the four girls."

"We're gone ta have a whole company if we keeps this up," Njondac said.

"Yeah, we'll have to rent a train if we are still doing this when our kids all get married."

"We could just drive down and rent a hotel," Mischal said.

"Hah. We could pay for all the campers outright for what we'd spend on hotel rooms anywhere near Clearwater Beach," Mista said. "We do have to think about riding arrangements, though. I guess we could farm the girls out, one to a car."

"That, or put them all in one of the motor homes," Mischal said.

"Yes, that would work," Mista said. "Molly, are you riding with us again?"

"Uh, well, I was not planning on going. If that's all right. I have a lot to do in the next few months."

"I guess I'm not too surprised," Mista said. "You could coordinate communications with Karl, if we need to talk to him. We have the telephones, of course, but that would be instant communications."

"I'll be glad to do that. But, don't forget, I won't be with him all the time. I might get an apartment in Atlanta, but basically, I will be living here. I can keep Sheila company."

"I think Sheila is coming with us."

"You bet I am," Sheila said.

"Hmmm. Molly, we could leave all the small children with you for company," Mista said.

She thought about that for a moment. Mista's four-year-old Sam, Chandri's five-year-old Tilly, Mischal's eight-year-old Cato and Njondac's eight-year-old Brut. "You just think you will. I don't need that much company."

Charly said, "I can drive our motor home, and Jeremy can drive the Rover. Em and the girls can all ride with me."

The girls had fun exploring the Internet and spent most of their free time chatting with new friends that they met on the net. Njondac took his truck to the new site, and parked his new trailer there, but Mista insisted that they return to the big house at night.

Janice was the first to get a hit. She was also the most bold, since she had been living on the streets for years. She was wearing a short mini-skirt and a white top when he came to the trailer. She had not actually invited him, but had given him the telephone number and the address.

She met him at the door, and went outside to talk to him while the other girls cleaned up evidence of more than one girl living there. She said, "Hi. I didn't expect you and my uncle is not home."

He said, "I just wanted to come and see if you looked like your picture. Could we talk inside?"

"Well, I don't know. Nobody's here but me."

Once inside, he came right to the point. "You said you had never had sex, but wanted to see what it was like. I can show you."

"Me, with a grown man?"

"Sure. Much better than with a boy."

"Well. If you're sure. Let me go change into something better." She stepped back into the trailer and he followed.

"Oh, I think that little skirt is just fine. Let me show you what I have for you."

"Sure. Lots of boys like to show off."

"Well, I'm not a boy."

"I'll say. I do need to change."

"Oh, no. I like you just the way you are." He walked over and reached for her.

Mista was waiting in the Range Rover, parked out of sight behind the trailer, listening on his audio bug. He was already out of the car and heading for the door when the man made his move. He inserted his key – although he knew that it was unlocked – and opened the door. "Well," he said. "What's going on, Janice?"

"This man has been talking to me on the Internet. I didn't know he was coming over. Really, Uncle Mista."

"Well." Mista scowled. "Go put some clothes on, girl."

When she left, the man said, "It was just a game, man."

"It didn't look like a game to me," Mista said. "Just exactly what did you have in mind, Mr. ....?"

"Ames. Jethro Ames. Nothing, man. She said she wanted some sex education and invited me over. So, I came."

"All right, Mr. Ames. Have a seat over there, please. I want to show you something. Sharra!"

Sharra stepped out from the back room. "Yes?"

"We have a live one, here." He went to the server and called up the chat logs for Janice. Mr. Ames, we have a complete record of all your on-line conversations with Janice. She did *Not* invite you over."

"Well, she gave me the address and hinted …"

"You might take it that way, but it certainly was not obvious." He pushed another button under the computer and a recorder whirred. The sound was for effect only. The actual recording was on his computer. Mista touched the playback button and the inside of the trailer came up on his computer screen. "We have a security tape running anytime Janice is here alone. Just in case someone like you comes calling. I think the police would be very interested in both of these pieces of evidence, Mr. Ames."

He bowed his head and covered his face. "Please. I didn't do anything. I have a good job and a wife and family. I'd lose everything."

"As opposed to an eleven year old girl only losing her virginity just as she is entering puberty? Ruining a girl's entire life is not nearly as important as satisfying your perversion, Mr. Ames?"

"Please. I'll pay you. I'll do anything."

"Well, since nothing happened – probably because I got here in time – I think I'll just put these in a safe-deposit box. I recommend that you forget that you were ever here, Mr. Ames. He's all yours, Sharra."

Sharra went into his mind and set up an illusion, similar to a post-hypnotic suggestion. Any time he felt any desire to have sex – even with his own wife – he would get a strong sensation of falling into a canyon. It would be much like a dream of falling and being unable to stop. He would also get a strong nausea like that which often accompanies motion sickness. He left hurriedly, not knowing that she had done anything until he went to bed that night. He was unable to explain to his wife what was wrong.

When he was gone, Mista called the girls out. "That was close, Janice."

"Whoo. I'll say. I was scared to death."

"Well, you see how quickly an encounter can turn dangerous. That little skirt was what really turned him on. Don't be afraid to flash a little view of underpants – or wear a bathing suit bottom under it, so you would not be actually showing anything you would not ordinarily show while swimming."

"Okay. I can do that."

Mista said, "Did the rest of you know what was happening?"

"Not really," Robin said. "We could hear them, but did not really know."

"Okay. Watch the tape."

After they had seen the tape of the scene in the main room, Mista said, "Now you see how quickly and unexpectedly something can go wrong. That's why I was here, and Aunt Sharra. Today, we just happened to be here when he came – unannounced. It could have been really ugly. If we had known that he was coming, then of course we would have been here. I told you that this could be dangerous. If you don't want to keep this up, just say so. I won't put you in danger against your will."

"Uncle Njondac was here," Candy said.

"Yes he was. And he is as good a man as you ever want to see in a fight. But he was not right on the scene, and he might have arrived too late. He would have killed that man after it was over. But you would already have been harmed. Just be very careful. Now, we are going to leave in a few days for Clearwater, Florida. Keep your chats going, but don't give out the address."

Chapter 12

They went back to the house early that evening. Mista did not want to risk another encounter. They all watched TV for a while after supper, and then the girls went up to bed at nine. When they left, Mista went into his office and leaned back in his big chair in the corner. He needed to review the incident and decide if he wanted to continue this experiment. He needed to ferret out the man who had taken Sheila, and he needed to shut down whatever operation was going on – assuming that it was still happening.

But maybe using the girls as bait was a bad idea. It was a lucky break that he had happened to be there when that man showed up unannounced. If he had not been there … he did not want to think about that. They had planned to schedule one man at a time, and he or Mischal would then be on the site, ready for action. This could go bad really quick.

No, this was still the best plan. But, now, they would have to have someone on the property whenever the girls were there. Perhaps they should have the girls do their school and computer work here most of the time, and only go to the trailer in the afternoons for a few hours. No, that would not work. They would be leaving for Florida next week. Then they would be in the trailer all the time. Perhaps a full time audio bug in the trailer. He'd have to tell the girls so that they would not think he was spying on them.

His thoughts were interrupted by the sound of small feet in his doorway. He opened his eyes and looked up. All four girls stood in his doorway. Janice walked forward slowly while the others watched. She walked up to his chair and kissed him, and said, "Thank you, Uncle Mista."

He could hear the other girls whisperings, "She did it!"

Mista said, "Would you like to sit in my lap and talk a few minutes?"

She did not answer, but climbed up and hugged him.

Mista looked at the other girls. "Anybody else want some?" Robin immediately ran and jumped up in his lap. Candy followed, a little slower, but Shawnah hung back. "There's always room for one more," he said.

Sharra stuck her head in the door. "What's going on in here? Are you under there somewhere, Mista?"

"Yes, I'm here somewhere. I think I need a bigger chair."

The girls scrambled around for a while, finding a place to sit and hold on. When they were finally set, Mista looked from one to another, and said, "I didn't expect this benefit when I signed on four girls."

They all giggled and snuggled closer. Mista said, "It's a good thing I didn't pick any fat girls. We'd be sunk." Then he sobered and said, "None of you have fathers, do you?"

Shawnah said, "I do, but he ain't there much. And I don't never want to see my uncle again."

Mista said, "I promise you that I will never do anything like that. I guess you were all a little afraid of what I might or might not do."

Janice said, "Yeah. But when you put that man out, we knew. What did you do to him, anyway? Anything besides send him out?"

Mista tried to stroke his chin, but his arm was captured by one of the girls, Robin. "Hmmm. You all know what love and sex is all about, don't you?"

They all nodded. "I would think so, from the homes you've come from. What he was going to do to you was terribly wrong. I know that you think so, too, but just so you know, I think it was terrible. It is the kind of thing that happened to my sister when she was your age."

"That's why you wanted us to be eleven?" asked Robin.

"Yes. That's why. Different men have different ideas. Normal men wait until they are adult and have sex with adult women. Some like to get their jollies on little girls. Some like babies, some like six-year-olds, some like teenagers. Some like girls who are eleven. It's all wrong, and it's all against the law. But they still do it. That man will not for a long, long time. Sharra messed with his mind. Every time he even thinks about having sex with someone, he will get sick to his stomach and feel like he is falling out of an airplane. Do you think he will be able to explain that to his wife?"

Janice said, "He can't tell her about me, and can't tell her why he can't have sex." She clapped her hands. "Great. Serves him right."

Mista said, "I've been sitting here thinking. I'm not sure it's a good idea to ask you to do this. I don't like the possibility that this might happen again."

Candy said, "No, we want to go ahead. We all talked about it. It's dangerous, but we know you will protect us."

"Yes. We will try. And I hope we are never too late. One of us will always be there whenever you have your chat sessions. I will have an audio link to a listening station, so he will know what is going on inside the trailer. I don't want you to think we are just spying on you, but if I had not been listening today, I would not have been there in time."

"We understand," Robin said, "and it makes us feel safer."

Mista sat in silence for a minute. Robin curled up against him and her eyes closed. Mista gave her a squeeze. "Don't go to sleep, yet. I have one more thing on my mind, and it is very important."

"What?"

"I just realized that none of you had any Christmas, did you?"

They all shook their heads.

"We were so busy setting things up last week and getting you the things that you need, nobody even thought about it. What would you like special for Christmas, even though the day has come and gone?"

Shawnah said without any hesitation, "I want an Ipod."

"You've got it. We'll go down and get one tomorrow."

Her eyes widened. "Really? I didn't really …"

Candy said, "Could I have a TV of my own?"

"With a DVD player built in?"

"Yes!"

"You've got it. Janice?"

"I don't know. I never had a Christmas present. I don't know what to ask for. I'm just glad to have a home."

"How about a fancy, beautiful dress that you could wear to parties and church, or anywhere?"

Her eyes got big. "Yes! I never had a dress before."

"Robin?"

"I don't know," Robin said sleepily. "I just want a home."

"Would you like a surprise?"

"Yes, a surprise." She was asleep.

He looked down. Janice was also asleep, curled upon his left shoulder. Mista said, "I guess you two better go on to bed before you go to sleep, too. I couldn't carry all four of you."

Candy jumped down and then came and kissed him. "Thanks. Good night."

Shawnah looked like she was afraid to come to him. He said, "Are you afraid still?"

"A little. But I trust you. Thanks for everything." She leaned over and kissed him lightly.

Mista kicked his chair all the way back, and the two girls stretched out, one head on each shoulder. Sharra came in and said, "How's it going. Oh."

Mista said, "I guess I'll have to adopt these two."

"You'll probably have to adopt all four."

"I'm afraid you're right about that."

Sharra left and Mista looked down at the two girls, wondering what he had gotten himself into. Robin was still a little chubby and had pearly white skin. She would probably lose the rest of her fat as she went into her growth spurt. If she did not, they then would have to watch her diet. If her mother was an alcoholic, then she had probably done most of the cooking. Would she have known to prepare balanced meals? Probably not. Probably ate mostly hamburger and potatoes. Cheap and easy to fix.

Janice had dark skin, rough from exposure to sun and wind. She was rail thin, but had probably had balanced meals, since she ate mostly in the shelters. Of course, who knew whether she ate everything served, or even how often she had a full meal. She would probably look a lot different when she had enough to eat.

At least when Jasmine had gotten the results back from the blood work, they found that none of them had any major problems. They didn't have to worry about allergies, and they knew all their blood types, in case of accident.

He dozed off, thinking about them. Sharra came in about midnight and woke him. "Aren't you coming to bed tonight?"

"Oh, yes. I must have dozed off. I'll be up in a few."

"Well, it's already after midnight."

"Already? Oh. Didn't know it was that late. I'll have to take these two up to bed. I don't think I can carry them both at once. I'll be there as soon as I get them to bed."

Chapter 13

The four girls stood behind Mista's chair waiting impatiently for him to finish breakfast. He took his time, looked at his plate when he finished, and then said, "I think I'll have another waffle."

"No!" Candy said. "You've had enough. You'll get fat if you eat too much."

"But I've only had two waffles."

"That's enough," Shawnah said.

"Are you eager for me to finish for some reason? This is Saturday. We don't have anything to do today."

"Yes, we do," they all chorused.

Robin said, "You promised to take us shopping."

"But it's probably still dark outside," Mista said.

"No, it isn't," Janice said. "It's almost nine o'clock. The stores are all open and people are buying up everything."

"Well, okay then. Don't you want Aunt Sharra or Aunt Em to take you? They know what girls like."

"No! You! You promised." They chorused.

"Okay, then, let's go. We'll probably be back sometime today, if they don't drive me crazy," he told Sharra.

"You asked for it."

When they got to the Range Rover, Robin said, "I get the front seat."

"No, me," said Candy.

"Me, me," the others said.

"Hmmm," Mista said, rubbing his chin. "There is only one seatbelt in the front, and three in the back. Logically, we should put only one up front and three in the back. I guess we could put all four up front and pull the seatbelt real tight."

"You cant' do that!" Janice said. "You'd squeeze us."

"Well, let's count off." He touched Janice on the head, and then Candy, Shawnah and Robin, chanting as he went, "Eeny, Meeny, Miney, Moe, Catch a tiger by his tail, if he hollers make him pay, fifty dollars every day. Well, Robin was the last, so I guess she gets the seat."

"I get it coming back," Candy said.

"No, me," Shawnah said.

"I called it first."

"Well, we'll see. Buckle up, now. I'm a terrible driver." He was not a bad driver, although the others teased him about it.

He started to pull into the Wal-Mart parking lot in Toccoa, but Robin said, "No! Atlanta."

"Yes, Atlanta," the others said.

"But that's a whole hour in here with you all. I don't know if I can stand it."

"You'll just have to," Robin said.

He came to the perimeter road and went on around to the Northgate Mall. "Is this good enough? There are several stores in here."

"Yes, hundreds," Janice said. "Sometimes I could sneak and sleep in here, but I usually got caught."

Mista went to the Toys-R-Us. The first counter he came to was a pile of monster trucks, some radio controlled. "Ah," he said, "these must be on sale."

"So?" Shawnah said. "We don't want trucks!"

"Oh. How about Legos?"

"No. That's for boys."

"Erector sets?"

"No way. Come on. I'll show you what we want," Shawnah said, pulling his hand.

The first stop was the Ipod counter. Shawnah immediately pointed to a pink Nano. She knew exactly what she wanted.

"Okay. Let's look around here, though and see what else there is." Mista noticed that Candy's eyes were riveted to the Ipods. Two cases down, he saw one about the same size as an Ipod, but cost less. "Look. This one has an FM radio and a mike built in. You could sing and record your own songs."

Candy stared. She had asked for a TV. Mista squatted beside her and said, "Would you rather have that than a TV? Maybe I could get a TV for each of your rooms in addition to these."

"Could I?"

"If that's what you want. I promised whatever you want. You aren't held by your first choice last night."

"Okay." Her friends had all had Ipods or MP3 players of some brand, but her mother never had enough money to buy her one. "We can download music, can't we?"

"Sure, but you can also listen to the radio and record whatever you want. How about it, Shawnah? Rather have this or the Ipod?"

It was a tough choice. The Ipod was what she wanted. But the radio ... "Ipod."

Mista flagged a clerk down and got one of each for them, and then took them around to another shelf and let them pick out cases for their MP3 players.

Janice had tagged along, wondering if she had made the right choice. Yes. She had never ever had a pretty dress.

Robin had wandered off. Mista found her at the game cage, watching a boy playing the demo on the Wii. Mista stooped down beside her and put his arm around her. "Is that what you want?"

"Yes. I never had a game. All the other girls had them but almost never let me play. Could I have a Wii?"

"Well ... it costs a lot more than what the others are getting."

"I was afraid of that." She looked away and tried to hide the tears standing in her eyes. She never got the really nice things.

"If I got that for you, you would have to share it."

"Then it wouldn't really be mine?"

Hoo boy. Now what do I do? I have to get it. "Look, part of learning about life is learning how to share. It would be yours, just yours. But you would have to share. I have money, and I am sharing it with you all right now. I could say that we need it for food and stuff, and we do. But I am willing to share with you. That make sense?"

"Yes, but if I am playing, they would take it away."

"You've never had anything that you could really count on keeping, have you?"

"No. I always had everything taken away."

"That's sad. Look, I'll get this for you and a few games."

Her eyes brightened and the put her arms around his neck. "Really? Just mine?"

"Yes. But you have to promise to share. Not on demand. But you can't play all the time, and when you aren't playing, you could let someone else play. Okay?" She nodded.

"You know, when I started out on this little job, you all were just something to get the job done. But now that you are here, I'm glad that we found you. You went to sleep in my arms last night, you know."

"I know. Is that all right?"

"You can do that anytime you want to. But normally, you should sleep in your own bed."

"But, I'm so lonely. Janice did too, didn't she?"

"Yes, she did. It must have been really hard, not having a daddy."

"Yes. All the other girls used to talk about what their daddies did all the time. Will you be my daddy?"

"If you still want me to after our job is over and done. I'll be glad to be your daddy."

"Thank you, daddy," she kissed him on the cheek.

"Call me Uncle Mista for now. That way, if you meet one of the bad men, 'Uncle Mista' will come natural to you."

"Okay."

Mista stood up and called the other girls over. Janice was already there, taking it all in. We're going to get a game. I want each of you to pick out a game that you like, or think you'd like. The game console will be Robin's but she will share with you all. The games will not have names on them, they will be everyone's." It took a few minutes for them to decide. The clerk was hovering, seeing commission dollars rolling up in his mind.

"Okay," Mista told the clerk. "Put that in your counter – we aren't done yet. The Wii is no good without a screen. We need a portable DVD player or two."

He picked out two portable players with 10" screens, one for the front seat and one for the back. Or for separate cars, if they rode separately on the trip down. "Pick out six or eight DVDs that you can watch while we are driving. I'm going to find some TV's and DVD players for your rooms."

After they had everything, Mista looked at the pile and said, "We're going to have to make about seventeen trips to the car with all this. Maybe I'll just put it all back but the Ipods and a game or two."

"No, no, no," they cried. "We'll help carry it!"

The clerk looked it over. Two TVs, two DVD players, two Portable DVD players, a Wii console, four games, and ten DVDs. "Tell you what. I'll put it all on a cart and you can pick it up at the loading dock. Just show them your ticket. The girls can take the Ipods with them if they want. I'll mark the ticket."

"Works for me," Mista said.

Then he looked at Janice. She was looking at the pile. None of it was hers. She had asked for a dress. Mista said, "Alright, hon. Your turn. You wanted a dress, right? Do you know where to find what you want?"

She nodded, her eyes shining. She was afraid that he had forgotten. Mista said, "You've been here before. You already know what you want."

"Yes."

"Okay. Take me there."

She took him to a dress shop in the mall and showed him a dress on display. It had several layers of lacy chiffon skirts, and a silk bodice with pink ribbons worked into the silk. Her eyes were shining.

Mista stooped down and put his arm around her. "It's beautiful, isn't it?"

"Yes."

"And you would look beautiful in it."

"Really?"

"Yes, really. I mean it. You would be beautiful. But there is a problem."

"It costs too much."

"No. Well, it might. I bet it cost $1000 or more. But that's not the main problem. Where would you wear it? Maybe to the inaugural ball of a princess somewhere. But we don't know any princesses, and aren't likely to get invited."

"I know. But I could just look at it. Maybe wear it around the house and pretend."

"You could do that. But I think that would get old after a while. I have an idea. Why don't we get you a couple of really nice dresses that you could actually wear to church or wherever." Her eyes fell. "AND, then go down to the toy store and get a Barbie collection. A princess doll, two or three friends, dresses galore and a Barbie castle."

"Really? Okay." She was jumping up and down. "Okay. Let's go." She ended up with three Barbies. Two to play with, with different hair styles, and one fashion doll in a wedding dress, boxed in its own display case. She also got the Barbie Castle set.

They got the car and went around to get their purchases. Mista looked at the pile and said, "It's going to take the whole car, just for your stuff. You all will have to walk home."

"No, we can't."

"Well, we could put you all in the front and strap you down good. Or we could leave some of this."

"Oh, no," they said. "We'll help. We can get it all in."

Once they were loaded, Mista said, "Before you get too involved, lets stop at a Sonic and get hamburgers and fries, and then ice-cream."

Nobody argued with Robin for the front seat. She had her game out and one of the DVD players. They had the other DVD player in the back and watched a DVD. Janice held one of the Barbies and just looked at it. Mista looked back and said, "Hon, you look just like your Barbie." *I bet she's never had a doll before. Not a new one, anyway. Maybe somebody's old broken one.*

"No I don't."

"Sure, you do. Button nose, blue eyes and light brown hair. Just like her."

"My skin is all rough. And my hair is almost black. And my eyes are brown."

"Don't worry. Aunt Sharra and Jasmine will go to work on it, and it will look as nice as anybody before long."

She sat back in the seat and closed her eyes. She still couldn't believe it. It was just like Cinderella, and it was all too good to be true. But she actually had the doll in her hand.

The next morning was Sunday. Janice picked the most frilly dress to wear. When they were all in the common room, about ready to go, Janice said, "I've never been to church. What do you do?"

Shawnah said, "You sit on a hard bench for an hour and pretend to listen."

Candy said, "You can't talk and you can't close your eyes, or you might go to sleep."

"You can sleep," Robin said, "if you are careful not to fall over and make a noise."

"And you can't use any dirty words in church," Shawnah said. "It's BORING."

"It doesn't have to be boring," Jasmine said. "The church we go to is very nice."

Shawnah said, "A white church? They won't let me in."

"They let me in, honey, they'll let you in."

"It's still boring. Can I take my Ipod and listen to music?"

"No," Jasmine said. "I can take you to my home church. I'll guarantee it won't be boring."

"A black church?"

"Black as black can be. Whiteys that come don't stay. They can't stand it."

Chapter 14

Each family had a mobile home or travel trailer for the times when they were on assignment away from home. They spent the day Monday checking out all the equipment and vehicles. Mischal took the Range Rover in to have a trailer brake control installed. Mista set up his server in his trailer. He had built a cage that held the computer on gimbals so that it would always ride with the drives flat, no matter how the trailer turned or swayed the main drive was solid state, but still he wanted to hold it as immobile as possible. He made sure that his automatic satellite antenna was tracking and that he had good connection. Then he checked the computers in the other trailers and motor homes to make sure that they had wireless connection with the server. Next he moved two of the girls' computers into Charly's motor home and connected them to the server. The server would maintain Internet connection by satellite while traveling, and the other computers would have connection to the server and thus to the Internet. His server was also a mail server and internet server. The girls could continue their chat sessions even while riding, or stopped over night.

They pulled out of their home base about 10:00 Tuesday morning. It was a late start, but they had reserved parking places in a KOA campground near Gainesville, Florida for the night, so they only had a six-hour trip. Mista wanted to arrive in the Tampa area early the next day, so that he would have time to find a place to park for their search. If necessary, they could park overnight at a Wal-Mart, or rent parking spaces in a local park for a night or two.

They were about two hours south of Atlanta when Charly called Mista. "We need you over here."

"Now?"

"Yes."

"Okay. You okay driving, Sharra?"

"Sure. I won't drive as fast as you do, though. I don't like the way the trailer pulls the car when those trucks whiz by."

"Shouldn't be so bad this time. I had a Henley Hitch put on, remember? It is supposed to keep the swaying to almost nothing, and in fact it seems to be working quite well."

"Okay. I'll try it."

He pulled off onto the emergency lane and got out. The other four drivers pulled off behind him and he walked back to Charly's motor home. "What have we got, a fight?"

"No, no. Just get back there and see what's going on." She called Sharra. "Ready to go on whenever you are."

Traffic was heavy, and the trucks were slow on acceleration with the trailers behind them, so they had to wait for a break. Once they were all on the highway again, Mista called Sharra. "Why don't you pull off at the next rest stop, and we'll all take a break."

"Gotcha."

"All right, what's going on here?" he said.

All the girls were crowded around one monitor, watching as Shawnah worked. They had put the computers on the floor under the table and the monitors on the table, one facing each way. Shawnah was in a chat session with someone, and all the girls watched. Robin moved back so that Mista could sit on the bench, and then sat on his lap.

Just as he sat down, he heard a motor start up behind him. "Oh. Forgot about that." They had four large batteries in the back of the motor home feeding a heavy-duty inverter. It could provide up to 2000 watts of power. They also had a generator installed that kept the batteries charged. It kicked on automatically when the charge got low.

Shawnah pulled her top off her shoulders and refocused the camera mounted on the monitor. She framed the picture so that it looked like she had nothing on. She typed, "Sending a new pic. U wanna see more?"

"Yes. Move the camera down. (pant, pant)"

"Naw, I ain't a grown lady. I ain't got nothing to show."

"Sure u do. I like em tiny. New buds."

"Naw, I better not. My uncle might come in and u know what he'd say."

"He's not home, is he?"

"Naw, but he might come home any time."

"U act chicken."

"Can't get caught. He'd take away my privileges."

"Just a peek."

She moved the camera down a little, watching her monitor picture, until it just showed the top of her blouse.

"Okay, here's another."

"That's no better."

"Wait one."

She got up on her knees, pulled her skirt down a little and pulled her blouse up. Then she focused the camera on her midriff.

"Here u go. Best I can do. Not too bad for a skinny little girl, is it?"

"UR not skinny."

"U should see my mom." She sat back down.

"Come on, just one little peek."

"Naw. Not on the air. Somebody'd see it and I'd be all over the I-net. My uncle wd kill me."

"I won't share it."

"Tell u what. I'll take a pic tonight of my legs. U like underskirt?"

"Oh, yeah. Send that."

"How old R U?"

"27"

"I'm 11, you know that."

"I know. I like em young. You cum to Louisville, I'll show some real good times."

"Well, my uncle was talking about maybe going. I'll try to come with him."

"Oh, yeah. You send that pic."

"Okay. I'll try to be on tomorrow PM. After school. If I can."

"U B Here."

"See u later."

She cut the internet connection and sat back. "Whew. That was scary."

"You did very well," Mista said. "Are you going to send a picture of your legs?"

"I don't know. I could wear my bathing suit under my skirt and he won't know the difference. Oh, no. Mine has flowers on it. That won't do."

"You can wear mine," Candy said. "It's white. He won't know."

"Is that all right, Uncle Mista?"

"I don't know. Remember, you don't want to actually show too much. No porn."

"But we wear bathing suits all the time. That's nothing."

"I guess that's so."

"You said we should entice them," Candy said. "My mother always used to say that men don't think with their brains, but with their gonads."

Just then the motor home slowed. Charly called back, "Rest stop."

Mista said, "Why don't you sign on with a new screen name. No camera views, but send him an email picture. Say that Meena chickened out, but she showed you the picture, and you were sending it. Say her uncle caught her taking the picture and he wanted to know why, and then he suspended her privileges."

"Hey, I like that. You did catch me, sort of. At least you know."

Charly pulled into a parking lane and stopped. She got out to stretch, and Sharra came in. "What was the big emergency?"

Shawnah said, "I was chatting with a guy in Louisville, Kentucky. He wanted me to send pictures of myself naked. I teased him a little, but I wanted Uncle Mista to see what was happening."

"Oh. Well, that's good. Louisville. You going there, now?"

"Could be. You want to?"

"I don't know. Let me think about it. I wonder if my mother is still there."

"You don't know where your mother is?" Robin asked.

"No. I haven't had any contact with her in years."

"Why?"

"Well ... She was loving, but she let some bad things happen. My father died or was killed—I don't know which – and I didn't like my stepfather. When I went away to college, I never went home again. I didn't even tell her where I went to college."

"How did you pay for it if she didn't know?" Shawnah asked. "College costs a lot."

"I worked a full time job, and got student loans. When I got out, I lucked into a good job and paid off the student loans as fast as I could."

"Oh."

"I think I would like to go back. We'll talk about it later."

Sharra left, and Mista said, "You girls shouldn't be running around when you're moving. You really should have seat belts on, but I don't think there are any back here."

"Why seat belts," Shawnah asked. "This thing doesn't move much. It's real stable."

"You never know when something might happen. Somebody might change lanes suddenly and make her brake hard or something. When we came down last fall, somebody shot at us."

"Shot at you?" Robin asked, her eyes wide. "With a gun?"

"Yeah. You think with a sling shot?"

"No, but … for real?"

"Yeppers. Somewhere along here. Blew out my tires, and one of Uncle Mischal's. We managed to stop, but if you had been in his motor home you'd have been thrown all over the place. Come on, let's go outside and walk some."

They got up and followed him out. Robin took his hand, "Why did they shoot at you, Uncle Mista? Did they hate you?"

"No, they didn't even know me. They were terrorists and were trying to stir up trouble. They claimed that it was because we had a black woman riding with us. But that was just an excuse. It got pretty bad before we finally found them all and put them in jail. Here, look." He pulled out his collapsible staff and extended it. "This is a weapon, the one that I prefer to use if I have to fight. See that bent part there?"

They all looked. "One of them shot at me, and I managed to stop the bullet with this staff. Just a little off, and poof! No more Mista."

Mischal came up just as he said that. "Is he telling you how good he is with that staff? It was just blind luck."

"It could have hit him, though, Uncle Mischal," Janice said.

"Could have, but didn't. He's lucky that way."

"At least, it worked. You can't say that."

"Hah." Mischal walked off.

Mista said, "I think you better stay off the Internet the rest of the afternoon. Watch videos or something. That's why I bought you so many."

Robin said, "Can I ride with you, Uncle Mista?"

"Me too," they all said.

"Well, there are already three of us in the car and only four seats. I guess three of you could ride in the rumble seat and watch the trailer bounce up and down."

Robin said, "What's a rumble seat?"

"In old cars they sometimes had a seat installed in the trunk that popped up for extra people. You had to face backwards. But, we don't actually have one. You could stand on the back bumper."

"Oh," Candy said. "Let's watch videos."

Robin said, "I'm going to ride with them. I can play my game."

Once they were on the road again, Sharra said, "Why did she come? Little pitchers, you know."

"Sorry. Didn't know it would be a problem. Want me t…"

"No. We'll talk later."

Chapter 15

They rolled into the KOA camp that evening without further incident. Mischal unhitched his Jeep and went into town to get some fried chicken. After they had all retired to their individual campers, Sharra said, "I think I would like to go back to Louisville and see if mother is still there. I should mend fences if I can."

"Well, this trail might just lead there. I think that call this afternoon was just a fluke, but … you never know. What kind of business was your father in. Freight, I know, but …"

"I don't know, really. I was only six, you know. I remember him coming home from trips and giving me bear hugs, and then sitting on his lap while he watched TV. Like you do with your girls. They are getting a little old for it, though, don't you think?"

"No. They've never had fathers, and they are loving it. It will grow old after a while as they get used to us, and as they grow older."

"Well, just be careful. You'll teach them to want some boy to treat them the same way."

"Right now, they are lonely and scared, and missing the father they never had and their mothers too."

Just then the door opened and Robin and Janice jumped in, and said, "Boo! We came to be rocked to sleep again."

Mista gathered them up and said, "This is getting to be a habit."

"Yep."

"Can we sleep with you, Uncle Mista," Janice asked.

"No, I don't think that's a good idea. Bed's not big enough for four people, anyway."

"Can we sleep in here?" Robin asked.

Mista looked at Sharra. She shrugged. "You could do that, I suppose. You need to get a robe or something, though, and tell Aunt Em that you'll be here, so she won't worry about you."

"I don't have a robe," Robin said.

"I don't, either. We didn't buy robes," Janice said.

"Hmmm. It'll be daylight in the morning. You can't run around the campground like this."

"They can wear a couple of my robes in the morning," Sharra said.

Mista whispered in Robin's ear, "Go kiss your Aunt Sharra."

Robin jumped up, and Janice followed. They ran over and hugged and kissed Sharra. "Thank you, Aunt Sharra."

"Go tell Aunt Em," she said.

"Looks like they're keepers," Mista said, when they had gone.

"What about the other two?"

"I don't know. They didn't warm up this fast. Maybe they will. They have nowhere to go, though. We can't just turn them out."

"No, but maybe somebody else will take them."

"Yeah. Shawnah seems to be drawn to Jasmine. I don't know about Candy, though. I think she's trouble. I'm not sure I believe her story."

"I'll find out later. It doesn't really matter at this point."

The girls came back and jumped up in his lap. "We're back."

"I noticed."

Chapter 16

They did not find anything suitable on a quick sweep along the beaches, so he turned back toward Tampa at Tarpon Springs. He arranged for a week stay at the RV park near Temple Terrace, and they set up camp.

Next, Mista called Commander Moskeffet, commander of the special investigations division of the Florida Highway Patrol, and told him what he was doing. They had worked with him before, so he was willing to hear Mista out.

"Just be careful, son. Don't get illegal on this. Better keep the local sheriff informed, also."

"I'll touch base with him, but I don't want to tell him everything."

"I think you had better."

"Maybe. If any hint leaks out, my quarry will go to ground. I'll talk to him in the morning."

Mista made an appointment with the sheriff the next morning and took Mischal with him. All he told him was that he was looking for a particular sex pervert, and had followed his trail to the Clearwater area. They showed him their Georgia State Police ID cards.

"Why is this being handled by the Georgia police instead of Florida?"

"We first heard of him in the Atlanta area, and are following his trail. It might lead to him here, or we might go on to another place. Or, we might lose him completely. Also, we will probably turn up some other perverts. If I get any evidence, I will preserve it carefully and turn it over to you after we are done."

"Why not let us handle it?"

"If we move too soon, I'm afraid my quarry will bolt or go to ground. We will be discreet, and we will be careful to give you full details. If you need us later to follow up any prosecution, we will be available."

"Just don't break any laws. This sounds like a vigilante action to me."

"I assure you that it is not. I have informed Commander Moskeffet of our plans. We have worked with him before. Here is his office number – you might want to call him and verify that I am for real."

"I will do that."

On the drive back, Mista said, "The more I think about it, the less I like the idea of making a temporary camp. If we were only going to be here a few days, it would be okay. But we might be months on this trail."

"Yes, so?"

"Well, we'd have to arrange for an electric meter, water meter and sewerage. Let's see if there aren't more RV camps around. I just happened to know about this one, because it's near Camping World."

They asked the camp manager if there were other parks around.

"Of course. Do you find us unsatisfactory?"

"Not at all. The thing is, we need to work in and around Tarpon Springs, and that is kind of a long drive."

"Oh. Well, there is a KOA campground at Tarpon Springs, I'm sure. Let me see." He opened his directory and said, "Yes. It's in Palm Harbor. That's near Tarpon Springs."

"Yes," Mista said. "I know exactly where it is. It happens that I was born in Crystal Beach, about a mile away from there. Thanks."

Mischal said, "It's still early. Want to go check that one out?"

"Sure, let's go."

The campground was full until past the weekend, but they liked the location. Mista asked for six slots next to each other beginning the following Monday.

"Hmmm. I've got five right near the gate, here. And one more, but it's a ways off. Why so many?"

"We have five campers in our group, but I wanted one for vehicles."

"You've got room for two vehicles at each slot. How many do you have?"

"Let me see the map," Mischal said. "What is that, one block over?"

"Yeah, about a block."

"That's not so far. We could put Njondac's there. He won't be in it except to sleep. Then we could leave one open in the middle for tables and things."

"Works for me," Mista said. "You have a monthly rate?"

"Sure. Five days buys a week, three weeks buys a month. I lose a little on rent, but cuts down on traffic and setups."

"Okay. I'll pay for one month in advance. I'd like an option to take a second month if we need it."

"If you give me at least a week's notice."

"Done." Mista gave him his American Express card. "We might not come in on Monday, but hold the spaces. We will be here."

"You've paid for Monday; it's yours."

Chapter 17

Njondac had found some wood somewhere, and he and Mischal had built a fire. They had their roasting racks out, waiting for the fire to burn down to coals and then they would cook a batch of steaks.

Mista sat back in his chair and was talking with Sheila about possibilities. "You should have come with us this afternoon. We will be only a couple of miles from where we used to live. Do you remember it at all?"

"A little. It's probably changed a lot in 25 years."

The door opened and Candy and Robin came in. Candy was wearing jeans, and Robin had Janice's short skirt on and a halter top. Candy said, "Uncle Mista, she won't share her Wii with me."

Robin sat on the arm of his chair. "I do share. But I just started a game."

"So, what you really meant," Candy, "was that she wouldn't give it to you right then. Right?"

"Yes. She's supposed to share. You said."

"Yes, I did tell her to share. Does she share it sometimes?"

"Yes, sometimes. Only when she wants to."

"Well, if she does share it, then she has met her responsibilities. You can't just demand it anytime you want it."

"Well, take her side. I didn't really want it anyway." She stomped out and slammed the door.

Robin had the beginnings of tears in her eyes, but had not actually begun to cry. She said, "Uncle Mista, I do share it. A lot, really."

Mista put his arm around her and pulled her into his lap. She laid her head on his chest. "I'm sure you do. Don't worry about it."

"But she's always demanding that I give it to her. Especially just when I start a new game."

Mista squeezed her once, and then turned her so that she sat on his knees, facing him. "Don't worry about it. There are a couple of rules to observe here. One, the game is yours. Absolutely and completely. You could refuse to share it with anyone if you wanted to."

"But you said…"

"I said you would have to share as a condition for me to buy you an expensive toy. And you should. Let's think about this."

The door opened and closed, but he paid it no attention. *I guess Sheila went out.*

"First of all, it is yours. You control it. Stand up for your rights and don't ever let anyone bully you. Okay?"

"Yes, but…"

"We have a conflict of rules here. Learn from it. One rule says that it is yours. The other says that you should share. Both are right. If you are generous and kind, you will share, even if you don't have to. And you don't really have to, any more. The newness is worn off, and other things are happening. You still should share it, but now you will because you are a good person, not because I said. Does that make sense?"

"Yes. I want to get along with the others, and I don't mind sharing."

"Then you have the idea. Did your mother talk to you much about right and wrong?"

"Not really. She used to yell at me, if she was sober, -- and actually yell more if she was drunk. But she never talked about things. Just yelled if she didn't like something, and I never knew why she didn't. And sometimes she would yell and sometimes she wouldn't. I mean, some things just seem right, but I don't really know why."

"We will spend some time learning why things are right or wrong. Sharing is right and good, and you should not have to be told to share. Bullying is wrong."

"I kind of knew that."

Mista pulled her to him and said, "Good."

She lay there a minute, and then she sat up, sliding down on his knees until she was in his face. "Uncle Mista, I got a hit today." Her voice was very soft.

"You did? Good. What happened?"

"He wanted me to take my top off, but I wouldn't do that. I pulled it down a little and sent him a pic, but that's all."

"That's good. We don't want porn. You know what porn is, don't you?"

"Not really. Dirty pictures."

"When a girl or woman takes some of her clothes off and has pictures made just to make men get aroused, that is usually called soft porn. Partially undressed. Taking all your clothes off is porn. Having sex and taking pictures of it to show is hard-core porn. There are a lot of things in between, but you get the idea?"

"Yes. Well, I didn't want to, so I didn't. He wanted to come over and see me." She looked down and looked about to cry again.

Mista said, "And you are afraid to let him come over?"

"Yes," she said, almost inaudibly.

"But I guess I have to. You said that is what this is all about. They have to come over."

Mista waited a beat and then put his hands behind her back and laced his fingers together. "Robin. You don't have to do any of this if you don't want to."

"But, you said that the reason you took us was to get these men to come over."

"And you're afraid that if you don't, that I might send you away?"

She nodded.

Mista pulled her to him and squeezed her. "That won't happen. Yes, this project is to attract men and catch them. But none of you have to do anything that you don't want to. I'm glad all of you are here, and I won't send any of you away."

She relaxed and wiped away the one tear that had escaped.

Mista said, "Things have changed. I think I was wrong to set you girls up as bait."

"No, we don't mind. It's just that this man, he kept insisting and I got scared."

"Well, just cut him off. Put him in your blocked name list. He will probably change his screen name and try again when he realizes that he is blocked. If he keeps it up, I'll call AOL and ask them to ban him. I don't want you to use your body to entice anyone. I might have said that, but I don't think it is a good idea. If he asks for more, just tell him that you can't do that.

"Also, don't invite him over. I want them to come, but I want the log to show that they made the first request to come here, without any prompting from you."

"Okay. Thanks, Uncle Mista." She looked over to her right briefly. Mista looked there for the first time and was surprised to see two other girls sitting on the floor.

"Oh. When did you come in?"

"A long time ago. We were listening," Janice said.

"Where's Candy?"

"Playing with the Wii."

Robin started to jump up, but Mista held her down. "No, I'll deal with it later."

"But I didn't tell her she could play with it!"

"Of course not. You were here. Is it really a problem?"

"No, but she should have asked."

"Yes, she should. You should share, but she should always ask. I'll talk to her. How long have you two been here?"

Janice giggled. "All the time."

"Good, then you heard everything. I will give to you freely and generously. Not necessarily everything you ask for, because if you get everything you set your eyes on, nothing has any value any more. But what I do give you, I expect you to share. I do not demand it. You heard me say that. I expect you to because you want to be a generous person. Understand? There is a great difference in doing what is right because you want to and doing it because you have to. Make sense?"

"Yes," Janice said.

"All right. Now, as long as you are with me, I want you to think of me as father. Call me Uncle Mista, so that you will be in the habit of saying that if we have visitors. I will ask you to do certain things, and I will tell you to do certain things. I will tell you not to do certain things. Now, here is a difficult question. If I ask you to do something, and you really don't want to, what should you do."

"Do it anyway," Shawnah said.

"No," Janice said. "He said we don't have to do things just because we have to."

"No, he didn't," Robin said. "He said he wanted us to do things because we wanted to. But," her face screwed up, "if we don't want to, I guess we should do it anyway, because we want to do what he says. What should we do, Uncle Mista?"

"I want you to want to do it because I asked, and you trust me to know what is right. I can ask you to want to do something that you really don't want to do, but be willing to do it anyway – in good spirit – because you know that that is what I want. That make sense?"

"Yes, sort of," Janice said.

"Okay, now if I ask you to do something that you *really* don't want to do, what do you do."

Robin shrugged. "Just do it."

"Let me give you an example. Take this man you were chatting with today. Go ahead and entice him. He wants you to take of your top and send him a pic, go ahead. Do it. In fact, go ahead and take it off now."

"No!" Then she looked down at the top, closed her eyes and said, "Okay. If that's what you want." She started to pull it up. Janice put her hand over her mouth.

Mista put his hand over hers and said, "Whoa. Do you think it would be wrong to take it off now, in front of me?"

"I don't know if it's wrong, but I *really* don't want to do it. I'd feel real funny."

"Then, what should you do?"

"Uncle Mista, I'm confused. First you said do what you say, and now ... I don't know."

"Anybody else know the answer?"

Janice said, "Tell you that we really don't think that we should?"

"Exactly. Go to the head of the line."

"What do you mean?" Janice asked.

Shawnah said, "In school sometimes we line up and the teacher asks us questions. If you get the answer right, you get to go to the head of the line. Then you get something nice, like being first in the lunchroom."

"Oh."

"If you really don't want to do something, then tell me, and tell me why. As best you can. You are scared to, you feel funny, you think it's wrong. Whatever. I'm not talking about being willful or hateful. You understand the difference?"

"Yes," Robin said.

"Now I don't expect you to be perfect little angels. But I do hope you will try to do the right thing all the time. And, just for the record, I do

NOT want you to show me your boobs. That would be wrong. And do not send pics of them, even if they ask. Robin, you did exactly right this afternoon. You got scared and didn't want to invite him here. That's fine. Don't do it if you don't want to. You did one thing wrong, though. What was it?"

She pulled her top back down and said, "I don't know." She had not actually moved it up any, but she pulled down on it anyway.

"You were afraid to tell me that you didn't want to do it."

"But, you said that is what this is all about. I wanted to do it because you wanted me to, but I didn't *really* want to."

"Exactly. But you should not have been afraid to tell me. This is not the army or something where you have to obey orders. I don't want any of you ever to be afraid to tell me what you think about anything. I might not like what you think, and I might disagree with you. But don't be afraid to tell me. I won't yell at you and I won't punish you for your thoughts. I might try to change your mind, if I think you're wrong. But it is important for you to learn to think for yourselves, and not be afraid to express your opinions to anyone. Is that understood?"

"Yes, Uncle Mista," they chorused.

"You know, I think something terrible is about to happen," Mista said.

"What?" asked Janice.

"I think I am about to fall in love with all of you."

"Why is that bad?" asked Robin.

"Me too?" asked Shawnah.

"Of course, you too. I didn't leave anybody out. Even my sister sitting over there like a silent ghost. But, it will be too hard to let you go after this is over."

"You can't let us go," Robin said. "You promised."

"I promised? How?"

"You said that if we wanted to stay you would keep us and even adopt us. You promised."

"Hmmm. I did promise, didn't I? Well, it won't be hard to keep that promise. Both parts."

"Both? That's one promise …"

"I also promised to let you go if you want to. I don't want to turn you out into the street, but I can probably find homes for you if you want to leave."

"We *don't* want to leave," said Janice.

Mista said, "Well, that might change in time." Robin was shaking her head. "Living with us could be a hard life."

"Not as hard as living on the streets," Janice said.

"Maybe, maybe not. We are always going to different places and doing dangerous things. That's why we have a teacher. Aunt Em is our teacher because none of our children will be in regular school. You won't have any friends, because we don't stay in one place. And you will have to do hard things. Having these men come to the house is going to be hard, and it could be dangerous. Don't forget – don't ask them, and don't entice them. The kind of men that I want to catch will want to come simply because you are eleven. They don't really care what you look like, even though they do want pictures. Okay?"

"Okay."

"Well, I think maybe a trip into town is in order. Any body need new DVDs?"

"Yes, yes, yes," they all said.

"You've looked at all of the ones you have?"

"Yes, five or six times each," Janice said.

"Run along and play, now. I have to go talk to Candy."

He found her in the girls' trailer, playing with the Wii. "I thought you didn't want to play with that?"

"Oh. Well, Robin said I could."

"Candy, I want you to learn two things. One, do not ever lie to me again."

"Well, she did. I'm not lying."

"She has been with me and the other two girls since you left. She could not have told you that you could play with it."

Candy turned sullen. "Well, she would have, if I had asked her. You told her she had to share."

"She probably would have. I do want her to share with you, and I believe that she will. But you told me that she said you could play with it, and that is a lie. That's a problem, not the fact that you are playing with it."

"It doesn't matter. You know that she would."

"It does matter. The lie matters, and courtesy matters. Even though she should let you play with it, especially when she is doing something else, you still should always ask. Never assume. That is simple courtesy, and I do want you all to be generous and courteous with each other. Okay?"

"Can I still play with it?"

"You will have to ask her. It's not my toy."

That night Janice and Robin came over to Mista's trailer when they were ready for bed and climbed up in his lap. Mista said, "This is getting to be a habit."

They both giggled. "Robin said, "Yeppers." She started to snuggle, and then she sat up. "Uncle Mista. How do you know what is right and wrong?"

"Whoo! I could take a whole year and not answer that question properly. What did you have in mind?"

"Nothing. I just wondered."

"What did you have in mind. Don't be afraid to tell me."

"Well." She played idly with a button on his shirt. "When you told me to take off my top. I didn't feel right about it, but you said it would be wrong. Is it wrong to undress in front of people?"

"Hon, I can't give you a quick answer to that one. I think it would be wrong for me to ask you to put on a show for me, and I also think it would be harmful to you. I will not do anything deliberately harmful to you, just to be doing it."

"People do. Undress, I mean."

"Yes. Grown women do. In movies, in dances, sometimes on the beach. A lot of people think that it is wrong, and they make laws against it. But a lot of people think it is all right, and do it anyway. But adults can do pretty much as they like as long as they don't hurt someone. I do not watch movies with naked women in them. I do not find them amusing."

"Oh. Okay."

"Now, let me ask you something. Could there ever be a time when I would ask you to take your top off and it would be okay?"

"I don't know."

"Suppose you were riding a bike or something and fell and hurt yourself. It might have to come off for me to help you. Or it might be snagged on something. Or what if you got cut real bad, and I had to bandage it? If you see a doctor, he will ask you to undress and examine every part of you. That's important for him to know what might be wrong with you. There are times when it is the only right thing to do. But just to show yourself? No, don't do that."

"Okay."

"You know Miss Chandri?"

"Yes."

"You think I would ask her to take off her clothes?"

"Nooo."

"Well, I did, once. I told you that we do dangerous things sometimes. A man forced us off the road when we were driving one night. He wanted us to wreck and kill us. We did wreck, and ended up in a river in the car. We had to swim out, and I told her that she should take off her skirt so she could swim. Sometimes, you have to."

"Did you look?"

Mista smiled. Of course she had to ask. "No. It was totally dark."

"Oh." She snuggled into Mista's arm. "I love you, Uncle Mista."

"Me, too," Janice said.

"I love you two also, " Mista said.

Chapter 18

The rest of the week passed without further incident. The girls continued their chats, but got no hits. Their chat logs were normal for their age. They went into Tampa one afternoon for a shopping trip. This time, Mista insisted on taking Sharra along.

They picked out 13 DVDs, mostly romance stories and horse stories. Then Robin asked, "Could I have a Barbie of my own, Uncle Mista?"

"I suppose so. Doesn't Janice share with you?"

"Oh, she does, but I just wanted one of my own so we could play together."

"Okay. Let's go see if they still sell them."

She picked out the one she wanted and got some accessories to go with her. Then Shawnah said, "I want one, too."

"Okay. Pick one out."

When they had what they wanted, he turned to Candy. "You want one, too?"

"No. They are for little kids."

"Oh. I never played with dolls, so I wouldn't know. You can put them back, if you're too old for them."

"Nooo," Robin said. "I'm not too old."

Candy sulked around in the store, not finding anything that interested her. Mista said, "Would you like a game of your own for the Wii?"

"No. I want a PlayStation and some games for it. They have better games."

"No, I think that's a little too much money. More than twice as much as the Wii, you know."

Candy shrugged. "You can afford it."

"I can, but that's not the point. If you see something else, we'll buy that." She turned on her heel and walked off.

"Don't go far," Mista said. "We need to stay together."

Candy ignored him and disappeared into the mall.

Sharra said, "Now what do you do?"

"I don't know. That's the problem with taking on half-grown girls without knowing anything about them."

Robin took one hand and Janice took the other. "We won't leave you, Uncle Mista. She's a priss anyway."

"What do you mean?"

"She always wants her way anytime we are playing together. Won't share her Ipod, but demands things from us."

"Well, do the best you can with her. Like I told you, you control your own toys."

"She says she'll tell if we don't share."

"So? We've already been there. I know you do share, so don't worry about it."

Janice had not said anything, but was looking around the store with obvious longing. Mista said, "Do you want a PlayStation, too?"

"No, it costs too much."

"But your Barbie is no longer so special, now that everyone has one?"

"Yeah. But that's all right."

"Would you like something else?"

"No. Thank you."

She was quiet for a minute, and Mista asked Sharra if she could contact Candy.

"I'll try. I haven't read more than her surface, but that should be enough." She closed her eyes a minute and then said, "Yes, I have her."

"Okay, keep a mind's eye on her. If we have to, you can stop her, can't you?"

"Yes. Might be awkward, but …"

"Better than a police report."

Mista said, "Janice?"

"What?"

"You don't want anything?"

"Well, maybe a pretty new dress. They probably cost too much, too."

"Well, let's go see what we can find."

Janice tried on several dresses, but did not find one she liked. She wanted something special. Mista spotted a dark plaid dress with puffy sleeves and suggested it to her. He liked it on her, and Sharra said, "It picks up the color of her eyes."

Mista said, "I like that one, Hon. How about you?"

She stood in the mirror and turned around several times, looking at it from all angles. Mista said to Sharra, "How do girls learn to do that? I thought mothers taught them, but she didn't have one of them."

Sharra laughed. "It comes natural."

Janice walked over to Mista and Sharra. "What do you think, Uncle Mista?"

"I like it, but you have one little problem."

"What's that."

"You're getting fat."

"I am not!"

He smiled. "No, not really. However, you are putting on some flesh – and that's good. You needed to. I expect that you'll pick up a few more pounds, too. That dress is a little tight on you, now, and you would probably outgrow it in just a week or two. I don't know anything about girls' dresses, but do you think they might have it just a little bigger? Outside of that, I think it looks great on you."

Janice already had most of her height, but she was starting to fill out some. They did have a larger size. She took it, and then asked Sharra, "I'm not getting fat, am I?"

"No, darling. Uncle Mista is just teasing you. You are starting to fill out, like you should. You're fine. And the dress is beautiful."

"Thanks. Three dresses!"

Mista finished paying for the dress and came over in time to hear that. "At the rate you're going, you're going to have so many dresses that you can't wear them all."

She grinned. "That's all right."

"Well, let's go find our wayward member," Mista said.

They walked through the mall, looking. Mista stopped at a book store. "You all like to read? Get you something."

Janice said, "I can't read all that well."

"Well, we definitely need to get you something to read, then. Aunt Em will work with you on it. Pick out several books that you would like, and read, read, read. You have to be able to read in order to survive in this world."

"I can read, just not that well."

"Then, read until it comes easy."

They found Candy back in the toy store looking at the Barbies. Mista said, "Change your mind?"

"No. What else did you get your pets?"

"Nothing that I wouldn't have gotten for you if you had not run off. I asked you not to run off."

"Well, you said we didn't have to take orders."

"That's not exactly what I said. Well, I did say that, but I don't give orders. I do expect you to honor reasonable requests."

"Well, I chose not to. You give them everything that they want, and I get the left-overs."

"Candy, we both know that that is not true. Now, if you want to be selfish and sullen, no one can make you change. But you are hurting only yourself."

She tossed her head and started to walk out. Mista said, "We are leaving, now. Please come along." He walked out with Sharra, knowing that three would follow. He did not look back to see if Candy was coming.

Sharra realized that he was challenging her, and sent, *What if she doesn't come"*

"Then either we have to force her to come, or just leave her to her own devices."

We can't just leave her.

Why? She was never one of us, Sharra.

I think you are right, but we did bring her.

Can you control her?

Not easily. I could if we were in a battle situation, or were at home. In this crowd of people it would be quite a scene.

Well, we are in a battle situation, like it or not.

I could call Jeremy and ask him to join us. Or I could make an illusion of something and then force her to walk.

Well, let's see if she comes, first.

Candy watched them all leave. She was sure that they would stop and try to force her to come, also. When Mista kept walking, she called after him, "Don't you care if I come or not?"

He kept walking. She could not be sure that he even heard her. Suddenly, she realized that if she were left, she would be all alone in a strange city, with no idea where she was or where to go. She ran after them.

She caught them just as they were leaving the mall. "Didn't you even care if I came or not?"

"I care, but you made it clear that you only wanted to do what you chose to do. That being the case, I saw no reason to try to force you to do something that you did not want to do. If you want me to, I'll take you back to your home."

"I don't have a home any more."

"Wherever you want to go. Or, if you choose, you may stay with us and work on this project."

"I'll stay."

Mischal had steaks ready to cook on two of the grills when they got back. While they ate, Mista said, "Let's take a day off and go to the Fort De Soto State Park. It's supposed to be an interesting place. They have a playground there and beaches. The girls could go swimming."

"Swimming in January?" asked Candy.

"Sure. This is Florida. It should be in the seventies tomorrow."

Chandri said, "What if I want to go swimming, too?"

"Well, last time I checked, you were still a girl."

"Oh?" She raised an eyebrow. "When exactly and how did you 'check' me?"

"Oops. That didn't come out right. You are a girl, though, aren't you?"

Chandri said, "I thought you only asked Charly that question."

Mischal said, "I'd like to go swimming, too."

"Well, I didn't mean to limit it to certain people," Mista said. "I just thought it would be good to have an outing."

The outing did relax everyone. They had been there for nearly a week without much happening.

Chapter 19

They spent most of Monday morning getting the trailers and motor homes ready to travel. The adults were familiar with the routine of camping and knew that everything had to be in its place and be properly secured. It was a totally new experience for the girls. They had driven down from Georgia, but they had not done the preparations. They had not actually lived in a trailer, and the few possessions that they had were packed by one of the adults. It took an hour to get all of their clothes put away and all the new things stowed properly.

When they got to the new campsite, they discovered that one of the lots across the street from their primary five lots was now vacant, so they took that for Njondac.

When they had finished setting up the camp again, they went into Tarpon Springs for a seafood dinner. The girls had never eaten shrimp and had never eaten fresh scallops. "There is a rumor that a lot of scallops served in restaurants are really just little balls of meat cut from shark meat. I don't know if that's true, but my taste buds tell me that it is certainly possible. Real fresh scallops are like nothing else you have ever eaten," Mista told them.

The girls logged into the chat rooms when they returned. After about half an hour, Candy said, "Look. This guy wants to see more of me. Said take off my shirt and send him a pic. I'm going to, and see what he says."

Robin said, "Uncle Mista said not to. Said just being an eleven-year-old girl was enough enticement for the men he wants to catch."

"He didn't tell *me* that," Candy said.

"He told everybody," Janice said. "Weren't you there?"

"I guess not. He didn't tell me. You all have a private meeting?"

"No," Shawnah said. "Robin told him that somebody wanted to see her, and he said not. Said if he insisted, that she should block him."

"Well, he didn't tell me. Maybe that's because I have something to show." She took off her shirt and bra. "See? Anybody else got more?"

No one answered. "I guess not," Candy said. She turned toward her camera and took a picture and then sent it to the man she was chatting with.

Robin said, "I'm telling."

"Tattle-tale. You're his pet. You can do anything you like."

"I'm not a pet. Just because I do what he says."

Candy said, "He said we didn't have to do everything he says. Said he wanted us to think for ourselves."

Janice said, "He said that at the same time he said not to send pictures. You must have been there, if you heard that."

Candy had not been there, but had been listening outside of the door. She had been playing with Robin's Wii, but when the other two girls left, she followed to see if they were talking about her. When it became obvious from the conversation that they were about to break up, she went back to the trailer and resumed her game so that she would not be caught eaves-dropping.

None of the girls wanted to be called a tattle-tale, so no one left the trailer. Robin did say, "He also told us a long time ago that he wanted somebody to be with us when we were on line."

Janice said, "Yeah, that's right. I forgot about that." She signed off and went and got one of her new books to practice reading. She had never had opportunity to read for pleasure, and had been surprised at how the story caught her up.

Candy ignored them and went on with her chat, but Robin and Shawnah also signed off. After a while, Candy also signed off. She said, "Well, he liked what he saw and wants to see more."

"You still talking to him?" Shawnah asked.

"No, he had to go. Said he'd be back tomorrow. You're just jealous because you don't have anything up top."

"Am not," Shawnah said. The other two girls looked up but did not say anything.

Candy still had her shirt off. No one was in the trailer except the girls, so it did not matter whether or not they were dressed. However, Candy was pushing. "Let me see what you have."

"Why? So you can laugh?"

"No, I just want to see."

"Okay." Shawnah showed her.

Candy said, "Janice, how about you? You have anything?"

"I'm starting to fill out."

"Let me see," Candy said.

"Why? It doesn't matter."

"Sure it does. Girls with big boobs can get anything that they want. How about you, Robin? Let's see what you have. Maybe that's how you got to be the pet."

"Is not. I'm not a pet."

"Come on, show me."

"No. You just want to laugh."

"No, I don't," Candy said. "I won't laugh. Let me see them."

Robin reluctantly pulled up her shirt and bra. Candy said, "Well, you have more than I would have thought." She looked at her monitor. It happened that Robin was in the camera view. Candy adjusted the focus and shot a picture and saved it on her computer.

Robin said, "What did you do? Take a picture? You better not send that!" She yanked her shirt down.

"I will if I want to and there's nothing you can do about it."

Robin was near tears. "You better not send it."

"Or you'll do what? Go tell? Teacher's pet."

"You just better not sent it. You'll get us all in trouble."

Candy said, "You're acting like a little girl. Are you sure you're eleven?"

Robin colored and began to cry. "I'll be eleven next week. And you better not tell."

"Who cares? I'll be twelve in a month, so there. Go ahead and cry, little girl."

"Stop teasing her," Janice said. "She's done nothing to you."

Candy's lip curled. "Nothing except make sure she gets the best toys."

"That's not true," Janice said. Uncle Mista bought all of us something, and he offered to buy you just as much, but you didn't want any. That's nobody's fault but your own."

"Yeah, sure. What would he have bought me? A Barbie doll like little kids play with? A game machine for babies? I wanted a real game machine and some good games."

"You didn't even ask for anything else but an expensive game. Nobody else got anything that expensive."

"She got a Wii."

"That's less than half the cost of a PlayStation," Shawnah said.

"So?" Candy said. "He can afford it. I'm going to send your picture to my new guy and see who he likes better, Robin. I bet you don't get an IM from him!"

"Uncle Mista said not to send porno pictures, and I don't want mine sent out," Robin said. "You better not."

"And if I do, you'll tell? Tattle-tale." Candy turned away and went back to her computer.

Robin curled up in a ball in her chair, crying silently. Em and Sheila came in a few minutes later. Em said, "What's wrong, Hon?"

Robin glanced at Candy and then shook her head. "Nothing."

Em pulled Robin to her feet and then sat down in her chair. She took Robin in her arms and cradled her. After a minute, she whispered in her ear, "I love you, Little Bird. Would a dish of ice cream make you feel better?"

Robin shook her head, "No."

"Ah, I'll bet it would. Anybody like some ice cream? Come on. We've got some in Charly's camper."

When bedtime came, Janice started for the door as usual, but Robin crawled into her own bed and covered up with her sheet. Mischal had built two compartments into the front of the trailer for privacy and to give the girls a secure place to stay in case one of the girls had a visitor. Robin and Janice shared one room and Shawnah and Candy the other.

Janice put her hands on her hips and said, "Come on. Aren't you going over?"

Robin shook her head and pulled the sheet up over it.

Janice said, "Come on. He'll miss us."

"Unh-uh."

Janice pulled the sheet down and pulled on Robin's hand. Janice was bigger and a little stronger, but Robin did not resist all that much, anyway. When they were outside, Janice whispered fiercely, "Come on, don't be a baby."

"I'm not a baby. But …"

"If she does anything, I'll knock her down and punch her eye out. Ain't nobody can fight better than me."

"How'd you learn to fight?"

"If you don't learn to fight, you don't live long on the streets. I had to. Had to learn to hide in the shadows, and how to run. I'll teach you, if you want to."

"I don't like to fight."

"Well, you might have to some day. Charly's going to teach me how to use a sword."

"You're too young to use a sword."

"Unh-uh. She was eleven when she started taking lessons."

Mista was reading one of Janice's books when they went in. Janice clapped her hands and said, "Goody. You're going to read to us."

"Nope. You're going to read to me."

Robin curled up in his arm in a tight little ball, while Janice sat up and took the book."

"I can't read all that good yet."

"That's okay, it's just us. Do the best you can."

"But I don't even know all the words."

"If you come to one you don't know, just sound it out. You know how the letters all sound, don't you?"

"No, not really. Sort of."

"Then read. I'll help you if you need it. Nobody will laugh at you, and reading out loud is good practice."

Then he cuddled Robin and said, "What's wrong with you, dear?"

"Nothing."

"Yeah, sure. Let me guess. Somebody broke the Wii. No? They break the DVD player? Take your new Barbie? No? Hmmm. She discovered that you aren't quite eleven."

"You told him!" Robin said, looking at Janice.

"No, I didn't."

"She didn't. I knew you weren't eleven. That's all right. When's your birthday?"

"January 15th. How did you know?"

"Aunt Sharra knows everything. We've known all along. It's all right, you're close enough."

"Oh." She relaxed some, but Mista knew that something was still bothering her.

"What else, Hon?"

"Nothing."

"Uh-huh. Tell me."

Robin shook her head and burrowed deeper into his arm.

"Come on, you can tell me anything, remember?"

She just shook her head and set her jaw. Janice said, "Candy took her picture naked and is going to send it out on the Internet."

"Not naked. Just had my shirt up."

"I don't want you to send out pictures like that."

Janice said, "We told her that, but she said she was going to anyway."

"Where is the picture?"

"I don't know," Robin said. "She took it on her computer camera. I didn't know she was going to. I told her she better not send it out."

"Hmmm. I can …"

"If you say anything, she'll think we were tattling," Janice said.

"But you didn't tattle. I had to pry it out of you with a crowbar."

"She'll think so."

"Well," Mista rubbed his chin. "Let's see what we can do about that." He got up and went over to his computer, sat down and put Robin in his lap. Janice leaned on his shoulder.

He opened Candy's computer drive and searched for pictures. He found several that she had taken of herself, and one that she had named 'Robin'. "Is this it, Hon?"

"I don't know. I guess."

"Well, let's look at it and see."

"NO! Don't look at it."

Mista looked down at her and squeezed her. "Okay. You know how to open and close pictures, don't you? You open it and tell me if it is The Picture." He put her hand on his mouse and closed his eyes.

Robin looked up at him and then double-clicked the picture. She closed it right away. "Yes, that's it."

"Okay, stand over there and I'll take another picture of you. Make a face, look mad, do whatever you want. I'll get just your head. Then we'll save the new picture on top of the old one. If she does send it out, she'll get a surprise."

"Okay." Robin stuck out her tongue and put her thumbs in her ears. Mista showed her the picture and then copied it on top of Candy's picture of Robin.

"Happy now, Robin?"

"Yes, Uncle Mista. Thank you. I was afraid …"

"I know. But don't say anything at all to her, even if she finds out. You know nothing, right? You all know that I can look at anything on your computers, don't you? Remember that I read your chat logs, too. Not spying on you, it's for your protection."

"I didn't know you could look at everything," Robin said.

Janice said, "Me neither."

"Well, now you know. Let's go read."

He carried Robin over, and Janice followed and jumped up on him after he was seated. She read, slowly and hesitatingly at first, but as she gained confidence her reading improved. She missed some words, and stumbled on many, but she managed a complete chapter.

"Good," Mista said. "Practice makes perfect. Now let me read some of that to you the way you were reading. I'm not making fun of you, I want you to hear how you sounded." He read the way many people do when reading aloud, giving each word the same emphasis and reading word for word.

"Now, here is the way I would normally read that to you," he said. He read it with feeling, as if he were telling the story, not reading it. "See the difference? Try to do that. It will be hard at first, but give it a try."

She did, and improved a little. Mista said, "Good. That's better. When you read to us or even to yourself, try to make the story come alive like that. Okay?"

"Okay."

"Well, time to go to slee – uh-oh. Already lost one." Robin was asleep.

"Janice," Mista said, "I want to ask you something. You haven't had a home for a few years at least. Right?"

"Yes." She wondered what was coming.

"I don't need an answer, now, but I'd like to keep you after this is over. I like your spirit, and I like your spunk. I think you'll be a beautiful girl some day, maybe as beautiful at Charly. Maybe not quite as tall, but I bet you do grow tall."

"I like it here. I really, really would like to stay. I never dreamed that I could ever have anything like this."

"You don't have to give me a final answer. You will find that we are often in danger, and sometimes one or another gets hurt. We travel a lot, so you wouldn't be able to make many friends, and couldn't go to regular school."

"I don't go to school now. I wish I could. But I like the way Aunt Em is teaching us."

"Good. We'll see how it comes out. For now, I just want you to be secure and know that we already love you and want you to stay."

"Thanks, Uncle Mista." She leaned up and kissed him on the cheek. "I love you too."

She curled up in his arm. Mista thought that she had gone to sleep and was about to get up and put them to bed, when she suddenly said, "I was afraid to come at first. Somebody showed me your ad, but I didn't trust anyone. I carried a hunting knife that I had found for a while, just in case. I don't know when I started to trust you – and I never knew how nice it is to be able to trust someone."

A few minutes later, she said, "If I don't do what you say, you can spank me, okay? I don't want to mess up and make you not like me any more. So spank me to remind me to be good."

Mista leaned down and kissed the tip of her nose. "Hon, as long as you want to be good, you will do fine. Don't be thinking that you have to be a perfect little angel in order to get to stay. I like you just the way you are, warts and all. You will make mistakes, and you surely will do things that are wrong. I never knew a little girl that didn't. I promise you, I won't stop loving you just because you do something bad. Ask Charly. She was as naughty a girl as I have ever known. But never *really* bad. If you do something that is really bad, then we have to talk, and I will have to do something about it."

Her eyes popped open. "What is *Really* bad?"

"Something like doing drugs, sneaking alcohol, or stealing. Getting mad enough at Candy to cut her. I'm talking about really serious things. The other stuff – if you do something, don't ever lie to me about it. I cannot abide a liar. Tell me the truth and we'll figure out what to do about your mistake. Maybe nothing, maybe an extra task to make up for it. Maybe a spanking, if that is what you need. But if you lie about it and try to cover it up – or worse, blame it on someone else – then we will have a real problem."

"Can I blame it on Candy?"

"No, not anyone. Maybe Candy will learn to get along with you all too, one day."

"Okay." She curled up and was asleep in minutes.

Chapter 20

They had classes every morning and for an hour or two every afternoon. The next afternoon, Em left the girls alone after classes. "I'll be back in a little, if you want to go on line. Or maybe Sheila will come over."

Mista had asked her to stop by after classes. He said, "Are you enjoying your new teaching career?"

"Yes. They are mostly sweet girls. You'd think that with their backgrounds, they would be – well hard to get along with. Maybe they know how much they would miss if something went wrong."

"Yeah. Makes them value it more than if it were just routine. I always wanted to be a teacher, but it never seemed to work out. I did have a school for a few years, and taught some. But I was gone more than I was at home."

"Sure. Same now, except now you take the school with you."

"Yes. I didn't know I was going to take on four girls so soon, but your expressing an interest in teaching was one of the things that helped me decide to let you join us. How is Candy doing?"

"She's okay. She's smart and does her lessons. A little snotty at times, if you know what I mean. She acts like she is top girl, so I guess she actually is."

"How did that happen?"

"Girls always establish a pecking order, didn't you know that?"

"No," Mista said. "Not having grown up with a sister or sisters, and not getting involved with girls, I never knew that."

"Well, she's claiming the honors. It's not a vote, or anything verbal. It just happens."

"Hmm. Well, I had the impression that she did not get along with the others very well. Like they didn't like being bossed by her."

"No, they don't like it much, but nobody else has come out on top."

"Well, I was just checking up on them. It's been pretty quiet this past week. They are still going on line, aren't they?"

"Yes, every chance they get. I better get back over there. They want to get on line this afternoon."

Candy was already on line, talking to the man she had met yesterday. He had wanted to see more of her, so she pulled down her jeans and showed him a side view of her buttocks. "I wish we had cameras that ran all the time instead of having to click pictures and send them."

"Why?" asked Janice. "You want to send him a live show?"

"Yes. We could really get their attention."

"You didn't send him that picture, did you?"

"Yes, why not? He asked for it."

"Yeah, but Uncle Mista said not to," Janice said. "You're going to get in trouble if he finds out."

"How will he find out unless someone tattles?"

"He al –" Robin looked over at Janice. She shook her head slightly. "He could find out," Robin said.

"Only if you tell." She heard Em coming and sent "BRB" and signed off the computer. "I'm going to send him your picture when I sign back on. And you better not say anything, little girl."

"I –" she picked up a book and buried her face in it.

Em stepped in and looked around. She sensed a certain tenseness in the air, but it was not at all obvious what it was, so she went over and sat down in the easy chair in the corner of the room. Shawnah and Janice turned on their computers, and Candy signed back on. Robin took her book and curled up in Em's lap.

"Don't you want to get on line, Hon?"

"Not now. I'm reading." She really wanted to be somewhere safe if Candy did send that picture, and she did not want her face to show anything, so she hid behind her book.

After a few minutes, Candy typed, "I'm going to send you a funny pic. Tell me what you think."

He sent back, "Yeah, that's funny. It's not you, is it?"

"No, can't you tell?"

"I wasn't real sure."

"Well. It wasn't me." She signed off and looked around the room. Shawnah and Janice were on their computers and paying no attention to her. Robin was reading and she also was apparently not paying her any attention. She assumed that they did not know how her man had slighted her. She sat there looking at the blank screen for a long time.

After awhile Robin got up and went over and started her computer. She got a contact almost immediately. Someone she had chatted with several times IMed her as soon as she signed on. She did not know who it actually was, but he had said that he was a teen-age boy. None of their chats had anything of note in them. This time, however, as soon as she answered him, he asked if she had anyone else living with her. Another girl, that is.

She said, that she did share a room with another girl.

"What's her screen name?"

"I don't know. I shouldn't put it out, anyway."

"Ask her."

"No, I can't do that."

"You're one of Sam's girls, aren't you?"

"No. Why do you ask that? Who's Sam?"

"Don't play innocent. Your roommate sent me a pic of you. She didn't say who it was, but I recognized you."

"My roommate wouldn't do that."

"Well, she did. I even know the password. 'Allacalah', right?"

"No. I don't even have a password."

"Yeah, right. I'm coming over there. I want to see you, and her. She's sent me some neat pics, but you never send me anything but a head shot. I want to see what you look like. It's just a few miles. I'll be there in a minute." He signed off.

She sat there stunned for a minute, and then said, "He's coming over, Aunt Em. Right now. He'll be here in a few minutes."

"Who, Hon?" Em asked.

"I don't know. We've chatted a few times, but this is the first time he ever did anything. He said he's in his teens, but now I don't know."

"Well, let me get Mista."

She ran out and came back a minute later with Mista. Mista said, "All right, take your monitors to your rooms and scram. We only want one girl in here when he comes."

Robin said, "I had to tell him that I had a roommate."

"Oh. Well, Janice, leave yours set up."

He had set the computers up out of sight so that if someone did come over, they could quickly disconnect the monitor and keyboard and leave the room clean. The file server sat in a corner, but its screen was dark. Mista turned the monitor on and quickly checked her chat log. "Okay. I don't see anything in here. What picture did you send?"

"I didn't. I didn't send anything. I had just signed on. Ask Aunt Em." Here eyes were large and anxious.

Mista looked at her. "Okay. I believe you, Hon. I see you had only been on a few minutes. Could it have been the picture that Candy sent?"

Her eyes widened. "Yes, it could have been. I told her not to send it. You think it was the same man?"

"I'd bet on it. Okay, the sound bug is on, so I can hear what goes on in here. I don't want to be inside in case he decides to look in your rooms. Are you okay with this? If not, I'll wait with you and we'll see what he has in mind."

Shawnah and Janice had gone out, and Mista had assumed that Candy had also. However, she had closed her door behind her and stayed in the room. She wanted to see who was coming.

Robin gritted her teeth and said, "Yes. It won't be any worse than everything else I've had to do."

"Okay. Remember, I'm only two steps away. If he does anything at all, scream, and I'll be right here."

"Okay."

Mista started out, but paused in the door and looked back. He had a funny feeling about this. He did not like leaving a ten-year-old girl alone in this situation. Maybe he should abort this project and find another way to track down his man.

He closed his own door behind him and pulled the shade on the side opposite the girls trailer, darkening the inside of the trailer. He had a silvered sun-shade behind the window looking out on the girls' trailer, so that anyone looking in would see only a blank window, but he could see out.

He took a seat behind the window and waited. Sharra sat across from him and Sheila was in his big chair in the corner. He was just in time to see a car pull up and a young man step out. He appeared to be about 30 and was neatly dressed. He was not carrying an obvious weapon. Mista relaxed some, but stayed on the alert. He now took the time to call Mischal and alert him. "Robin has a visitor. Be ready for anything."

"He's already here? Why are you just now calling?"

"He didn't give us any notice. Just said he was coming and was here five minutes later. I had to get everything set up first."

"Oh. I'll alert the others."

The man entered the trailer and looked around. "Is that your roommate's computer?"

"Yes," Robin said.

"Where is she?"

"I don't know. She went out. Playing, I guess."

"Where are the rest of the girls? I know that Sam has more than two girls."

"I don't know what you mean. I only have one roommate."

"We'll see about that. They must live in the other trailers."

"Go see for yourself. Other people live in the other trailers."

"Hah!" He walked out and went around to the next camper, which was Mischal's motor home. He yanked open the door and started to enter, but found Mischal standing in his way.

Mischal said, "Can I help you, sir?"

"I'm looking for girls. You have any here?"

"Sorry, man, no girls here. Try the bars."

"I'm sure there are. The girl next door is lying." He tried to push his way inside.

Mischal picked him up with one hand and dropped him on the ground outside. "No girls in here, Mister. Try the trailer across the street."

He rubbed his shoulder and decided that it was not in his best interests to try to push past the giant. He tried the trailer across the street, Njondac's trailer. Again, he simply yanked open the door without knocking.

Njondac was not known for his courtesy. "What d' ya want, bud?"

"I'm looking for girls."

"Hah. I gots only one, an that's enough fer me."

"Let me see. I know that there are some girls here somewhere."

"Try tha bars." Njondac kicked him in the shins and then punched him in the stomach, sending him sprawling in the sand, trying to catch his breath. "An don't come back here."

When the man caught his breath, he went back across the street and tried Charly's door. Logically, he should have gone to Mista's next, but he was confused. He would never have thought that a fat little man could hit so hard.

The door opened before he touched it and Jeremy was sitting at his table studying. "Yes?" he said.

"I'm looking for girls."

"Oh. Well, I've got one and a half, but they aren't for sale."

"I'm not buying."

"Oh. Well, they aren't free, either."

"I mean, I'm looking for little girls. Sam's girls."

Jeremy looked him up and down. "What would a man your age want with little girls? Did you lose some?"

"No, I need to find them."

"I'm easily confused, sir. If you didn't lose them, how can you find them?"

"Oh, never mind." He headed for Mista's trailer. Sharra sent a thought into his mind and he walked by it without seeing it. He returned to the girls' trailer. "Well, I didn't find any, but I'm sure he has more stashed somewhere. But I can take care of you, anyway. No girl who does the things you girls do deserves to live." He pulled a switch-blade knife out of his pocket and flipped it open. Robin's eyes widened, but before she could scream, he lunged for her, slashing down with the knife.

She did scream then, and jumped back. She avoided the killing blow, but he still cut her from shoulder to waist, laying her open to the bone. She fell back into a corner, trying to hold back the blood.

Mista started to move as soon as he heard the man's comment about girls like her not deserving to live. He flung open the girls' door just as the man slashed at Robin. Mista raised his staff and struck the man a stinging blow across his shoulders. The man turned to face Mista, and Mista could see Robin cowering in the corner and Candy standing in her doorway, petrified with fright. He yelled at Candy, "Go get Jasmine. Go!"

Candy did not move, but continued to stare. "Go, girl! Go get Jasmine!" But Candy was too frightened to move. Meanwhile the man turned on Mista and charged at him. Mista blocked his lunge, and tried to fight back, but the man fought like he was possessed. He slashed and jabbed, seeming to know where Mista's staff would be. Mista assumed that he was a trained fighter, perhaps ex-military. Mista parried blow after blow, and the man struck so fast that Mista was hard-pressed to keep up with him. Mista struck him a few blows, but he ignored them and continued to slash at Mista. Mista took time to send to Sharra, *Get Jasmine. Hurry,* and continued to fight. The man continued to take damage but ignored the pain. His knife hand moved so fast that Mista could hardly follow it. Twice he managed to cut Mista.

Sharra opened the door and the distraction caused just a second of inattention for Mista; the man slashed him across the stomach. Sharra realized that Mista was in trouble and sent a bolt of energy into the man. He reeled back, but quickly recovered and lunged for Mista again. Sharra caused a sheer wall to form in the air in front of him and he slammed into it. He stepped back, dazed, and Sharra began the process of heating his knife. She knew that it would take several seconds for the knife to get hot enough to hurt him and was not sure that he could ignore that pain just as he had ignored Mista's attacks. She could only hope, but she also called Jeremy. *Need some help, Jeremy. Be quick. In the girls' trailer.* Sharra had not taken her eyes off the attacking man until now. She had not dared. Now she ran to Mista's side to see how badly he was hurt. She dropped to her knees beside him, heedless of the blood there, and touched his stomach. Her eyes widened in shock and fear. *JASMINE! Get in here NOW!*

Jasmine came running in. She saw Robin first and started toward her, but Sharra pointed to Mista, who was now sitting on the floor in a pool of blood. "Oh, my," Jasmine said. She laid her hands on him and prayed for healing, just enough to stop the bleeding. She made sure that he was still conscious, and then ran to Robin. She laid her hands on Robin's chest and prayed again for healing. Robin did not know what was happening. She had not had time to feel pain, yet, but she knew that she was seriously cut. She felt the warmth of energy flowing from Jasmine's hands into her body, and watched in amazement as the cut stopped bleeding and then closed.

Jasmine ran back to Mista to finish his healing. His cut was deep and potentially more serious than Robin's. Her cut was a flesh wound, the knife stopping at her ribs. Mista was cut through his abdominal muscles all the way across his stomach. The wound knitted together, but Jasmine knew that he would take a while for the healing to be completed. Then she wondered if he might have internal bleeding. She had not taken time to check the extent of the damage. "Sharra, we better get him to a hospital, and fast. He might have cut something inside, an organ, maybe. Do you think Jania could take a look long distance?"

"Hold on." Jeremy had arrived on the scene. Sharra said, "Hold him. I can't."

Jeremy nodded and wrapped the man in a blanket of hard air. That was not literally what happened. In actuality, he used mental energy to bind him and prevent his moving anything. But it was more convenient to think of it has hardening the air and making a blanket of it. He nodded. "I've got him."

Sharra called Jania. *Jania, Mista is hurt. He's been in a knife fight and cut pretty bad. Take a look inside. I'll link you.*

Wait a minute. She was in class at the moment, and she jumped up and ran out into the hall. Okay. I'm ready.

Sharra sent to Mista, *Jania is coming in.*

Jania sent, *Daddy! Let me see. Yes, your large intestine is cut and leaking. I'm closing it, now, but we need to clean you out. Can't leave that stuff in there. Can you do it, Mom?*

I can't see inside him.

Can you see what I see? Jeremy can, if you can't.

Yes. She followed Jania's interior sight and collected all the blood and feces in one place and then used telekinesis to move it onto the ground outside.

Mista sent, *Thanks, Kitten. I feel better, but I feel really weak.*

You'll be weak for a while. Your muscles need to knit and you need to rebuild the blood that you lost. If you're too weak, you might need to get a transfusion. I could take your pain from you – I can stand it – but I can't put the blood back.

Thanks, Kitten. Can you come home for a little?

I will come. I don't care what they say.

We'll log on and get you an E-Ticket. Thanks, Hon.

By this time, everyone had gathered outside the door, there not being room inside for any more. Janice squeezed through and ran to Mista, kneeling beside him. "Are you all right, Uncle Mista?"

"Yes. Just a little weak."

She touched the welt across his stomach. "Are you sure? If he hurt you, I'll kill him."

Sharra stood up and tried to raise Janice to her feet. "He's hurt pretty bad, Hon."

She resisted, looked up and asked, "Is the cut bad?"

"Yes," Sharra said. "Very bad."

"Who did it? That man?"

"Yes …"

Janice lurched to her feet and drew a long pocket knife out of her jeans. She snapped it open and lunged at the man standing there. She hit

Jeremy's invisible wall and bounced back. "Let me at him! I'll kill him!" she screamed.

Jeremy said, "No, little one. You can't reach him and he can't move. He cannot do anything at all right now. Let him go."

"NO! He tried to kill my new daddy, and I'm going to kill him."

Mista smiled. "Come here, honey. I'm all right. Two wrongs don't make a right. Just sit with me for a minute."

She backed up slowly, and sat down beside Mista. She put her arm around him. "Are you sure?"

"Yes. Your big sister healed me pretty much. She is coming home, too, to make sure that I'm all right."

She frowned. "I don't have a sister."

"I adopted her a long time ago. That makes her your sister, if you still want to stay after this."

"Oh, yes. More than ever. I'll never leave you. You need me to help protect you. Can I call you Daddy, now?"

"Yes, dear. If you feel that strong about it, call me Daddy. I'll try to be a good daddy for you."

Janice suddenly noticed Robin sitting in a pool of her own blood. She said, "I need to see about Robin, okay?"

"Yes, dear. Go see about her. I'll be all right."

Janice ran across to Robin and sat down beside her. "You okay, too?"

"I guess. Look, my cut is gone." She pulled her blouse open to show Janice, and then snapped it closed, suddenly remembering that there were a lot of people in there.

Chapter 21

Sharra said, "Jasmine, help me, please. We need to get him out of here and cleaned up." Each of them put an arm around Mista and helped him stand. They supported him while he walked slowly out and back to his own trailer.

In the trailer, they stripped him and helped him stand in the shower while Sharra washed the blood off. About halfway through, she said, "I might as well get in with you if there were room. I'm about as wet as you are. And here I thought we were going to get through a quest without me getting wet. I should have known better."

Mista laughed. "Come on in. I'll make room."

"No, I don't think you need that distraction in your present condition."

Jasmine said, "We need to get you dressed and get you to a hospital to have you checked out thoroughly."

"Why? Jania is coming."

"Yes, but it will be a while. Chandri is getting her a ticket. I don't know when she will arrive, but it will be hours at the very least. We're going *now*."

"Okay, okay. You're the doctor."

Janice watched them leave her trailer, and yanked at Robin. "Come on. You need to get cleaned up, too."

Jeremy said, "What do we do about this one?"

Mischal stepped inside. "I'll tie him up for now. Anybody call the police?"

"No, I don't think so," Mischal said. He stepped into a bedroom and ripped a sheet off the bed and tore it into strips. Then moved to bind the stranger. Jeremy released his hold as Mischal reached for him. As soon as he realized that he could move, he turned on Mischal and raised his knife. The hot knife had burned his hand down to the bone, but he was ignoring pain. However, Mischal was not Mista. He snatched the man's knife arm, spun him around and deftly tied a sheet strip around both wrists. He wound the sheet around him several times to make sure that it would hold him. Next, he kicked the man's feet out from under him and bound his ankles, and then tied another strip from his wrists to his ankles. "Hog-tied," he said. "Now let's see you move. You probably should call the police, now, Jeremy. Why don't you search his mind first, though, and see what he was thinking."

Jeremy nodded and entered the man's mind. All he could see at first was a driving desire to kill the girl and anyone who helped her. Suddenly, that thought vanished. Jeremy heard the door slam, and realized that the girls had just left. Now the man was lying on the floor, limp and confused. He did not know where he was or why he was there.

Jeremy went deeper. The man's name was Regis Campbell, and he lived at 4448 91st Street, Clearwater. Jeremy backed out. "He's sane, now. I'll call the police. We need to leave him tied, just for show, but he's harmless at this point."

Then he saw Candy sitting in her doorway behind the man and out of his sight. She had not moved since the affair started. He was afraid that if the man saw her, he would go berserk again. "Candy, get in your room and close the door."

She didn't move. Jeremy shook his head and sent a mental urge to obey, and to hide in her room. That overcame her fear, and the scooted backwards into her room and pushed the door closed.

Janice and Robin ran across to Mista's trailer and burst in. Sharra took one look at them and said, "Oh, my. Well, you're next. Let me get Mista into the bedroom and then we'll get the blood off of you two." She closed the door between the living room and the bath, got a towel down and helped Mista into the bedroom. Then she got him some dry clothes and helped him dress. "Lie down, dear, while I clean the girls up."

She closed the bedroom door and went back out. "Okay, girls, you're next. Into the shower. No, leave your clothes on. We'll rinse the blood out of them while you're wearing them."

She ran the portable shower head up and down on them, getting out as much blood as she could. "Okay, strip. Just pile them in a corner. We'll need to wash them later. Sneakers, too." She handed them each a bar of soap and a wash cloth. "What do you want to put on?"

Janice said, "All our clothes are over there."

"I'm not going back over there," Robin said.

"You'd look funny going over like that, anyway," Sharra said. "I'll get you a couple of Mista's tee shirts. They'll be big enough that they will look like dresses. Then we can get someone to get you some clothes. Robin, you better come to the hospital with us and let them check you out."

"Whatever. But I don't even have a scar."

Janice said, "I'm coming, too."

"Okay. If you want to."

They all went out and were getting in the Range Rover as the sheriff's deputy drove up, lights flashing, but no siren. He immediately stepped out, gun in hand, and said, "Okay. What's going on?"

Jeremy was waiting, and said, "I called you. We have an attacker tied up in here. He isn't talking to us."

"Show me." To Mista, he said, "Don't be going anywhere just yet."

Sharra said, "We're taking him to the hospital. You can talk to him there." She put Mista in the front seat and went around to the driver's side.

Jasmine started to get in so she could support Mista, but Janice beat her in. She scooted in beside Mista and said, "You can lean on me, Daddy."

"Thanks, Hon."

Jasmine shrugged and closed the door. She got in the back with Robin.

The deputy said, "Hey, you can't leave."

Sharra ignored him and drove out. At this point she did not even want to wait until the girls had proper clothes to wear.

Jeremy said, "Come this way, sir. I'll explain it all to you, and you can go to the hospital later. I guess they're going to Clearwater." He called Jasmine. *Where are you going?*

Clearwater, I think. We are going south, anyway.

Okay. I'll keep a link open. Tell me what hospital when you get there, so I can send the dumbhead.

The deputy followed Jeremy inside the trailer. All he saw was blood everywhere and one man tied hand and foot. "What happened in here? And why do you have him tied. Who are you, sir?"

"Regis Campbell. I don't know why they have me tied up."

"Whose blood it all this?" the deputy asked.

Jeremy patiently said, "This man came in, tried to kill one of our girls, and then attacked George Mictackic. They are taking them to the hospital. Both of them lost a lot of blood."

"They should have called an ambulance."

"They'll be there before an ambulance could get here."

"Yes, but the EMS workers could have stabilized them on the way to the hospital."

"Well, they didn't want to wait. We have a doctor, and she went with them."

"Well, I'll talk to them later. Untie this man."

"If I do, he is your responsibility," Jeremy said.

"He is my responsibility anyway. Untie him."

Jeremy shrugged and checked his pockets. He did not have a knife. Mischal had been listening at the door and handed Jeremy his Leatherman Army knife.

"Let me see that!" the deputy said. "Is this the weapon used in the attack?"

"No, sir," Mischal said. It's left over from my Marine days. He is still holding his knife."

He examined it and then handed it to Jeremy. Jeremy took a while to find the blade and then cut Campbell's bindings. He stood back quickly. "Check his knife," he said.

The deputy noticed the knife in the man's hand for the first time. "Let me see that, sir."

"I can't. It's stuck to me."

Candy opened her door and came out just then. Campbell said, "Oh, there you are. I didn't see you earlier."

Jeremy stepped back further and went into Campbell's mind again. He wanted to sample his thought again, now that he was no longer confused. All he got were normal thoughts. The man had enjoyed talking with Candy and had wanted to see her in person.

The deputy said, "How did you get the knife stuck to you?"

"I don't know, but it's starting to hurt like the dickens. Did you do something to me?"

"Not me," Jeremy said. Looks like you held on to it after it got too hot to hold safely."

"And how did it get too hot to hold," asked the deputy.

"You'd have to ask him," Jeremy said. "It's his knife. But his whole hand seems to be burned. Maybe you better take him to the hospital, too."

"Yes, I better do that. Don't touch anything in here. I'm calling in the crime scene investigators. Somebody has already tracked it all up."

"Well, yeah," Jeremy said. *They were having a hum-dinger of a fight.*

Jasmine called Jeremy, *We are at the Clearwater hospital. It's déjà vu all over again. Like when we took Charly in. They don't believe that they were wounded today.*

"They just arrived at the Clearwater hospital. If you take this man there, you can talk to the other people involved."

The deputy's eyes narrowed. "How do you know that?"

"I –" Then he remembered the radios that they all had installed. Although he had not used them, he said, "We all have sub-vocal radios installed. We often need to communicate."

"Oh. Come on, sir. Let's get that hand looked at."

Jasmine was not having a good night at the hospital. They simply did not believe that Mista had been wounded that day, or that Robin had been wounded at all. "We have other patients to see that have real emergencies," the doctor on call said.

Jasmine drew herself up to her full height, which was slightly taller than the doctor. "I am a Nurse-Practitioner, sir. Here is my ID card, and my license is hanging on the wall of my office. They were both in a knife fight this afternoon. The outside skin has healed, but I don't know how deep their cuts were. I want you to take x-rays, sonograms, MRI scans or whatever you want, but I want to know if there was any internal damage. Her ribs could be cut, and his internal organs could be bleeding inside. And I want it before they die on you."

"I understand that you are trained, but this man's wound is old."

"It is not old!" She turned to Sharra. "Do something."

Sharra looked into the doctor's eyes and sent a suggestion to his brain. *Check them out quickly.* "This man is my husband, sir. If he dies on me, I'll slap a lawsuit on you that will shut you down, for neglect of your sworn duty."

The nurse stood by watching. At the venom in Sharra's voice, her mouth dropped open. She recovered and said, "We will need your insurance card, Miss."

"It's not 'miss', and we do not have insurance. Don't worry, you will be paid."

The doctor shrugged. "Let's see what we can see." He planned to run every test that he could, and charge them the full price. He was surprised when the x-rays showed a scar on Robin's ribs.

Jasmine watched over his shoulder. "Satisfied now, Doctor? It that life threatening?"

"No, but it should have healed more that it has."

"In just an hour or so? I don't think so."

The doctor said, "Does it hurt, honey?"

"It's starting to hurt real bad."

"It will hurt for several weeks while the bone sleeve heals. I'll give you something for the pain."

X-rays did not show any damage on Mista, so the doctor said, "I'll need to run an MRI if there is internal damage."

"Do it," Jasmine said. "What is his blood pressure?"

"Dangerously low, but his heart is steady. Why?"

"Then get him some blood. I suspect that he lost more than two pints before I could get the bleeding stopped."

"I can do that, but the MRI will have to wait until I have staff on duty tomorrow. You can leave him overnight, if you are that concerned."

"I'm not leaving him anywhere," Sharra said. She called Jania. *Hon, look into your daddy and see if he is bleeding again.*

But, I fixed him.

His blood pressure is low. Better check.

Can it wait? I'm on the road to the airport, now.

No.

Okay. Let me pull over. She pulled off the road and closed her eyes. *Okay, I'm looking. No, no bleeding. If his blood pressure is low, give him some blood. The doctors there should know that.*

Hah! Sharra sent. *Remember when we took Charly in? They don't believe that he was actually wounded.*

But he was!

Oh, I know he was.

I remember. More dumb doctors?

Yeppers. You're flying to Tampa, right?

Yes, wherever that is.

Someone will pick you up. You should have listened to your geography lessons when you could.

The pilot knows the way, I'm sure.

They gave Mista one pint of blood and checked him again. "It's low, but it's in the normal range. I don't think we should give him any more."

"Put that in writing, please," Jasmine said.

"You better not be wrong," Sharra said.

"There is no way to actually measure the quantity of blood while alive," he said. "Blood pressure is high enough that everything seems to be within acceptable range. Notice also that his color is much improved."

"All right. Sign your treatment write-up and give me a copy," Jasmine said, "and we will be on our way."

"How much will this cost, doctor?" Mista asked.

"Admitting will have a bill ready some time tomorrow," he said. "I have no idea."

Mista handed him his American Express card. "Charge $1000 on this for now, and send us a bill for the balance. We have no intention of trying to cheat you."

"Oh, that won't be necessary..."

"Do it. I do not carry insurance – I am self insured."

They walked out to the main room and the doctor handed the card to the admissions clerk. "Run a charge of $1000 on that against his bill."

The sheriff's deputy was waiting with Campbell. He said, "This man needs treatment. Treat him as dangerous. And I need a room where I can interview these people."

"Use one of the admissions rooms."

They put Mista in a wheel chair and rolled him into one of the rooms. The deputy said, "Tell me what this is all about."

Mista handed him his card. "The sheriff knows who I am and what I am doing. This man was chatting with my niece on the internet today, and suddenly came to the house and attacked her and then me. I'm sure the sheriff will be interested in what happened. You can either report it in the morning or call him tonight."

"Maybe I better call him." He called and said, "Roberts, here, sir. Sorry to bother you at home, but I have a man says he was attacked by some guy from the Internet. He ..."

"Where are you?"

"Clearwater hospital. He ..."

"I'll be there in five. Take his statement."

He looked at the receiver a minute before he hung up. "Well. He's coming over. Asked me to take your statement. Tell me exactly what happened."

Mista gave him a verbal account of what had happed from the time the Campbell appeared at their door until the deputy arrived. Deputy Roberts wrote it all out, and then went out to see about his prisoner. The man had seemed docile enough, but after hearing Mista's account of events, he thought he better pay more attention to him.

When the sheriff came in, Mista told the story again, this time starting from the time when Robin started the chat with Campbell. The sheriff grunted. "You did not do anything to provoke an attack?"

"Nothing. I promised you evidence. I have the chat log on my computer and I have surveillance video. I will give you copies of both. I would appreciate it if you would consider it 'eyes only' for now. If you need to charge this man, and need the evidence, then of course do what you must. Call us in to witness, if you need us. You know where to find us."

"You telling me how to do my job?"

"Not at all, Sheriff. However, I think that this might be my first real lead on the man I am hunting. If the wrong ears hear of this, I might lose him."

"All right. Are you going to press charges?"

"No. There is something really strange about this. He does not remember coming over or making an attack. Literally. He does not remember. My guess is that he was acting under some kind of post-hypnotic suggestion or something like that. As far as I am concerned, he did not willfully do us any harm. And, as you can see, no real harm."

"All right. I'll send him home with orders not to leave the area. I will need your documentation."

"If you will follow us to the RV park, I'll get it for you right now."

Chapter 22

Charly picked up Jania at the airport at 3:15 the next morning. Jania immediately ran to Mista's bedroom when she got to the trailer and laid her hands on him. Mista stirred sleepily, but did not come fully awake.

Sharra said, "That's a sign of how bad he is. Normally, he'd be awake at a touch."

"I know," Jania said. "Let me see inside him and make sure nothing else is wrong." After a few minutes, she said, "I found a little more damage inside, and fixed that. He will take a while to get his strength back, though."

"Yes, we expect that."

"Where is the little girl?"

Robin was sleeping in the upper bunk in the bunkroom, but she was not asleep. Jania said, "Hi, hon. I'm Jania. I need to see how bad you were hurt."

"Okay. What do you want me to do?"

"Nothing. Just lie there." Jania laid her hands on Robin's chest and looked inside. "Oh, boy! You were cut with a knife, right?"

"Yes."

"He must have hit you pretty hard. All your ribs are scarred. They hurt, don't they?"

"Yes. It hurts terrible. I can't even sleep."

"Just a minute." She prayed for healing. Robin felt the energy flow from Jania's hands into her body and the pain went away. She breathed a sigh of relief. "Is that all better?"

"Yes. How do you do that?"

"It's a gift from God. I don't really do anything, but I can see inside the body and see what's wrong. Then I pray for healing, and God heals."

"Does he always obey you?"

Jania laughed. "I don't presume to tell God what to do. I ask for healing power, and so far he has granted my request. I suppose if I asked and he didn't want that person healed, then he would say no."

"Oh. My mother used to pray sometimes, but she never got answers."

"Yes," Jania said. "Prayer is not a command to God. He is not our servant."

"Yes, I guess that's true. But my mother always said that if she had enough faith, then God would have to give her what she asked for."

"Did it work for her?"

"Not that I could tell."

"Well, I don't think faith works that way. Ask Daddy about it. He has all the answers. Go to sleep now, little bird."

They went back into the main room, and Jania said, "Hmmm. Where can I sleep? There's somebody in the bed in here."

"We can make room for you in my motor home," Charly said.

Janice was awake and watching. "Who are you?" she asked.

"I'm Jania. Mista adopted me about two years ago. Who are you?"

"I'm Janice. He's going to adopt me, too. Then I can protect him."

Jania laughed. "You protect Mista? I'd like to see that."

"If I'd been there, I'd have fought that man off," Janice said. "She's going to teach me sword-fighting."

"You will probably be a natural. We need to get you a sword first, though."

"Yeah. You can sleep here. I'll sleep on the floor."

Charly said, "That couch folds out and then two can sleep on it."

"Oh. Okay. Show me how. I didn't know it would fold out. Really, though, I don't mind sleeping on the floor. At least it has a carpet on it."

"And that helps?" Jania asked.

"Sure. I used to sleep on the ground or the street. If I was lucky I could find a piece of cardboard or a newspaper to lie on."

"Wow! This must seem like hog heaven."

"Yeppers."

Sheila brought two breakfast trays in the next morning. She set one on the table and took the other in to Mista. He started to get up. "I can eat at the table."

"No. Save your strength. I don't mind doing this for you."

When she went back out, Robin was already eating. "Hey, Hon, I was going to take it in to you."

"That's okay. Jania fixed me last night and now I'm all better."

"Well, okay, then." She turned to leave just as Janice came in with her own tray. "I'm eating in here with them."

Sheila went back out to the picnic table where the rest were eating. She thought, *Boy! What I've missed, not being able to raise my own children.* Jania had been taken from her when she was one, and Gary at five. She had had another girl, Rose, who had also been taken from her when she was a year old. She had no idea where Rose was, or even if she was still alive.

Sheila prepared a tray for Sharra, so that she could eat with her husband, before eating her own breakfast.

Sharra helped Mista walk out to join the others later. Janice jumped up and opened the door for them and then took his other arm to help support him.

Mista said, "Thanks, but I can stand okay."

"No, you can't. You need me."

Mista smiled and said, "Okay, then K ..." *oops can't call her Kitten. Especially with Jania here.* "I need to find a pet name for you."

"Janice is fine."

"We'll see, Janice."

Jania watched while he found a chair and then said, "Did they give you enough blood last night?"

"I wouldn't know. Ask Jasmine."

Jasmine said, "I think so. They didn't want to give him too much."

"What happens if I get too much," Mista asked.

Charly said, "It squirts out your ears."

Janice said, "It does not! Does it?"

Jasmine said, "No, dear. She's just teasing you."

"Well, if you need more you can have my blood," Janice said.

"What if I need all of it and more, too?"

"I'd die if I gave it all to you, wouldn't I?"

"Yes. You can't live without blood."

"Oh." She looked over at him with big, solemn eyes. "Well, if you need it you can have it."

"Thanks, Tanker, but I would never take it all."

"Tanker?" Janice asked.

"Yes. You're my tanker. You know what an army tank is, don't you?"

"Yes, I've seen them on TV."

Mischal nearly exploded trying not to laugh. Mista said, "Now, there is my real tanker. A tank driver sits inside his big steel shell and thinks nothing can touch him, so he charges ahead no matter what is there. Trees, rivers, guns, nothing gets in his way."

"That's not quite true," Mischal said. "They know their limits."

"Of course," Mista said. "But there is a certain mind-set that ignores danger. They feel invulnerable, even if they know in their mind that they really aren't. When you charged that man with a knife, yesterday, Janice, did you really expect to win a knife fight with him?"

"Of course. I'm good with a knife."

"But he is a grown man and he is good with a knife, too. Still, you ignored all that and charged ahead. You ignored the danger of loss of blood and offered all of yours to me. You're my little tanker. You set your mind on your goal and charge right in. I like that."

Janice tried to sit on the arm of Mista's chair, but it was a canvas camp chair, and its canvas arm did not support her at all. She sat on the ground beside him.

Mischal said, "Well, what's next? Can we stop messing around with the Internet stuff and go find this man?"

Mista grinned. "Well, Big Tanker, just charge off. Draw your sword and go fight the darkness. I know you are impatient for action, but we have to find this man first. The man who came last night might be a lead to him."

"I'm just tired of sitting around doing nothing."

"Yes, I know. You could teach Janice sword fighting. She wants to learn."

"Janice? You're a little young for that, aren't you?"

"How old was I when I started," Charly said.

"Eleven. But ... Okay. We'll go buy you a sword later today."

"Hold on, there, Bigun. She'd cut her own hand off. Ya can buy her one, but first let me make some practice swords so she doesna kill nobody."

"Okay, that gives you three something to do. But there is a deeper issue, here. Do you girls still want to stay, after that attack yesterday? If you don't, we'll take you back home. I don't want to risk you."

Janice said, "I want this to be my home. I never had another home to go back to anyway."

Robin walked over to Mista and said, "I don't have a home to go back to. Can I stay?"

"Yes, Little Bird, you can stay." He put his arm around her and pulled her to him.

"I'll hurt you."

"No. I don't hurt, I'm just weak." She climbed up and lay back against his shoulder.

Candy said, "I think I would rather go back."

"Okay. Get your stuff together and well fly you back this afternoon."

"I don't have anything. We threw away my old clothes."

"You have everything we've given you. It's yours to keep."

"Even the Ipod?"

"Even the Ipod. I don't take gifts back."

"Okay, thanks. But…"

Sharra said, "Put them in plastic bags for now. We'll get you a suitcase on the way to the airport."

"Okay, Shawnah?" Mista asked.

She was standing, shuffling from foot to foot. "I don't know. I want to stay, but, what if we have another attack? What if it's me this time?"

"You can stay if you want to. I cannot promise that we will not have another attacker. After all, we are trying to get the wierdos to come to us. Some of them are bound to be like that guy yesterday. That's why I had the audio link set up and the camera recording whatever happened. And I cannot promise that nothing will happen to you. Robin was very lucky that she was not hurt worse."

"Don't worry, Robin," Janice said. "If he hadn't made me leave the room, I'd have been there to protect you. Next time you have to let me stay, too, Uncle Mista."

Mista smiled. "I appreciate your courage, Tanker, but I don't think you could beat a grown man. However, it probably would have been better if you had been there."

"You just wait till Charly starts teaching me how to use a sword. I'll show you how good I can fight."

"Okay, Tan -- I think I'll change that to Tinker. I like that better."

Shawnah said, "Can I stay for now and change my mind later?"

"Sure." Mista said, "no problem."

Chapter 23

Mista looked around. "We still have not made any plans. I don't like putting the girls at risk, but I don't know any other way to find these people. Maybe we just need to modify our reception procedure."

"We need a back door on that trailer," Jeremy said. When you get a visitor, I'll come in the back door, into one of the bedrooms, and see what's in his mind. If he starts any violence, I'll be already on hand to hold him. I'll need to be able to see him, so I guess a one-way mirror would work."

"What about the legal aspects?" Mista asked.

"I don't know enough law yet to answer. But if the law is logical – and I assume that it is – then I don't think observing a person without his knowledge is against any law, so long as you don't use that observation to initiate action against him."

"Sounds like a lawyer already," Jasmine said.

Jeremy grinned. "Maybe a little. Goes with the territory. Since there is no way he can prove, with your present technology, that I can see into his mind, I believe that reading his mind is a safe action. Again, absent the use of information obtained in that way against him."

"And what about Mr. Campbell?" Mista asked.

"Since we can prove that we did not entice him or suggest to him that he should come here, and since he initiated the action without any provocation at all, you have grounds for a suit against him."

"And you know for a fact that we did not entice him?" asked Mista.

"Well, I don't. I assumed from what you have said …"

"I have not looked at Candy's chat log," Mista said. "It might contain some damaging statements and/or pictures."

"She said she was sending pictures of herself half undressed to someone," Janice said.

"And she said she sent someone a picture of me – the one she had on her computer. That man said that my roommate sent him a picture of me, but I know Janice wouldn't do that."

Mista rubbed his chin. "So. You think maybe this man was using different screen names to contact each of you. Could very well be. And then he assumed that Candy was your roommate, since you only admitted to one other girl. Yes, I think so. I'll need to check her chat logs."

"That can wait, Mista," Sharra said. We need to get that trailer cleaned up first. Besides, the sheriff taped it off yesterday."

Mista smiled. "I don't have to go there to do it. They are on my Internet server in our trailer. I'll show you where they are and how to access them later. Now, I just had another thought. If he chatted with the two of you, maybe he also chatted with Janice and Shawnah. I'll have to pull those logs, too, and see if we can spot a pattern. It also occurs to me, that his conversations with you, Robin, were just routine, but he wanted pictures of Candy. Maybe she indicated willingness to show them?"

"Could be," Jeremy said. "Janice, Shawnah, has anyone asked you for pics lately?"

"Not me," Shawnah said.

Janice said, "I had one request yesterday. I sent him a face shot and said that was all I could send. He didn't mention it again."

"Did he specifically ask for nude pictures," Mista asked.

"Not exactly. He wanted to see more of me, but like I said, I told him that I couldn't send pictures like that, and he did not say anything else about it. Check my logs."

"I will. Later."

Jeremy said, "I will send a query to AOL and ask them to identify his screen names."

"You'll need a court order," Sharra said. "That is something we can do this afternoon. We'll take the logs down and a copy of the video and tell him we need to track down any other activity he has been into." Sharra smiled. "Your first bout with the system."

"But, I thought you did not want to be a lawyer," Jeremy said.

"I don't. I have had some experience obtaining legal records. It's been a few years, but I remember some of the things I had to do. If necessary, we'll get our lawyer in Atlanta involved in it. I know he could, but I'd like you to try first."

Mista said, "One other thing. One of you should search through his mind and see if you can find out what he meant by his reference to Sam's girls."

"There was nothing about any of that in his mind after he reverted to his apparently normal personality," Jeremy said. "It's as if he had two distinct personalities inside of him, and neither knew about the other."

Mista said, "Some psychologists swear that multiple personalities exist, and others swear that it is just a mechanism by the defendant to protect him or her from prosecution."

"I don't know about the theories, but I know what I saw. When he was raging, he was intent on killing all of these girls. After it was over, he really did not know where he was or how he got here."

"Well, the knowledge must be in there somewhere. See if you can find it."

"It is stored, yes. But I can only see what he is consciously thinking about. Probably something like the way a computer works. You have pictures and data stored on your computer, but the computer has to open it before a person can see what is actually there."

"Data can be read."

"Only because the computer reading it knows how it was stored. Pictures could be opened by an outside computer also, if that computer knows how the picture is stored. But you cannot personally look at the storage and read data or pictures."

"That's true. Well, see what you can find."

Chapter 24

Jeremy stood up and said, "I'm going inside so I won't have any distractions."

Mista said, "Good idea. I need to get inside, too. I'll show you how to access the chat logs, Sharra."

Chandri said, "I'll go get some tickets. Who wants to take her to Atlanta?" No one responded. She shrugged, "I'll do it, then."

Sheila said, "No, I'll take her. This is all about me, anyway, and you have children here." She went in with Chandri to arrange tickets.

Janice and Robin went in with Mista. Jasmine looked around. "Shawnah, let's you and me have a good girl talk. Let's take chairs over there in the shade."

Mischal said, "Stubbs, let's go shopping. What do you need to make practice swords?"

"In this world? I don't really know. Wood, lead."

"Let's try Home Depot or another building materials place. I'm thinking an ax handle or a maul handle. Long and straight, and tough wood. Hickory, probably."

"Yeah, that'll take tha punishment. But tha weight's not right."

"We'll get a really long drill bit, and maybe an extension or two, and drill a hole all the way through it. Then put in a steel rod. Should be enough weight and give it some strength, too."

"Sounds good. Let's go."

Charly went to their motor home with Jeremy and then left him to himself. She went to help Candy pack, but found her standing in front of her trailer door, not sure what to do. It had police 'do not cross' tape on the door. "Hey, we forgot about that," Charly said. "I guess we can't pack you up until the police clear this scene. Let's go make sure that they don't schedule you out before you have a chance to pack your stuff." They joined Chandri and Sheila.

Jeremy leaned back in his easy chair and closed his eyes. Having made contact with Campbell before, he knew that he could find him again. It only took a few minutes. By his thoughts, Jeremy was pretty sure that he was at work as a computer programmer. The task at hand did not take his full concentration, and his thoughts wandered from time to time to other subjects. He wondered how many on-line 'friends' he would contact tonight after he got home. He wondered idly what his wife would fix for supper, or if she would want to get some fast food. From time to time his mind would shift to the strange experience he had had yesterday afternoon. He had found himself in somebody's trailer, tied hand and foot, and had no idea how he had gotten there. His wife was not at all satisfied with his statement that he had no idea how he got there. He had also had a knife in his hand, a switch-blade, and he didn't even own one. The police had taken that. Just as well – he certainly didn't need it. It had been hot, because it had burned his hand severely. Good thing he didn't have a lot of typing to do this day. Most of the job at hand was reviewing what he had written last week and making a few corrections.

Jeremy lurked in the man's mind for about half an hour. That was about the limit of his own energy, the energy required to maintain a contact. He saw nothing that indicated that the man had any conscious knowledge about the events of the day before. He did not name any of his own screen names or any of his friends. *Well, I'll try tonight. I think I'll be in the room with the girls when they go on line, if they do. I don't think it will do any good to listen in unless they are also on line. On the other hand, he might have other contacts. I better sleep this afternoon and rebuild my energy level.*

Mista showed Sharra how to access the chat logs and then printed out the logs for Candy for the past week. Janice leaned on one shoulder, watching, and Robin leaned on the other. "You girls forget what you are seeing," he said with a smile. "If I catch you erasing any of your own logs you're in deep trouble."

"I wouldn't think of it," Janice said,

Robin said, "Me neither."

Mista found that Candy had invited the man over several times. Each time she did, he would ask for another picture, which she promised.

She had also invited other people over, but no one had taken her up on it yet. Mista wrote out the other screen names and gave them to Janice. "See if you can talk to any of these, and let's find out what they are like. Remember: Do not invite them over, do not suggest that they come over, and do not send pictures other than your face or full body – fully clothed."

"What kind of clothes?"

"Anything you have, I think. If you have any doubt, ask Sharra or me."

"Okay. … Uncle Mista, could we have some bicycles so we could go riding?"

Mista looked at Sharra. She shrugged. "Sure, why not. Sharra might take you today to buy some. Stay in the park, though. And whenever you ride, somebody must know that you are out. Sharra or Jeremy should always know, so if you get in trouble they can find you."

"We'll be careful," Janice said.

"It's not just the general risk. You might have attracted somebody like that man who came last night, or he might even come back. Just let us know."

"Okay. Thanks, Uncle Mista."

The sheriff stopped in a few minutes later. "How are you feeling, Mr. Mictackic?" he asked.

"Not hurting any more, but I am pretty weak. I was just going to take a nap. What can I do for you?"

"Well, have you got a minute to talk?"

"Sure. Girls, scram."

"There are some really strange things about that encounter last night. Mr. Campbell swears that he does not know how he got here, and has no memory of attacking the girl or you."

"I believe that, Sheriff," Sharra said. "I believe he has multiple personalities, and sometimes does things that he does not remember, as in the old story of Dr. Jeckyl and Mr. Hyde."

"Well, he also swears that he does not own a knife like the one he held. One of you did not put in into his hand, did you? And how did it burn him so badly?"

"You saw the video, Sheriff," Mista said. All I know is that he tried to kill one of my girls, and when I heard her scream, I ran in. Then he attacked me."

"There are some strange sequences on that video tape, also. Like he suddenly stopped and never moved again."

"If I told you, you wouldn't believe it, Sheriff."

"Try me."

"Okay. Some of our family can use ESP. One of the tricks they can do is to hold someone like you saw. Don't ask me how it works, but you saw it in action."

"Humph. I do find that hard to believe. I've heard of some strange things, but ... Nevertheless, it does fit the facts. I'll leave it as a working theory. How about the knife?"

"He brought it with him. Maybe it was already hot when he picked it up? He did not seem to feel any pain. I'm pretty good with my staff, but I couldn't seem to hurt him at all."

"Well, I'll leave it for now. There is nothing else for us to do here. If you don't press charges, then I cannot hold him. Please let me know if you get any more like him."

"You will be the first to know, Sheriff," Mista said. "I have asked the girls to be really careful what they say on line, and to be sure not to invite anyone over here, or even hint at it. You know that I want to find the root of these activities, and that I expect more men to come here. But if I am right, they will be the ones to make an overture to the girl. If they don't, then they're not the ones I'm after. To get the ones I want, all the girls have to do is be here and give him our address if he asks for it."

"Just be careful. Some of these men are vicious and dangerous."

Mista grinned. "I noticed."

CHAPTER 25

When the sheriff left, the girls came back inside. Janice came up to his chair and put her hand on his arm and said, "Are you still sick, Uncle Mista?"

"Not sick, exactly, but not well, either. Just weak, mostly."

"I'll give you some of my blood if it will make you feel better."

Sharra said, "Jasmine could set up a transfusion. She should have their blood types from the blood tests we did on them when they first came."

"I'll try. Call Jasmine. Thanks, Tinker. I need to find a better name. That's not good enough."

"Janice is fine."

Sharra called Jasmine. Mista wants you to set up a transfusion. I do, too. He's still too weak. Janice wants to give him some blood, if they are compatible. Robin probably will also, once she sees it.

Okay. I'll bring Jania with me to help.

Jasmine and Jania came in a few minutes later with their equipment. Jasmine had been issued a full field medical kit by the Georgia State Police when they went to work for them, but had used very little of it. She had found an emergency blood transfusion kit on the bottom of the storage case.

"You want to give your blood, Honey?" she asked. "You ready to die?"

"I won't die. Uncle Mista said he wouldn't take it all."

Jasmine smiled. "You're right. He will only take a little."

"Will I be weak like he is when we're done?"

"No. You might feel a little weak, but we won't take much. Not enough to hurt you."

They folded out the dinette seats to make a bed. Janice lay on one side and Mista on the other. Jasmine watched carefully, and stopped when she had half a pint. Robin stood by the bed wide-eyed the whole time, with her hands on Mista's other arm. Janice sat up when Jasmine disconnected her.

Mista remained on the bed and said, "I guess that makes me a blood father, now. A long time ago boys used to cut them selves and mix their blood and then called themselves blood brothers."

"That's okay with me. That means that you can't send me away, now."

Robin did not move until they had finished. Then she said, "I want to give you some of my blood, too, Uncle Mista. I want you to be my blood father, too."

Jasmine only took a little of Robin's blood because Mista was showing signs of not accepting any more. She disconnected the equipment and Robin sat up. "That didn't hurt."

Mista said, "No, and I feel much better. Thank you both. Now I think I better take a nap and let the change take effect." His voice rose higher and higher as he spoke, until at the end it was about the same pitch level as Sharra's.

Sharra said, "Stop it, Mista. You're scaring the girls."

"Oh. Didn't mean to scare you," he said in a normal voice.

"It won't make you into a girl, will it?" Janice asked.

"No. It isn't the blood that makes the difference."

"What does make us different. These?" She fingered her budding breasts.

"No. They are signs of the difference. It is chemicals inside your body called hormones that make the difference. You have a lot of female hormones, and they make the breasts grow, make you beautiful, and prepare you to have babies. Male hormones make hair grow on your chin, make you ugly and mean."

Janice slapped his arm. "You aren't ugly or mean, Uncle Mista. And I'm not beautiful."

Mista grinned. "Maybe I need more male hormones so I can be ugly and mean. And don't worry about you. You will be beautiful one day. You, too, Robin."

He sat up and drew a girl into each arm and hugged them tightly. Janice said, "Does this mean that we are now your daughters?"

"It does if you want it to be. It is still voluntary on your part. You can change your minds at any time. If you still want to, when we get back to

Atlanta we'll have official adoption papers drawn up and then it will be official and permanent."

They hugged him back. "Okay."

Mista said, "That also means that I can spank you if you need it."

Janice looked up at him solemnly. "If that's what it means, then I'll take that too."

"Me too," Robin said.

Mista said, "Ever been spanked?"

They both shook their heads. "Well, it's no fun. But you know, the funny thing is, it hurts me as much as it hurts you. I am going to take a nap, now. You run along and play. Maybe somebody will take you to buy bicycles."

Sharra brought his supper in about six o'clock and woke him up. "You want to eat in here or at the table?"

"I'll go to the table. I feel pretty good, now."

Sharra joined him for supper. When they had finished, she asked, "You ready to go for a drive?"

"Sure. What do you have in mind?"

"You have to go buy some bicycles."

"Me? Nobody was willing to take them this afternoon?"

"A lot of people were. But the girls were having none of it. You promised, so you had to buy them. End of story."

Mista smiled. "Looks like I'm stuck with them. Dear, I want them to be as much your children as mine. I know you miss not being able to have children."

"Not as much as you do. They'll be your shadows whatever you do, from now on. It would drive me buggy, but you eat it up."

"Well, I like children. I like working with them, teaching them. But, Sharra, I'm in love with you. They cannot replace you, so don't even begin to think that."

Sharra smiled. "I think I'm over all that. You love your girls – no matter how old they are. But I finally have realized that I should not ever be jealous of them. Maybe that's one of the reasons that I love you so."

Mista said, "Well, let's go see about the girls."

He changed into street clothes and went outside. All three girls ran to him. "Are you all better, Uncle Mista? I mean, Daddy?" Robin asked.

"Pretty much. That young blood did the trick. Where are your bikes? And where's Candy?"

Charly said, "Sheila has taken her back to Atlanta."

"You have to take us. You promised."

Mista said, "Well, I don't know if I feel that well. You might have to wait a few days."

Robin said, "But y—"

Janice said, "Shhh. Okay. We'll wait. Come on."

They walked over to the fire and sat down in the chairs there. Mista watched for a minute and then sent to Sharra, *Now what?*

I think they have figured out how to wrap you around a little finger, dear. You ready to go?

I think I can still play that game.

He walked out to the Range Rover and got in, shut the door and started it; then he backed out without saying a word. All three girls ran after him, shouting, "Hey! Wait for us!"

Chapter 26

Jeremy checked on Campbell again after supper. Once again, he found no indication that he knew anything about the attack or the phrase 'Sam's girls'. At one point, the man seemed to change in character. Jeremy sensed something different about the way the man was looking at his screen. He was on line at the time, and talking to a friend. He glanced at the list of his buddies who were on line at the same time, and thought, *Well, looks like no fun tonight.* Then the mind reverted to what Jeremy had come to accept as normal. Jeremy withdrew after half an hour.

No one slept in the girls' trailer that night. Robin absolutely refused, and since she had been the one attacked, no one tried to force her. It did not matter that Chandri and Em had spent a long time cleaning the trailer up. Janice would have gone, but not alone. And Shawnah was not about to sleep alone in the trailer. Em would have been there, but Sheila was not back.

So Em slept on a fold-out bed in Charly's motor home, and Shawnah slept with Jasmine. She had been feeling somewhat left out until Jasmine took her under her wing. Robin and Janice had quickly become chums, but Shawnah and Candy did not get along all that well. Candy had not gotten along with anyone, but Shawnah had assumed that the problem was because she was black. Shawnah was surprised to be included in the bicycle trip – she had not asked for one and had assumed that only the other two girls would get them.

Mista just looked at her and raised one eyebrow. "Ask Jasmine. I have no color prejudice. I treat all of you the same, so I would not buy bikes for two and not also include you."

They had to ride around the park a few times before they would settle down to lessons, and then again that afternoon, as soon as Em released them. After a few minutes of riding, they came in and went to work on the computers. It was a little scary at first, but after a while, they settled down and enjoyed their surfing. Nothing unusual happened while on line. Jeremy was attentive, and specifically searched Campbell's mind while the girls were on, but he was at work and remained unaware of them.

They went back to work after supper, and again Jeremy listened in. Jeremy had gotten the girls' screen names, and recognized all of them in Campbell's buddy list when he signed on. *Hah! I won't need that court order after all.* There was only one name that he knew in the list that came up when Campbell first signed on. He chatted with a few people, but did not attempt to call Candy. In fact, he showed no reaction at all to her screen name. Then he switched screen names and Robin's screen name showed up. There was a flash of recognition and a brief glimpse of the other personality in his mind, but it was quickly gone. Campbell himself did not reply when Robin sent him a query. Jeremy committed the list to memory.

Campbell changed names several more times while Jeremy was observing. Shawnah's name was on one buddy list and Janice's on another. Jeremy committed these lists to memory, also, and as many of the other names as he could. In all, Campbell went through seven screen names. Jeremy had no idea who any of these people were, of course, but he wrote out each list while it was still fresh in his mind. Campbell showed no reaction when Shawnah's and Janice's names popped up, nor did he respond to their calls to him.

As Jeremy watched, he realized that there were several people on each list that Campbell ignored when they IM'ed him. He thought that that might be significant, so he made a note of the names that Campbell ignored.

Jeremy had to withdraw after half an hour, again. That was as long as he could maintain that level of energy drain on his mind. He took his lists over to discuss them with Mista.

Mista sat up in his recliner and studied the lists. He had a lap desk handy, and spread the lists out side by side. "Sharra, ask Mischal to come over, please."

Jeremy said, "I could call him."

"I know, but you have to be pretty tired. Let her do it. ... Hmmm. Looks like each list is a discrete list."

"Discrete?" Jeremy asked. "What do you mean?"

"No names are on more than one list. No. This one is also here. And here. And also on this list. And this name is on those four and one more. Sharra, would you put these names in an Excel spreadsheet? Or ask Chandri to, if you'd rather."

"I can use a computer."

"I know you can, dear. I was just suggesting an option. Thought you might want to participate in the discussion."

"Oh. Well, okay." She called Chandri. She knew that Chandri was better at computer work than she was, but she did know how to create a spreadsheet.

Mista explained what he wanted. He also asked her to put blank spaces in the columns as appropriate so that the repeated names would line up across the page. While she was working, he said, "It looks there are at least several names under each screen name that he does not recognize in this persona."

"Not necessarily," Jeremy said. He might have recognized them but not wanted to talk to them so close to his brush with the law."

"Perhaps. But what then is the common denominator?"

"They are all under-age girls," Sharra said.

"Possibly," Mista said. "Likely, in fact. But you did not even see a glimmer of recognition."

"He must have known them," Jeremy said. "They were on his buddy list."

"No. He might have names on there that he only chatted with once and then forgotten. In that case he would not show any recognition when they signed on. However, he certainly should have known Robin. And Candy." Mista stroked his chin as he thought.

"Yes," Jeremy said. "Looks like the alternate persona is a good explanation. So, now, who are these people that Campbell Nr. 2 talked to?"

Mista said, "I think I'll ask the girls to contact them and see who they say they are. It'd be interesting to find out who they really are."

When the girls came in to say good night, Mista gave them a hug and rocked them for a while, and then asked them to sleep in their own trailer. "Shawnah will feel lonely and slighted."

"Aunt Sheila is back," Janice said.

"Yes, so you will be safe there, but I think it best if all three of you sleep there tonight."

"Okay," Robin said.

They really did not want to go, but they obeyed. Mista watched them go. I have a feeling that they won't sleep well tonight. Well, maybe none of them should sleep there. Put Shawnah in with Jasmine. They seem to be bonding. He also wanted the girls to not be around while he did some work on the computers. He had to review all the chat logs, now that he had screen names that they had talked to.

Chapter 27

About midnight, Robin awoke, screaming. The trailer was full of smoke and was apparently on fire. She had been dreaming moments before that that horrid man, Campbell, was in the trailer trying to kill her again. She had tried to run, but her nightmare held her in place. Her legs wouldn't move. He was coming closer and closer with his knife raised. Suddenly the trailer burst into flame right where he was standing, igniting his clothing. He turned and ran, and she woke herself up screaming.

She saw that the trailer was on in fact burning, and she was suffocating from the smoke. She jumped up and ran for the door, still screaming. But this time, her scream had words. "Oh no. They'll think I did it again. Fire again."

Sharra had set a danger link to the girls' minds. She, too, was worried about them being alone in the trailer after the attack by Campbell. She had met them at the door as they left and kissed each one on her forehead, and then said, "I have set a watch on you. I know you don't understand, but if anything at all happens, I'll know immediately and we'll come running. We want you to be safe. We love you."

Janice said, "Good night, Au – can I call you Mom, now."

"If it pleases you. As Mista told you, we will make it official and permanent when we get back to Atlanta, if you still want to."

Janice hugged her and kissed her. "Good night, Mom."

Robin also hugged and kissed Sharra, saying, "Good night, Mommy."

Now, at midnight, Sharra was jolted awake. Something was wrong. Then she smelled smoke. "Mista! Wake up! Get the girls. I think their trailer is on fire. I *know* something is happening there. HURRY!"

Mista woke instantly. It had been awhile since his wife had set an alarm and called him to danger, but it had happened enough times in the past that he was out the door before he even thought about it. "Call Misch!" he called over his shoulder.

He hit the ground running toward the girls' trailer across the parking area. Smoke was boiling out of it. He got to the door just as Robin burst out. He caught her in his arms, "Hold on Little Bird. I've got you."

"No.no.no.no. Let-me-go! Let-me-go! You'll think I did it." She struggled and twisted in his arms, trying to get free. "Let me go!"

"No, no, Robin. I've got you -- you're safe now." She continued to struggle, and he knew that there were others still inside. *Sharra! Get everybody here, QUICK!*

Mischal was already running, Chandri right behind him. Charly burst out of her door moments later, followed by Jasmine and Jeremy. Mista tucked Robin under one arm and dived into the burning trailer. He banged on the bedroom door to wake up Em and Sheila, and ran through the trailer to the girls' rooms in the back. *Wish Misch had put the door in back here already.* He flung open Shawnah's door and yelled, "GET OUT!" and then Janice's door. She was just lying there, too still. He snatched her up and ran for the front door, trying to hold his breath all the way. His pajama legs caught fire, but he made it out with the girls, gasping for breath.

Robin was still struggling to get free, but Janice was limp. He dropped her on the ground and said, "Breathe her, Jaz!" He took a breath and yelled, "Get the others! Mischal ran for the trailer, just as Em and Sheila came staggering out. He charged inside, and ran to Shawnah's room. She was trying to breathe smoke, and coughing, but so disoriented with panic that she could not move. Mischal snatched her up, tucked her into the pit of his stomach, ducked his head and dove through the wall. He had already cut a hole in the outside wall there, preparing to put in a door, and he knew that the inside wall was thin plywood. He also knew that it would hurt, but it was better than trying to run back through the fire.

Outside, Jasmine was trying to give Janice mouth-to-mouth artificial respiration. Mista said, "You have oxygen?"

"YES!"

Mista said, "Get it. Chandri, take over."

Jania was faster. She leaned hard on Janice's chest, and reached inside her lungs and pushed out the smoke and CO_2, then relaxed and let her chest suck in fresh air. That push, along with Chandri's mouth-to-mouth brought Janice back, just as Jasmine arrived with a small oxygen bottle and mask. She quickly fitted the mask and turned on the oxygen. "Breathe, Honey." Janice sucked in a deep breath of pure oxygen and then another. The cherry red color gradually left her face.

Robin finally quit struggling and threw both arms around Mista's neck, holding on like her life depended on it. She began to cry, and her little body shook with great sobs. "You'll think I did it. Another fire, and I was in it, and you'll think I did it, but I didn't! I didn't do it!"

"There, there, Little Bird. I've got you and I'm not letting you go. We love you. Be still now."

Sharra sent, *I looked. She was asleep and dreaming that Campbell was chasing her and suddenly the trailer burst into fire. Then she woke up and it was burning. So, no, she did not do it*

Gotcha. Thanks.

Sharra got up and went into their trailer, but Jania suddenly noticed that Mista was burned. "Stand up, Daddy. You're burned. Let me see."

He stood up, still holding Robin and crooning to her. Jania said, Daddy, you're burned all the way up your back. And you were sitting in the dirt! You'll get infected. Stand still." She laid her hands on his back at the top of the burn and prayed for healing and then slowly drew her hands down his back all the way to his feet. Behind her hands, his charred skin and flesh turned a healthy pink.

Mista said, "Thanks, Kitten. I hadn't had time to realize that I was hurting."

Sharra came out with a robe. "Here. Put this on. Your pajamas are burned completely away in back."

"Well, hey! I didn't do it on purpose!"

Janice sat up and took the mask away. Jasmine closed the oxygen valve and asked, "You okay now, Honey?"

"Yes." Her eyes were on Jania. "How did she do that?"

Jasmine said, "It is God's gift to her. She prays for healing and he heals. She healed Robin's cut and Mista's, remember?"

"You healed Robin."

"Yes. Well, God did. I prayed. But Jania came in behind me and finished the job."

"I want to do that."

Jasmine laughed. "It wasn't something that either of us asked for, Honey. If God gives you the gift, then you can heal, too."

"How can I get it?"

"You get to know God and then ask him. If he wishes, then he will give you a healing gift."

"But, I don't know anything about God. I never even went to church."

"Well, you stick with us, and we'll teach you everything we know about God. Not a lot, really, but it's enough."

Mista sat in one of the camp chairs with Robin. Janice went over, opened up his robe and ran her hand up and down his back. "It's like new skin."

Mista smiled. "She does a nice job, don't you think?"

"Yeah. I want to be able to do that."

Mista turned his attention back to Robin. He pulled her more upright, and sat her in his lap. She buried her face in his chest, saying, "Please don't send me away, Mista."

"What happened to 'Daddy'?"

"I was afraid."

He took her shoulders and tried to push her back some. She clung tight. "Please don't send me away."

"Look at me Sweetheart. Look at my eyes."

He pushed, and she finally looked up at him.

"We're not sending you away. You hear? You see the truth in my eyes? We don't ever want to send you away. We know you did not set the fire. Okay? We *know* it. We know it in a way you cannot understand, but we know absolutely that you did not do it. We know that you were asleep."

She buried her face again. "I was afraid. I was afraid that you wouldn't believe me."

Fire trucks started arriving about that time, and they soon had the fire out. The fire marshal came over and asked Mista if he had any idea how it happened. "Not a clue. Something woke me up and it was on fire. I ran in and got two of the girls out and my sister, and my friend there got the other girl. They were all asleep."

Jania looked at Mischal when Mista named him and said, "You've got blood all over you. What happened?"

"I had to finish making the back door in their trailer. The hard way."

"Well, let me fix you."

"Not now. Not in front of them."

"Oh. Will you be all right?"

"I've had worse wounds."

Jeremy had his own task. He was listening to the thoughts of Campbell, and this time he was in the adversary state. He was driving somewhere in Clearwater and thinking. *I almost had all of them. I got inside the trailer without waking anyone, and they had a candle burning, so I could see. I must have knocked it off or something, suddenly the whole place was on fire. Barely got out. At least the fire should finish them off. Another job well done.*

Jeremy said, "We had an intruder, and I believe that he accidentally started the fire. He ra—must have run out when it started."

Chandri went to the door and looked at the ground. "Look. There are some boot tracks, going in and coming out, running. All of us are barefoot."

"Good eye, Miss. I believe you are right."

Jeremy said, "You girls have a candle burning?"

Janice said, "Yes. We like to be able to see at night. It's Robin's idea, but I lit it. It was safe in a glass bowl."

"Well, your attacker came back. He was inside and must have knocked it off."

"And just how do you know who was here, sir?" the fire marshal asked.

"It only makes sense. Who else would bother them?"

Sharra sent, *Careful!*

Yeah!

The fire marshal said, "Well, the fire is completely out, and the trailer has cooled some. Enough to be safe from a flashback. I'll be back in the morning to try to determine the cause. Please do not touch anything inside until I've finished. Are you going to take these people to a hospital to check them out?"

Jasmine said, "No. I listened to their breathing and don't hear anything wrong. We are close enough that we can run in if they develop problems later."

Mista made a snap decision as the firemen were leaving. He said, "Sweetheart, you can sleep with us the rest of the night, if you want to."

Robin looked up at him. "Really? But you said, ..."

"I know. But I think this one time will be okay. I want you to feel completely safe with us."

"Thank you, Daddy. I love you."

Sharra sent, *Mista, are you sure about this. She's nearly eleven.*

Just this one time. She's scared that we don't really believe her and will send her away. I'll sleep in my sweats. You can hold her in your arms, if you like..

Okay. But I suspect that she won't let me.

"Robin, I want to show you something. It'll hurt a little."

"Okay."

He took her inside and put a small drop of crazy glue on one of his fingers and then pressed one of hers against it and held it a few seconds. "Okay. Now, take your finger away."

"I can't. It's stuck."

"If you pull hard enough, it'll come off. It might hurt a little."

She pulled it off and then cried, "Ow! That hurts."

"Yes. Nothing dissolves that kind of glue. If you get it on your fingers, it stays. If they stick to something, the skin comes off. Love is like that. When you love somebody, like I love you, you can't dissolve that love. You can break away, but if you do, you will leave some of yourself behind. I just want you to know that's how much I love you. I won't let you go, unless you decide you want to break away. But if you do, you'll take some of me with you, and leave some of yourself behind."

She looked at him with solemn eyes. "I'll remember that."

Jania had watched, remembering some of her lessons from Mista. He had not had crazy glue where she grew up, but he still make his lessons stick. She said, "I can heal that for you."

Mista said, "No. Put a Band-Aid on it, but let it heal by itself. The lesson will be more effective that way."

Chapter 28

Jeremy came in a little later, after everyone else had found a place to sleep. Mista had the girls in his arms. Robin was already asleep, but Janice opened one eye and looked to see who it was, then closed it and went on to sleep.

Jeremy waited a minute and then said, "Isn't it odd that a girl like that, so street wise, trusts you so completely?"

"Not really. Every girl wants someone to love her, someone she can depend on no matter what. But, if I made a single wrong move, you better believe that she'd have that pocket knife out in a flash."

"Yeah, I guess that's true."

"This one is the one that surprises me," Mista said indicating Robin. "She missed her father when he left, but managed. But when her mother died, she was devastated. She had no one. She didn't trust me at first, but when she gave up and placed her trust in me, it was like a dam bursting."

"Well, she's a cute little thing. She'll be a heartbreaker one day. I wanted to talk to you about Campbell, but I don't think I should talk in front of them."

"It's all right. They're asleep."

Sharra came in quietly and sat on another chair.

"Well, you know I followed Campbell while he drove home. Mentally, that is. He's cagey. He might have sensed the intrusion – he did not go straight home."

"We have his address."

"Yes, but this is the bad one. He might not know that. Or maybe he was just taking precautions. I don't know what triggers the persona change, but he was definitely thinking about our girls and the fire. He was here, and had planned to kill them in their sleep. He was surprised when the fire erupted at his feet, and assumed that he had knocked the candle off."

"You don't think that he did?"

"He wondered how he could have done it, since he was being so careful. I wonder ..." he nodded his head at Robin.

"Yes. I had wondered."

Jeremy shifted to thought transfer. I have heard of people who could start fires under stress. I can, of course, and so can Sharra. But we have control of our talent. Could it be that hers is just breaking through? Could she have reacted to a threat and started the fire without being conscious of it?

She certainly could have. I'll talk to Sharra about it tomorrow, and then I want to talk to Robin about it. It will be an interesting conversation, but not much fun.

Be careful. You might set something off. "Also, while Campbell was driving, his thoughts turned to other people he talks to. Some of them are girls, and he wants to eliminate them as well. By the way, he assumes at this time that the girls must have died in the fire."

Mista said, "I would have thought so. Any idea who the other girls might actually be?"

"No. Just names. He doesn't have their addresses yet. Most interesting, though, are the people he talks to who aren't girls. Some are just Internet acquaintances. Others ... He appears to belong to a group dedicated to eliminating Internet sex offers. They eliminate it by eliminating the girls offering."

"Interesting logic. He's found the goose that lays golden eggs, but he destroys the eggs an lets the goose live."

"You could say that. He gets names from someone else, apparently a sponsor of the girls, and contacts them. Then he passes their name and address to someone else in the group. He makes sure that he is publicly visible while his friend eliminates the girl. Or he does the same for someone else who supplied him with a name. He did our girls because he came on them quite by accident. He only assumed that they were some of 'Sam's girls'."

"So what's next?"

"We need to find out who he talks to. I need to be listening when he contacts either a sponsor or one of his ring."

"Yes. We, too, are trying to eliminate the practice. But we go after the perps pushing the girls. He assumes that the girls are willing conspirators. Some of them might indeed be."

The next morning Mista called the girls in about 10:00. Sheila and Charly came with them. "It's time you girls learned who we are, what we are, and what we do. This situation has gotten a lot more dangerous that I would have predicted. So. One. We are crime fighters. Sometimes we work independently – like now. Sometimes we have contracts from one of the states. It is often very dangerous work, since we are chasing criminals who like to kill their enemies. Namely, us. I did not expect this one to be deadly, but perhaps I should have. Any questions?"

No one answered.

"All right. We have become a group like a family. We have traveled and fought criminals for about 12 years. We did not plan to create a group like us, it just happened.

"Now. How. You have seen some of the things that we do. Mischal and Charly and Njondac are our primary fighters. Chandri is able to talk to animals, so she is a scout and many other things. Animals can't talk, of course, but she can somehow communicate with them. Sharra and Jeremy have mental powers. ESP. They can do things with their minds, like hold someone still, talk with them, and other things. Jasmine and Jania are healers. You have seen that at work. Any questions, now?"

Janice said, "What do you do?"

"Nothing. I'm the philosopher and teacher. I just sit and think. Sometime, I cook a little."

"A VERY little," Charly said. "I ate something he cooked once."

Robin asked, "Can Sharra read minds?"

"Yes."

"That's how she knew that I was not eleven. And knew I was not lying about not setting the fires."

"Yes, that's correct," Mista said.

"That's scary," Janice said.

"She does not read anyone's mind unless they ask her to, or there is danger. If we are fighting an enemy, then she can see what they are planning. When you came, Robin, you would not talk to us, so she listened just to the surface thoughts, in order to find out who you really were. Normally, your thoughts are private, and she respects that."

"She doesn't read our minds all the time?" Shawnah asked.

"No. Only when danger threatens, and rarely even then. She will read enemy minds and fight them with her mind." Mista smiled at them. "No one wants to have someone constantly watching every action and every thought. You can be sure that she doesn't do that."

"How do we know that?" Janice asked.

"You just have to trust us. There is a thing called ethics, which we will teach you as time goes by. It can be a very complicated subject, but basically, it means that we do what is right simply because it is right. We could use our powers to hurt people, but that would be wrong. We do not do that. We could steal and be sure of never getting caught. We do not do that."

He looked at the three girls. "Now, I want you to know about us before we go any further on this project. We intend to catch the man that stole my sister so many years ago. When we do, he will probably die. He might fight back, and then some of us could be killed as well. If you want out, just say the word. We'll find some place to take you. If you want to stay and help, or just stay and not help, you are welcome to stay. You might get hurt. Again."

Robin said, "Do we have to get on the Internet and help find him?"

"No. You do not have to be involved in any way. If you want to stay anyway, you are welcome. But remember you could get hurt just being here."

Robin looked at him with wide eyes. "I'm scared. He has tried to kill me twice. But I still want to stay."

"Good. Janice?"

"I'm staying. I'll help, too."

"Good. Shawnah?"

"I think I want to stay, for now. I'm not sure about getting on the Internet, though."

"Good. Like I said, you don't have to. However, Shawnah and Robin, if you want to get on just to play around, you have permission. Only one thing. We know that this man thinks that you all died in the fire tonight, and he's happy about it. I have killed your screen names. You can't use them again. So when you want to get on again, we will have to make you new screen names."

"What about him," Janice asked. "Did he get away?"

"For now. But we know exactly where he is. We will use mind control to find out more about him, and hopefully find out who is behind him. He won't like what we do to him."

"Will he come back after us?" Robin asked.

"I don't think so. He will not know that we are doing things to him. If he does come, we will know, and he won't be able to sneak in or hurt anyone."

Mista looked around. "No further questions? Go play."

They left quickly. Mista said, "They will probably do something or think something and see if we know about it by reading their minds. Not knowing, or at least not admitting to knowing, is not proof that we didn't, but I think that they will take it that way."

"Probably," Sharra said. "I've been a little more in Robin's mind that I would have liked. But it had to be done."

"Yes. Don't worry about it. Jeremy, where is our friend right now?"

"He is at work. In his normal persona. I guess that is the normal one."

"Okay. Sharra can you send him an illusion? Like Robin walking by his desk. She should never be there, of course. And if he thinks she is dead …"

Sharra grinned. "How about I make her a ghostly figure? Yes. Hold on."

She made the mental contact, and then sent him a vision of Robin walking past his desk, stopping and turning back, and then looking into his computer screen. She appeared to be insubstantial – he could see the walls through her. Then she turned, waved to him and walked through the wall behind him.

This version of Campbell did not know who she was. But somewhere in his mind, he did know, knew that he had cut her badly, trying to kill her, and then had seen her trailer burn while she was asleep. She had to be dead, and she looked like a ghost.

He froze. He was in the middle of a telephone call from his manager, but he put the phone down and looked at the wall where she had disappeared. After a minute he shook his head, decided that he really was not crazy, and picked the phone up. "Hello? Mr. Avery. Sorry I was distracted."

"What would distract you when I am talking to you?"

"Sir, this is hard to believe, but I thought I saw a ghost."

"Bah. There are no ghosts."

"I know. But I saw her. I think it was someone that I knew, but I can't place her. But I knew somehow that she was dead. And she walked right through the wall. I can't explain it."

"Are you hallucinating? Are you on drugs?"

"No, sir. I don't drink and I don't use drugs. I can't explain it. But I know that I saw her."

"You want the rest of the day off?"

"No, sir. I think I'll be all right now."

Jeremy laughed. "That ought to rattle his cage. I'm surprised that Campbell Nr. 2 did not come out, though."

"Well, we'll try something else tonight, when he is at home. Sheila, would you ask Robin to come back in? Just Robin, and the rest of you should not be here, either. Just Sharra and me. I think that she started the fire last night. But we know that she was asleep. I think we have a fire starter, and we need to address it and get it under control. Jeremy, you should stay, too, since you are a Psi teacher."

Chapter 29

Robin came in a minute later, looking scared. "What did I do?"

Mista said, "We need to talk about that. Come here, Little Bird."

He picked her up and put her on his knees, facing him. He took her hands in his and said, "First, I want you to know that nobody is mad at you for anything. You are not in trouble, so relax."

"Okay," she said, but did not relax. She knew that something was wrong.

"You know about psionic things, ESP and stuff, right? Not just what we just told you, but you have heard people talk about it."

"Yes. But most people don't think that it really happens."

"That's true, but you know that it does. You have seen us use it."

"Yes."

"What would you think if you had that kind of power?"

"I'd be scared. I don't."

"I think you do. Tell me again how the fire started last night."

She started to cry. "I really didn't do it."

"Don't be afraid. You are not in trouble. This is one of the times that Sharra thought it best to read your mind. We know that you were asleep. Just tell me about it. You were dreaming, right?"

"Yes. I was dreaming that that man was chasing me. And I couldn't run."

"And then what happened?"

"I don't know. I screamed at him."

"Screamed what?"

"I don't know. Just screamed. And then I woke up and the trailer was on fire, and I was afraid that you would think that I set it."

"Why would I think that?"

"I don't know. Because of the other fire."

"But, you didn't set that one either. And we knew that. So why would we think you set this one?"

"I don't know." Her eyes got big, and she started to cry again. "I was just scared."

"All right, Robin. Let me tell you what I think really happened. You dreamed that the man was chasing you. In fact he was in the trailer, coming for you. Somehow you knew that, even though you were asleep. And the part of your mind that knew that tried to wake you up, and made you dream that he was chasing you. When you didn't wake up, that part of your mind caused a fire to burst out right under the man's feet. Then you did wake up."

Robin was silent for a minute. She wanted to run, but Mista was holding her by both hands. And he didn't seem mad. "But that would mean that I did set the fire."

"Yes," Mista said. "But without knowing it."

"But, if I did …"

"It was an unconscious reaction to danger. Unconscious and uncontrolled. That could be a very dangerous thing."

"It might be what killed my mother?"

"We don't know about that. It might have been, yes."

"Now what?"

"Jeremy teaches people how to use their psi power. Their ESP. He tests them to see what all they can do, and then he teaches them the right way to use it and teaches them how to do different things. That was his job before he met us and married Charly. He will teach you, and then it won't be uncontrolled and wild."

"You're not going to send me away?"

Mista shook her hands up and down and smiled. "No, Sweetheart. We are not going to send you away. I've already told you that a dozen times. We want you to stay with us. And we want you to learn how to use that talent of yours, and how to use it properly."

"Jeremy taught me a lot of the things that I know," Sharra said. "He can teach you the same way."

Robin blew out breath. "Phew. You really aren't sending me away? You're not just saying that?"

"I'm really not. We love you and you have a home here."

"Okay. When do I start?"

Jeremy said, "Do your normal lessons this morning, and then I'll start giving you special instruction after lunch. Okay?"

"Yes. Can I go now?"

"You're not going to run away, are you?"

"No. I don't have anywhere to go."

"Okay." Mista kissed her on the forehead. "Go join the others."

Chapter 30

Robin did not join the others like she was told. Her mind was in turmoil. She saw her bike and decided to ride around the park for a while. Maybe she would run away. Again. But she had nowhere to go, and she was in a totally strange place. When she came to the front gate, she thought again about just riding out and not coming back, but once again, she had nowhere to go. She thought about going down to the beach, since she had loved the one time that they had gone. But she didn't know where it was. She'd just get lost.

The real question was whether she could really trust them or not. Maybe she was reading her mind right now, even though she said that she wouldn't. *Well, if she is, then she will find out how I really feel. Uncle Mista had seemed so nice...* She didn't want to call him Daddy right now. But it would be nice to have a daddy. And he never yelled at her. Of course, he had said to go to class, and she hadn't, so now he might yell at her. But that would be okay. She was used to being yelled at.

She sighed. It was nice while it lasted. She came to the playground and decided to swing for a while and think. She parked her bike off to one side and pumped up a swing until she had a good rhythm going. But she couldn't think.

She swung and tried to think for about an hour, and really did not solve anything. It would be nice to be able to burn down the man who attacked her. If she knew where he lived and could control the fire starting, if she really could do that, then she could burn his house down and him in it. But she had no idea how to do it. If she really did do it when she was asleep and mad at someone, then maybe the other fires … no better not even think about that. But what if she got mad at Mista and burned down their trailer. No, that would be terrible. He had been so good to her. Sharra she didn't know about. She wasn't mean or anything, but just not very warm. But Uncle Mista had thought she had set the trailer fire, and still let her sleep with him and Sharra, just so she would not be scared. No, she had to find out how to control this, so she wouldn't hurt anybody she liked. So, she had to stay and let them teach her.

She slowed the swing and jumped off. Then she stopped short. Her bike was gone. She had left it right there by the swings, and now it was gone. She'd never see it again. Probably either a kid who wandered in and took it, or someone only here for the night and would be gone. Now she was in trouble. She'd have to tell them, when she got up the courage. She walked home, just in time for lunch.

After lunch, she went and found Mista, and crawled into his arms. As she had hoped, he was in his big chair. He said, "Well, Sweetheart, what brings this on?"

"I just wanted to tell you that I love you."

"Okay. I love you too. Did Aunt Em fuss at you for being late to class?"

"No." Now she had a problem. Tell him that she didn't even go? He'd probably find out sooner or later. He said never lie to him, and he'd know. "I didn't go. I just rode around on my bike."

"Oh. Did you work out your problem?"

She sat up. "How did you know?"

"Know what? I understand how people think. If you didn't go to class, you must have had a good reason, and since we talked about ESP and your possibly being a fire starter this morning, I assumed that you went off to think about it."

She curled up against him and put her arms around his neck. He felt wetness and waited until she was ready to speak again. Finally, she said, her voice still muffled by his shirt, "I don't want to leave, but I'm afraid to stay."

"What can I do to make you less afraid?"

"Nothing. It's not you that I'm afraid of, Uncle Mista."

"Who then? What can we do?"

"I'm afraid of them reading my mind, and making me do things I don't want to do. I'm afraid of what I might do."

"Hmmm. I see. You don't really know what you are getting into, do you? Well, first off, one of the things that I teach my students is how to know what is right and wrong, and how to always try to do what is right.

Now, nobody is perfect, but when it comes to something like mental control, mind reading, or magic, you must always do what is right. Magic doesn't work here, but we have been places where it does. When you have that kind of power, you must always use it correctly. If you don't learn to do things right, then someone with more power than you will take your power away."

Her eyes got big. "They can do that?"

"Yes. That was one of Jeremy's jobs in his home country. He examined every Psionic user and made sure that they were not hurting people. He also had to be examined by someone with more power than he has."

"He's going to examine me? Like reading my mind?"

"He is going to examine you. I'll go with you if you want me to. It's not like reading your mind. It's looking at your mind to see what you can do. Before we let him come with us, Sharra examined his mind. She just wanted to be sure that he was not going to hurt anyone. We didn't know him then. Now we know that he would never hurt anyone."

When Jeremy had first met Charly, Sharra wanted to be sure that he meant her no harm. If he did intend harm, then she would make sure that he never saw Charly again.

"You can come with me."

"Okay. You understand that we fight the bad guys. People who murder people, steal their cars and things, people who look for little girls on the Internet so that they can hurt them. If you were to use your power to hurt people, you would be just like them. You don't want to be like them, do you?"

She shook her head. "Then you wouldn't like me any more?"

"Right. Then we would have a *biiig* problem, because we love you. You like Charly?"

"Yeah, she's cool."

"Ask her what she thinks of Jeremy."

"Okay. Let's go."

Jeremy took his time and Robin sat very still and held Mista's hand the entire time. Finally, Jeremy said, "I see a lot of potential here, but the only thing that has happened so far is the ability to heat things up. More will come in time. Basically you have the ability to change things at their molecular level. That's how you start fires. We will teach you how to use that power whenever you want to, and how to control it. We also need to teach you to use it wisely. I see a basic desire to be good in you. You should be easy to teach."

Robin visibly relaxed. "Okay. When do we start? I don't want to accidentally start a fire in one of the other trailers."

Chapter 31

Janice was waiting impatiently when Robin came out of the motor home after her lesson. Robin was tired. She had no idea that working the mind like she had been trying to do was actual work. She raised a hand in a weak gesture. "Hi."

"Hi. What were you doing in there so long?"

"They're teaching me to use my brain better. Let's go swing, and I'll tell you all about it."

"Oh. I wanted to go riding. Let's ride awhile first."

Robin grimaced. "Can't. Somebody stole my bike."

"What? When?"

"This morning. When I cut class, I rode for a while and then swung for a while. When I was ready to come home, my bike was gone."

"Whooo. What'd Uncle Mista say?"

"Haven't told him. I guess I'll have to, though. He'll probably ground me."

"Yeah. Well, you can't get a new one 'til you tell him."

Robin kicked sand. "I know. Let's go swing."

Janice laid her bike down and they walked over to the playground. One other girl was swinging when they got there, so Robin would only talk about little things. She shook her head and changed the subject when Janice asked her about her new classes.

When the other girl jumped out of the swing and left, Janice immediately asked, "So what's the big secret?"

"They think I started the trailer fire."

"WHAT? But you were asleep. It was an intruder, the same man who tried to kill you."

"Maybe. But they think I have some untrained power in my mind that starts fires when I'm scared. You know, like they can read minds and stuff, and they think I have a talent like that. They don't say power, they say talent."

"Well, that's crazy. ... And they're going to teach you how to use it?"

"That's the idea. Jeremy is a teacher and he says that he can teach me. So now I have afternoon lessons. I guess I won't have time to get online much. I don't really want to, right now, anyway."

"Yeah. It is kind of scary. I know they said right at the first that this might be dangerous. But I never expected anybody to try to kill us. And tried twice!"

Robin was silent for a while, pumping her swing. "You know, if I really can start fires ... and they can teach me how to control it. I could find out where that man lives and burn him up."

"Yeah. Wouldn't that be cool. Then you wouldn't ever have to worry about people hurting you again."

Shawnah came riding up then. "I've been looking all over for you guys."

"Come join us," Janice said. "Robin has a secret."

Shawnah parked her bike and got a swing. "What's your secret?"

"They think that I started the trailer fire. Somehow my mind can do that even when I'm asleep."

"No way! Really?"

"Yep. So now I have classes every afternoon to learn how to control it so I don't burn somebody up by accident."

"Cool! How long will it take?"

"I don't know. No one seems to know how long. Guess I won't be online with you for a while."

"Sokay. I'm not doing anything online anyway for a while. Maybe not ever. I don't want somebody coming for me."

After supper that evening, Robin searched out Mista. He was relaxing in his chair, so she went up to him and stood for a while, and then began to pluck idly at his pants leg.

"What's on your mind, Little Bird? Did the afternoon go well?"

"It was okay. I never knew how tiring that could be."

"Still scared?"

"No. Just ..."

Mista held out his arms, but Robin shook her head.

"What's wrong, Sweetheart?"

She looked down at the ground for a long time before answering. Two tears rolled down her cheeks, and she wiped them away quickly. "Something happened to my bike."

"Oh? Care to tell me about it?"

She wiped her eyes and looked up at him. *This is too hard. He's not even yelling at me.* "This morning I went down to the swings and swung for a long time thinking about all this. Then when I was ready to come home, my bike was gone. I guess somebody stole it."

"Well. You want me to yell at you?"

"Yes."

"I'm not going to do that. Were you careless with it?"

"Not really. I laid it down by the swings, but I was not paying any attention to it. I was just thinking about all that has happened and nothing else. Then it was gone."

"Come up here."

She climbed up, but sat stiffly upright. Mista said, "Did you consider lying about it?"

Robin looked up sharply and caught her breath. *How did he know? Should I just tell him? Or pretend that I didn't. Better tell.* "Yes." Her voice was almost inaudible.

"Good. You must always be honest with me. I would have been very surprised if you had not considered it. But I am glad that you chose wisely. Now, what should we do about it?"

"Can we get another one?"

"I want you to think about it tonight. You decide tonight whether we should or should not get another one. I can afford it – we are not talking about money. The question you have to answer tomorrow after all your classes is whether or not we should. Not whether or not you want one. Obviously, you do want one. Okay?"

"Yes."

"Okay. You can go play, get on line, or whatever."

"Can I just sit here with you and watch TV?"

Mista squeezed her. "Yes. What would you like to watch?"

"I don't care. I just don't feel like doing anything."

She watched whatever he selected, and didn't even talk. She just sat quietly in his arms. After about an hour, Mista said, "You still aren't sure about all this, are you?"

"No. I will do whatever I have to. But I'm not sure that I like it."

"Don't like having a talent, or don't like living with people who do?"

"Both. What if I hurt somebody? What if I had lied to you earlier? You could have read my mind and known."

"One. I can't read minds. I don't have that talent. I can read people from the outside, though. I can pretty well guess what you are thinking. Now, bear in mind that a guess is just that – a guess – and it could be wrong. If I could read your mind, it would never be wrong."

"How can you look at me and see what I'm thinking?"

"Not really see exactly what you are thinking, as in the words that are going through your mind. I just know you well enough to guess. Now, Sharra can read, but won't unless she has to. You understand, the only two times she read you was when you first came – we had to know what really brought you to us, and who the woman was who brought you. And then the fire. If you had started the fire deliberately and then lied about it … that would make you an enemy within the camp. You understand?"

"You wouldn't have let me stay."

"Yes. We couldn't have let you stay. So, we had to know. She couldn't see everything, but she knew that you were not lying. So, we were relieved. We do love you and did not want to lose you. Okay?"

Robin nodded, not knowing quite what to say.

"Now, if she had not been able to read your mind, what could we have done?"

"I don't know. You'd just have to believe me."

"We would have had to guess whether or not you were lying. And, if you were lying and did set the fire, then we could not have kept you. And we probably would not be willing to take the risk. You understand?"

She nodded.

"So, since we did not want to lose you, she made sure that you were telling the truth and did not deliberately set it. Now what did I know about you? That you were scared to death. So, to give you the most comfort that I could, I suggested that you sleep with us, since I know that you had wanted to before."

"Yes. I wouldn't have slept at all if you hadn't. Can I sleep with you again tonight?"

"No, honey. I don't think you should. That was a one-time gift. You are getting to be a big girl, now, and we don't want to start something that should not happen. Sitting like this is all right, but you need to sleep in your own bed."

She sighed. "Okay." It did settle one fear that lurked at the back of her mind. What if Mista turned out to be like Shawnah's uncle? She snuggled closer, glad that she did not have that worry.

After her classes were over the next day, Robin went to find Mista. She found him in one of the camping chairs, watching Mischal prepare fresh fish to cook for supper that night.

"Uncle Mista."

"Yes?"

"I have decided that you shouldn't buy me another bike. It wouldn't be fair to the others for you to buy me so much more. Maybe I could do some chores and earn enough money to buy my own?"

Mista rubbed his chin. "Hmmm. A wise choice." Her face fell. She had hoped that he would buy one anyway.

"Part of your training will be to learn to put the needs of the group before purely personal desires. For example. Look at Mischal there. Do you think he wants to be here doing nothing for weeks while we try to catch a criminal?"

"No, I guess not."

"But he does not complain. You have made a good start in that direction. After supper, we'll go buy you a new bike anyway. Not because I should, but just because I love you."

Robin was stunned at first. She had already given up. Then she threw her arms around his neck and said, "Thank you, Uncle Mista. Daddy."

Chapter 32

The rest of that week and the following week passed slowly and uneventfully. The girls spent very little time on the Internet, and only talked with people of their own age. Mista had blocked the old screen names so that Campbell would not see them online, so they were starting with fresh names.

Jeremy spent the mornings doing homework for his legal classes, the afternoons with Robin, and then tried unsuccessfully to catch Campbell communicating with any of his buddy list people who did not seem to be girls.

Mischal, Chandri and Charly did some fishing, but that began to pale after a while. Mischal and Njondac scouted the area and found a vacant tract of land on the Hillsborough River and bought it. They hired a bulldozer to clear a road into the center of the land and make a small clearing there, as if for a house. They also asked him to push dirt and trees into a berm between the clearing and the river. They did not tell him that they were setting up a target range and a sword training area.

Njondac made practice swords and Charly began teaching Janice how to fight with a sword. Mischal also bought three 22 caliber pistols and taught all three girls to shoot. He did not give them the guns, but did tell them where they would be stored, in case of need. He held classes on safety on the range, and made sure that the girls practiced safety as well as weapons handling.

Nevertheless, by the end of the second week tensions were high. The investigation had stalled, and no one had anything essential to do. They were just marking time and getting thoroughly bored. They might as well be at home, and everyone knew it, but no one would say it.

They had found a church in Sulfur Springs that was comfortable for all. Even the girls enjoyed the Sunday School classes. Sunday afternoon, Mista asked Mischal to take a walk down to the beach.

When they had left the park behind, Mista said, "We're spinning our wheels here. The girls are afraid to work, and we haven't turned up anything else. We might as well be at home."

"I think we all agree with that," Mischal said.

"I still think we need to be here to find and corner the man I want. But nothing is happening right now. We have paid for the park sites for next week. We need to pay for the next month if we stay here."

"We could have electricity and water run to our little acre and move the campers there."

"Yes, but that would take time. Why don't we go home for a while. I'll pay for the next month, to reserve our spaces. You can arrange for power and water drops on the land, and we can take necessary vehicles back for a while."

"Works for me. I'll arrange it sometime tomorrow. Might take me a day or two."

"Fine. I'll take the computer equipment out and leave the trailers here. You probably want to drive the motor homes back. Plan for a month or so at home?"

"Sounds good. There are things that we need to do there. Work, but at least it's not busy work."

"All right. I have decided to adopt the two girls. We can get that done, too. Then if something happens to them we don't have to worry about any legal consequences."

"Two? Janice and Robin, I presume. What about Shawnah?"

"I don't know." Mista rubbed his chin. "Let's talk to Jasmine. She seems to have bonded with her. I don't know if she wants to keep her. If not, then I suppose we should send her home."

"Yes. She did have relatives, didn't she?"

"Yes. She came in with an aunt, who signed papers giving us permission to travel with her. However, she might not be willing to sign her over for adoption. We'll have to ask. And Jasmine might not be interested in adopting her, anyway."

That night when Robin and Janice came in for their nightly loving, Mista was reading. They had taken all the girl's personal possessions out of the burned trailer and then towed it to a junkyard for salvage. Janice slept in the bunkroom with the baby, Samantha, and Robin slept on the couch in the main room. She would go to sleep on Sharra's bed and then Mista would move her when he was ready for bed.

Janice asked, "Are you going to read to us, or do I have to read?"

"Hmmm," Mista said. "This is an adult book, but you can try it if you want to. It's about ethics."

"I'll try it." She settled herself on his lap and took the book, while Robin curled up in his right arm. "There aren't any words in here!"

"Sure there are. I was just reading."

"Here, then, you read it."

The book was a Greek reproduction of the Nicomachaen edition of Aristotle's Ethics. The part he was reading was Aristotle's discussion of the goal of all rational creatures as being ευδαιμονια, pronounced efdemonia, the word usually translated happiness. Mista read the next sentence, in Greek.

"Wait a minute," Janice said. "I don't understand what you are saying."

"Oh, well, this is book written in Greek a little over two thousand years ago. Let me translate it into English as I read."

"Two thousand years? We are learning about a man named Jesus who lived about 2000 years ago. He was a real good man. Was Aristotle good?"

"Yes, I think he was good. By the way, do you know why this year is called 2008 AD?"

"No."

"It is supposed to be 2008 years after that man Jesus was born. We know now that this is probably not the exact year, but you can't change the calendar now."

"What does AD mean?" asked Janice. "Some people call it CE. What does that mean?"

"AD stands for two Latin words, Anno Domini. It means in the year of the Lord. That is Jesus. CE means Christian Era or Common Era. People who are not Christians don't like their calendar to refer to Christianity, so they tried to change the system."

"Now. Aristotle is talking here about happiness, but he is careful to say that happiness is not the same as pleasure. Let me read." He read and translated.

"You understand what he is saying? That happiness, or well being, or being good and content is the end of life, or the goal of living. Happiness is something you do."

"Yes. What happens if you are bad?"

"Then you won't be happy. I'll find a story written by another philosopher about the same time. This one was called 'The Ring of Gyges'. He had a magic ring that made him invisible. He could do anything he wanted to and know that he could not be seen, so could not be caught. It did not make him happy. Read the story."

Mista closed his book and then said, "Enough about this tonight. We are going to go back to Toccoa sometime this week, as soon as we get things ready here. I need to replace your trailer, and we have some other things to do. None of you are working on the Internet trap anyway, so we are going to take a break."

"You said we didn't have to," Robin said.

"Yes, that is true. And you don't. But since you are not, we are not making any progress here. We will figure out something else and come back later. Now, the most important thing for you two. You both said that you wanted to be adopted. If you still want to, we will do that while we are in Toccoa."

"You betcha," Janice said. "I can't wait."

"Me neither," Robin said. "But then you'll find out who I really am."

"You mean that you aren't Robin?"

"No. I mean yes, but I might have aunts and uncles. They might not let you."

"It's possible that they could stop it. I'll contact my lawyer in Atlanta and let him find out. He would have to do the legal work anyway for the adoption to go as planned. You have a birth certificate or anything to prove who you are? We know, but the courts will want to see paper."

Robin shook her head. "It all burned up in the fire. I guess. Since I ran away, I really don't know what happened. The police might want to put me in jail, too."

"Well, we'll just have to be careful. Did you have a social security number?"

"Yes." She gave it to him.

"Good. A lot of children are registered with social security at birth. That will make things a little easier. Now, Janice, did you ever have anything on paper? Like a birth certificate, social security number, or anything?"

"Nope. My mother's name was Ruby and I barely remember her. I think my last name is Stormes. It's been so long since I've used it that I'd almost forgotten it. She was killed in a street fight when I was six. I've been on my own since then."

Mista shook his head. "She was homeless?"

"Yes. We came from Topeka, Kansas, but I don't know what happened. I don't even remember my father. I think maybe he was killed when we got to Atlanta, or maybe we went to Atlanta because he was killed. I don't remember anything before Atlanta, and mother would never talk about it."

"How did you ever survive?"

Janice shrugged. "You learn how, or you die."

"How about school?"

"She got me in school in the first grade, and then she was killed the next summer."

"What school?"

"I don't remember the name. Somewhere in Atlanta."

"Okay. We might be able to find out."

Mista called his lawyer the next morning. "A girl named Janice, last name Stormes, entered a school in downtown Atlanta in 2003. See if you can find out anything about her. Her mother's name was Ruby. She has been living in the homeless community in Atlanta for more than six years, but I believe she was born in Topeka, Kansas. I want to adopt her. Do whatever you can to identify her, and even if you can't find out who she is or was, I will adopt her anyway."

"Hah. You have plenty of money to spend, right? Send me DNA sample, fingerprints and footprint. I'll get somebody on it. I suppose you want this right away?"

"Yes. We will be back in Atlanta next week for a month. I want to adopt her officially in February. Also, another girl. This one is more difficult."

"More difficult than a homeless orphan, or supposed orphan, who claims not to know her last name? Let me have it."

"Discreet inquiries. Her house burned down in December and she ran away. We found her and took her in. I want to adopt her, also. We believe that her mother died in a fire. I don't know if she has any other relatives. If police are looking for her, we might have to wait until the heat dies down. Her name is Robin Smith. She was born on January 15, 1998. Atlanta, I believe."

"Fortunately, not a common name. Should be a piece of cake." He sighed. "All right, I'll see what I can do. You are prepared to pay for a lot of time, aren't you?"

"Yes. I know it won't be easy, but that's what I need you for. I'll give you another call when we get back."

"You need to be aware that we have to be able to prove identity – birth certificates – and prove that the parents are deceased. Then we have to file a petition for adoption in your home county and then wait 30 days before it can become final."

"Well, it might be March, then. If we have to wait, we'll just have to wait."

Chapter 33

After the afternoon classes, the girls went down to the playground and swung for a while. Then Robin jumped down and said, "I'm going to ride down to the beach."

Janice said, "You better not. You'll get in trouble."

"No I won't. It's not far. I asked the man at the gate and he told me how to get there. I'll be back before supper."

"Okay. But, I'm telling you, you better not. He said not to go off anywhere."

"It's not all that far."

Robin was careful to follow her directions exactly, and sure enough, the beach was not far. No one was there, but she was not surprised. Not many people went to the beach in January. However, today was a little warmer than usual, and it was her last day here. Well, maybe one more day, but they were leaving, and she might never get to come back. She loved the water and the way the waves came in and crashed on the beach.

She sat on her bike for a long time just watching the waves come in and thinking about all that had happened to her. It seemed like a year had gone by in the last few weeks. Losing her mother had hurt terribly at first. She had been an alcoholic and rarely did anything for Robin. Robin had learned to wash clothes and how to cook. She had cooked almost every meal that they had eaten for the past year. Robin had even missed school many times to stay home to take care of her mother. *Whatever happens to me, I don't want to grow up to be like that. I'll never touch a drop of drink. For all her failings, though, I still miss my mother.*

However, that loss had propelled her into another situation. Now she had a real mother and father ready to take her. They had been good to her, and seemed to really care about what might happen to her. It seemed too good to be true. And yet, several times they would have had the right do dump her or punish her, and they had not. They had bought things for her. Pretty much what she had asked for. Of course, she had not asked for a lot, but they had never refused. Especially this skirt and blouse, her favorite of all. It was a wool plaid skirt that cut off just above the knees and a white blouse.

She looked around again. Still no one. She propped her bike on a palm tree and ran the lock through the rear wheel spokes like Mista had shown her. It could be taken, but they would have to lift the rear wheel and carry it while trying to steer the front. Then she walked down to the edge of the water. She stepped back when the waves started creeping up. *Tide coming in. Wonder what makes the water come up and then go back down?* Mista had told her it was tides, but had not told her what made tides. She'd have to ask him. He knew everything.

Suddenly a bigger wave came in and the water ran up onto her sneakers. Oops. *Oh well, they aren't very wet. Water won't hurt sneakers anyway. And since they are wet, I could wade out into the water a little. Maybe knee deep. It feels so good.*

She waded out a little further. *Should take off my sneakers and socks, but then I'd get sand in them when I put them back on. They're already wet anyway.* Then she noticed the minnows swimming around her legs. The waves rose and fell as they came in, rising just over her knees on the big ones. She leaned over and put her hand in the water and watched as the minnows all scurried away. They came back after a few minutes, though and nibbled at her legs and her fingers as long as she was still. The minnows fascinated her. She moved her hand a little, and the darted away and then came back. She did not notice the rising water, even when the tops of the waves began to brush her skirt hem.

Then a bigger wave raised her skirt quite a lot, and she did notice that the hem was wet. *Oh, well. It doesn't really show on this dark wool, though. Nobody will notice.* She played with the minnows a while longer.

After a while she thought about her bike. It should be safe, but … She turned to look, and saw a boy examining the lock. "HEY!" she called. "That's my bike." A much bigger wave rolled in, making a secondary breaker right behind her, and the water rose all the way to her waist.

She hardly noticed. She ran splashing out to get her bike. The boy saw her coming and ran off. *Phew. Thought I'd lost another one. That would never do.*

She unlocked her bike and rode back to the camp. The wind was cold while riding, reminding her of how wet she was. Can't go back like this. They'll know right away that I've been down to the beach. I'll just swing a while till the skirt dries some, and nobody can see that it is a little wet. Still be home in time for supper.

Chapter 34

When supper was served, Robin had not come home. Sharra looked at Mista and raised an eyebrow. "What do you think?"

"I have no idea. She's never been late before. You want to check on her?"

"No. I told her that I would stay out of her mind. I did set a danger link with her, though, and if she were in trouble I would know that."

"Doesn't keep her from running off, though."

"No. Do you think she would?"

"No," Mista said. He rubbed his forehead. "I can't believe that she would run off now. A few days ago, maybe, but not after all that has happened. She knows that we plan to adopt her, and she wants that."

Janice and Shawnah were sitting close enough to overhear them. Both girls looked steadily at their plates as they ate. If Mista asked them if they knew where Robin was, they would have to tell, and neither wanted to tattle on their chum. Mista did not ask. He decided that the best thing to do was wait and see what happened.

After supper, Mista retired to his big chair to read. A few minutes later, Robin poked her head in, and then tip-toed into the room, heading for her bunkroom. Mista said, "Where are you going, Hon?"

"I'm ... uh ... going to my room to change. Am I in time for supper? I'm starved."

"No, I'm afraid supper is over. Why do you need to change. Come here."

She tried to walk softly, but her shoes still squished. "Hmmm." Mista put his arm around her. She tried to step back, so he wouldn't feel her wet skirt, but he did not release her. "Skirt, too. What happened?"

"I … I fell and got dirty. I washed off in the outside shower, but I guess I got too much water."

"Oh." He rubbed a finger on her leg. "Salt. Salty water in the shower now?"

"I don't know. Whatever." She could not look at him.

Mista reached over and lifted her chin, forcing her to look at him. "Salty water is only in one place. You went to the beach, didn't you?"

"No. You said not to …"

Two tears rolled down her cheeks, followed by many more. "You said not to, but we were leaving and I wanted to see it one last time I didn't mean to get wet, I just wasn't paying attention I'll work hard on extra things and buy new clothes if they're ruined." Her words tumbled out like one long sentence.

"Hon, I'm not worried about the clothes. Doesn't hurt them to get wet. The salt will scratch a little, to remind you, and then we'll wash the salt out. I'm worried about you."

"I'm all right."

"Why did I tell you not to go to the beach?"

"I shouldn't be out alone. But it's not that far. And I didn't go far out in the water."

"What if a big wave had come along and carried you out to sea?"

Her eyes got big. "It can do that?"

"Yes. You never go to the beach alone."

"You didn't tell me that."

"I shouldn't have to. In time I would have given you proper warning, but it should be enough that I asked you not to."

"I know. But I wanted to see it one last time."

"Why didn't you ask? I would have taken you down."

"I was afraid you'd say no. Is it all right now? Can I go change?"

"Not yet. The clothes will dry. Maybe you should wear them until they do dry. But that's not a problem. You didn't get hurt or lost. I do love you and am glad nothing happened to you. Maybe you learned something. But there is something else. What did I say is the worst thing you can do?"

She didn't answer at first, and the tears came harder. "Lie?"

"Did you lie?"

"Y – yes."

"Why?"

"I didn't want you to know that I went to the beach."

"Going to the beach I will forgive. Don't let it happen again. The lying, I cannot let go."

"You're going to send me away?"

"I thought about it."

"But, Uncle Mista, I don't want to leave!"

"Then you should obey."

"I will! I promise I will!"

"What should I do to make sure that you remember that?"

"I don't know. Yell at me! Take my bike. Send me to bed without supper. Anything. I don't want to have to leave."

"Little Bird, I don't want you to leave, either. But I have to be able to trust you. Once you lie, you break trust, and then it is ten times as hard to trust you again. I don't yell at you. I won't ever do that. Taking the bike – no that's not appropriate. I think the only thing I can do is spank you. I don't think you'll forget that."

Robin gulped. She had never been spanked. Her mother had hit her, slapped her and hit at her. But spanking – well, she had told him that he could. "Okay. Does it hurt bad?"

"Supposed to." He set his knees together, feet flat on the floor. "Bend over my knee. She leaned over against his knees. "Pull your skirt up. No insulation."

"Oop!" She reached back and pulled it up and waited, eyes screwed shut.

Mista placed his left hand on her back and raised his right hand. "This hurts me worse that it hurts you," he said.

Sure it does. Just get on with it.

He slapped her hard on the bottom. She yelped and then snapped her mouth shut. *I will not cry. I will not cry. I don't care how bad it hurts or how long it lasts.* Tears came anyway, but she did not cry out. She waited for the next blow, but it did not come.

Mista said, "I can't do this. I love you too much."

Sharra sent, You have to now that you've started.

No. Let's see how this works out.

"Sit up, Robin. Look at me."

She sat on his knees and looked at him, her bottom still stinging. He placed his hands on her sides and said, "I cannot allow a person in my household to be a liar or a thief. I don't ever want to hurt you, even in punishment. But I must be able to trust you."

"You can, Uncle Mista. I'll never do it again, I promise." She leaned forward and put her arms around his neck. "Just don't send me away. Please don't send me away."

Mista hugged her. "I promised to take you in and adopt you. I keep my promises. I don't want you to worry about being sent away. There is much more to worry about. But if you continue to lie, or if you steal, then I will have to reconsider. And I don't want to have to do that."

"You won't. I love you and Sharra. You can trust me."

"All right. I'll give you the chance to prove that. Now get ready for bed and go on to bed."

Robin left and came back a few minutes later in her nightgown. "Where? There are still people in here."

"Go to sleep in our bed. I'll move you later."

Jania said, "Honey, you should have seen what he did to me. I'll never forget."

"What?"

"He took his belt off and told me to spank him."

Robin's eyes were wide. "Did you?"

"I couldn't. No way could I hit him. But I'll never forget that night."

Robin went on and crawled into bed. She was hungry, and she was cold. Mostly she was afraid that Mista now hated her. She could not sleep. Later she heard Janice come into the main room and talk with Mista. She read to him. Robin cried. She should have been there, but he had sent her to bed. She heard Janice kiss him good night and walk out.

When Sharra came in a few minutes later and went to bed, she pretended to be asleep. Sharra stroked her hair and kissed her, but Robin pretended still to be asleep.

Everything grew quiet. She knew that Mista must be reading, but she still could not sleep. Even when he came in to carry her to bed, she pretended to be asleep. He laid her on the couch and covered her. He stood over her for a minute, and then kissed her lightly on the forehead, and went back to his chair.

Robin lay still for a few minutes, but then she could stand it no longer. She got up and walked over to his chair. "Uncle Mista, do you hate me now?"

Mista picked her up and set her in his lap. "No, honey, I don't. I love you very much and that's why your breaking my trust hurts me so much."

"Are you just mad at me, then?"

"No. Not even that. Just disappointed."

Robin wrapped her arms around his neck. She was crying again. "You didn't even say good night or anything."

"I know."

"I can't stand it if you're mad at me."

He pulled her up tight and rocked a few minutes without speaking. "In everything you do, for the rest of your life. Remember, you cannot build a relationship with someone if they can't trust you. I would have forgiven you for going down to the beach. I would have taken you if you'd asked. I'm hurt because you didn't trust me enough to believe that."

"I didn't know. But, I won't forget."

"Okay. Good night, Little Bird."

"Good night, Uncl – can I call you Daddy, now?"

"If that's what you want. I'd be proud if you do."

She tingled all over. "Good night, Daddy." She kissed him and went to bed. This time she was asleep before Mista went over and covered her.

When he went to bed, Sharra said, "I don't know how you do it, Darling. But I don't think she will ever forget this night."

"And if I'd just spanked her?"

She took his hand and squeezed it. "You know she'd have forgotten it sooner or later."

Chapter 35

Two days later they were on the road north. They had left all the trailers in place and told the camp manager that they would probably bring a replacement trailer with them when they returned. Jania was on her way back to school.

Sometime during the morning Mista became aware that the murmur of voices in the back seat had dropped to a whisper. He glanced in the mirror. Sheila was asleep in one corner and the two girls had their heads together. As he watched, their voices raised a little in volume and their heads parted. He could now make out most of the words.

Robin was saying, "He does not! I know he doesn't, because he said he didn't."

Janice said, "How do you know you can trust him?"

"Because he doesn't lie."

"How do you know that? Most adults do lie about things. Especially about things that they do and don't want you to know."

Robin shook her head. "He doesn't. After that fuss he made about me lying? I don't know how he knew, but he *knows*."

"Maybe Sharra told him?"

"No. She said she would not go into my mind again unless there was some kind of danger. She doesn't lie, either. Besides, she wasn't even in the room."

"How can you be so sure?"

After a minute, Robin said, "I don't know. Maybe it is part of whatever is in my mind that can start fires. But I know. I don't think anybody in the family will lie about anything. And for some reason, Mischal and Charly *can't* lie."

"Anybody can, and most people do lie when they feel like it."

"Yeah, I know. But, I don't think these people do."

"Ask Uncle Mista. He knows everything."

Mista could not help smiling when Robin said, "Yeah, I know. I'm not going to ask him. He'll want to know why."

Janice said, "I'll ask him. I'm not afraid." She tapped him on the shoulder. "Uncle Mista, is it true that Mischal and Charly cannot lie at all, even if they wanted to?"

"That's true, but not accurate," Mista said.

"What's the difference?" asked Janice.

"What is a lie?" asked Mista.

"I ... saying something that is not true."

"Okay," Mista said. "I'm telling you now that we will be in Atlanta by 3:00 this afternoon. What if something happens and we don't get there till four? Is that a lie?"

"No ... you didn't know the future."

"But I did say it. And it wasn't true. Why is it not a lie?"

"I don't know. Because you didn't mean to be wrong?"

"Yes. Lying is intentionally deceiving someone. What if I were able to read minds, and I told you that I could not? That would be a lie. What if you asked me if I could, and I said something like I didn't have to read minds, because I can tell pretty well what people are thinking without reading minds. Would that be a lie?"

"Can you tell?"

"Pretty much."

"Then, no. You didn't say you couldn't."

"Wrong. I would be intentionally deceiving you. The technical word for it is dissembling. Leading you to believe something by an action or by giving an answer which while true in itself, still leads you to believe an untruth. What if I did not answer your question, but Sharra said that she didn't think so. What then?"

"No. You didn't say anything."

"No. I would be lying. You asked the question, and someone answered wrongly, and I did not correct them, therefore causing them to think something untrue by my action. Or untrue. Now, if I tell you that Robin's birthday is tomorrow and it turns out that I was wrong – that it is in fact today – is that a lie?"

Janice thought about that. "People say it all the time when they are wrong. 'I lied.' No, I don't think so."

"Correct. I would not be intentionally deceiving you. I would simply be wrong. Now, to answer your real question about me, I cannot read minds, but my father taught me to read the little things that people do and guess pretty well what they are thinking. I will always know if you try to lie. Ask Robin."

Robin said, "Told you."

Mista smiled. "Mischal and Charly have taken a vow to God. It is more than a promise. They swore an oath to God that they would never lie. If they do break that vow, then God will punish them. He helps them fight when they are in battle. They would lose that special help. They could lie, but the binding of that vow to God is so strong that for all practical purposes, they cannot lie, and they certainly would never want to. They might be tempted, but never actually want to."

"I don't ever want to, either," Robin said.

"That was a promise to me," Mista said. "I certainly hope that you keep it. But a vow is much, much stronger. Ever jump off something just to see if you could? Like a porch, or something?"

"Sure."

"Would you jump off a ten-story building?"

"NO! I'd die."

"That is about what it would feel like if Charly or Mischal were asked to lie. And because of an experience that Mischal had, he probably would die. At least he thinks he would."

"Wow," Janice said. "What happened?"

"Long story. I'll tell you sometime. Or ask Mischal. He might tell you. Why did you ask? Did one of them say something about lying?"

"No," Robin said. "I don't know how, but I knew that they can't lie. I had no idea why they felt like that, I just knew that it was so."

"Hmmm," Mista said. "Be sure to tell Jeremy. It might be another power beginning to manifest."

Later, Robin said to Janice, "Try to tell him a lie and see if he doesn't know."

"No way. I believe you. And I don't want to get in trouble. He sent you to bed without supper, didn't he?"

"Yeah. Without anything. No stories, no loving, no rocking. Nothing. I couldn't sleep."

Janice said with a knowing smirk, "He spanked you, didn't he? You should have worn two or three pairs of jeans."

"I was going to put on both of mine and one of yours over them, but I never got to my room. Anyway, he didn't really spank me."

"Oh?" she raised an eyebrow. "Either you got spanked or you didn't. You can't get sort-of spanked."

"It was weird. I'll never forget that. He started to. He hit me once – and that *hurt*. Then he quit and said he couldn't do it. I'll tell you this. I don't ever want him to get mad at me."

After supper that night the girls came to Mista with a request. "Daddy," Janice said, "since we are going to belong to you, do we have to sleep way on the other side of the building? Can't we have a room near you?"

Mista smiled. "Yes. We'll make room for you over here tonight. Let's go find one."

Since the building had been built with rooms for 50 people on each side of the main hall, each family had taken a set of connecting rooms to make a personal suite. The room next to Mista's bedroom was empty, so Mista asked, "Since this already has a double bed, can you sleep together or do you want separate beds?"

They looked at each other. "We'll sleep together," Janice said.

"Okay," Mista said. "It's yours. Put your things in it."

Then he led them to the room two doors down the hall. The door was open and Mista said, "We call this our family room. You see the chairs and TV in here. I'll be in here when you are ready for bed."

Sharra was waiting with him when the girls came in. Mista said, "I need to ask you a few questions and I think I want Sharra to read your minds and make sure that the answers are completely accurate. I don't mean that you would lie, but you might have made a mistake."

"Okay," Robin said. "I've learned my lesson."

Janice was not so sure. "What is it about?"

"About your parents and your birth and early years."

"Oh. I've told you everything I remember. But go ahead. You think I might have forgotten something?"

"Could have. Let's start with you, Janice. You were born in Topeka. Do you remember your father's name?"

"No. I think it was Topeka, but I don't really remember. I don't remember my father at all. His last name must have been Stormes, since that is my name."

Sharra sent, True, so far. She has no active memory of Kansas or her father. Just some remarks that her mother made.

"All right. Do you have any aunts or uncles or any grandparents?"

"Not that I know of. I might, but I have no way of knowing."

Sharra nodded. Mista said, "Okay. You understand, when we go to court, if we are wrong we could all get in trouble. Might even go to jail. I don't want that, and I'm sure you don't either. Or they might just set aside the adoption and send you to somebody else, or even have the state take you and put you in foster care, thinking that we lied and so aren't going to be good parents. We have to be absolutely sure."

"I understand," Janice said. "I've told you all that I know."

"Okay. Robin. You didn't bring your birth certificate with you, did you?"

"No. You know I didn't have anything."

"Well, you didn't have anything when I first saw you, but you ran away a few days before that. Your mother's and father's names?"

My mother was Mary, but I don't remember my father. I think he was in the Army or something."

You were born in Atlanta?"

"I think so. Atlanta or somewhere near."

"Okay, Georgia, at least. Aunts and uncles and grandparents?"

"I have two aunts, but we haven't talked to them in a long time. I think that they will be glad to see me gone. I don't know about grandparents. Mother never talked about them."

"Well, we will see what happens. I need to call and schedule a visit at the lawyer's office. Do you think a new dress and shoes would make the visit more interesting?"

Their eyes lit up. "Oh, yes!" they both said at once.

"Okay. We'll go early enough to find you something nice. You can change in the store, and then we will go on. However, before anything else happens, let me give you a set of rules that you must agree to. I don't expect you to be perfect angels, but these are rules for expected behavior. Understand?"

They nodded.

"Then you agree?"

Robin said, "Yes."

Janice said, "You didn't give us the rules."

Mista smiled. "Smart girl. Don't ever agree to anything unless you understand it."

Robin said, "But we know you wouldn't give us something bad. Would you?"

"No, I wouldn't. But still, never agree until you hear what it is. You both know the Ten Commandments, don't you?"

Robin said, "Yes. But nobody keeps them all the time."

Janice said, "I don't know what they are."

Mista said, "We try to keep them all the time, but of course, no one is perfect. Read them later, Janice. They are in the book of Exodus in your Bible. There are many little rules and interpretations of what to do, but these are the basis of everything else. One, we don't really keep like it was written. The Sabbath Day was Saturday. We worship on Sunday. It is still every seven days, but we are not quite as strict as it was written. However, we do believe that there is only one god, we do not swear, and we do not have idols. It is the next six that form the basis for your rules of conduct. Honor and obey your parents. That will be us. They will issue a new birth certificate with our names on it as your official parents. Okay?"

"Sure."

"All right. We have talked about lying and stealing. Adultery is not something you are likely to be interested in for a long time. However, when you do get interested, remember that you have agreed not to do it."

"Okay."

"The last two are pretty important. The last commandment is covetousness. It is not simple. It doesn't mean that you can't want something like somebody else has, but that you cannot want to take it if it belongs to them. Like lying, it has a deeper meaning. It really means that you should not want anything that you should not have. The old Greek people had two sayings that pretty well summed up the ancient Greek way of life. Gnothi seauton is Greek for 'know thyself'. That means that you must know who you really are and know your limits. Put the other phrase with it, 'nothing in excess', and you have a good guide. Coveting means wanting something that you should not have and wanting to be something that you are not, and a lot more. Wish for things, but do not demand them. Ask me for anything that you want, for example. But, if I say 'no', then I have a reason. Accept that."

"Okay."

"Now, murder. Many books say, 'thou shalt not kill'. The actual word means murder. We are going after a very bad man, as you know. Depending on what happens, we might kill him. If we do, it will not be murder. You have to understand that. Some people call any killing murder, but that is wrong. Murder is kin to coveting. It is taking a life that does not belong to you. We do not murder, but we have had to kill some people in battle. We do not like to, but sometimes, people will not listen.

"Well, all this come down to a few simple rules for you. No lying, stealing, coveting. No drugs, no alcohol, no sex. Anything else we will talk about, but these things are absolute."

Robin said, "I already agreed."

Janice said, "That sounds okay to me. I agree."

"Well, then, time for bed. Cuddle up."

Chapter 36

They finally got their court date on the last Friday in March. The girls were dancing with anticipation, Robin in a new white dress and patent leather shoes, Janice in a blue and white check and white sandals. Before they went out to the car, Mista said, "I have one more requirement before we take the final step."

He produced two white buttons about two inches across. They had a point behind them designed to be punched into a bulletin board, and the front had a red circle around the edge, with a diagonal line across the button, and the words, "NO WHINING" in large letters.

"I need to stick these to your chests so you won't forget."

Janice backed away. "You mean stick that point into my chest? Just like that? No way."

"Why not? The marines like to stick medals to their recruits so that they can prove how much a man they are. You are better than Marines, aren't you?"

"Yeah, but you can't stick that into me. I'd bleed all over my new dress."

"So? Then the judge would know you were serious about this."

Robin said, "Do we have to?"

"Yep."

"Will it hurt?"

"Not for long."

She sighed. "Okay. Maybe it will quit hurting by the time we get there." She closed her eyes and stood ready.

Janice, not to be outdone by the younger girl, said, "Well, if she will, then I will. Stick it to me."

Mista put one hand behind her back and raised a button in the other hand. Janice looked him square in the eye, waiting. Mista dropped his hand and laughed. He stooped and put an arm around both girls. "I can't do that to you."

Charly said from across the room, "You better learn when he's teasing, or you will never know which end is up."

Mista gave a button to each girl and said, "I do want you to have the buttons to remind you that in this family, we do not whine. If we don't like something, we try to change it. If we can't change it, then we just go on and accept it. No whining."

Janice said, "We haven't been whining."

"No, you haven't," Mista said. "And that's a good thing. Just remember, we never whine."

The process did not take long. The judge handed Mista new birth certificates with his and Sharra's name on them as parents and ordered the old ones sealed. He said, "Robin Mictackic and Janice Mictackic, you are now part of a new family. I trust that you will make your new parents proud."

When they returned, Mista said, "I have one more button for you to wear." He pulled two buttons from his pocked and pinned one on each of the girls. "This is your official ID button."

Janice was the first to take hers off and read it. "Property of Mista and Sharra Mictackic. If found wandering loose, please return. $5.00 reward for safe return."

"Property?" she said. "We're property? I thought we were supposed to be daughters."

"Daughters are property," Mista said. "If you don't perform, I can sell you to the highest bidder."

Robin's eyes got big, and she looked like she was about ready to cry. "I thought we were here permanent."

Janice said, "Five dollars? Is that all I'm worth?"

"Yep. I've already spent a bundle on you. I figure another five is enough to ensure that I don't lose my investment."

Sharra had to turn her back to keep from laughing. He had done something similar when he adopted Jania.

Janice studied the button. "Well, if I'm property, I should get an allowance, anyway."

"Okay," Mista said. "Is a dollar a week enough?"

"One dollar? No way. At least ten."

Mista rubbed his chin. "Well. If ten dollars keeps you from running away, I guess it will be worth it."

He turned to Robin. "I suppose you want an allowance, too."

"Well, it would be nice."

"How about if I split the ten dollars, and give you five apiece?"

Janice said, "No way. You promised it to me."

"Oh, well. That leaves you nothing, Robin."

"That's okay. I don't really need it."

Sharra said, "Mista, you better stop teasing them or they won't know what to think."

Mista dropped to Robin's level and took her shoulders in his hands. "Robin, honey, if I teach you anything at all, I hope to teach you to stand up for your rights. There is no way I would give Janice an allowance and not give you the same thing. The real question is, is that enough?"

"Sure," Janice said.

Robin said, "More than enough."

"Of course, you have to buy your own clothes, now, and ..."

"Mista!" Sharra said.

Mista grinned. "No, it's yours to spend any way you want. I'll buy your clothes, your ice cream, your major toys and everything you need. As for the buttons – you are NOT property, and this *is* permanent. You are now family, officially and permanently. You can't back out now, and I don't think there is any way I can cancel it, even if I wanted to. And I'd pay a whole lot more than five dollars to get you back if something should happen to you. There is no way to put a value on your lives. I'll pay whatever it takes, or do whatever it takes."

Robin said, "What if we make you really, really mad?"

"Then I'd have to hire Mischal to spank you, since you know that I can't do it. And I bet he can spank good. But put out any fear that I would ever throw you out, no matter what you do. You are mine, now. Not as property, but as family, and nothing can change that. Not ever."

Robin put her arm around his neck and closed her eyes. "I was afraid ..."

"Don't be afraid, Little Bird. I shouldn't have been teasing at this time. I love you – love you both – and nothing can make me stop loving you. I don't think you can do anything to make me really, really mad. And even if you did, remember, I don't whine. You are safe here."

Janice came over to his other side and put her arm around his neck. "I was afraid, too. I never had a home, and I was afraid that it was not really true."

"Don't you be afraid, either, Tanker. It's real. There is no risk that you would be thrown out, or sent away ever again."

"Hmmm. That means I can be bad, now? And you can't do anything about it?"

Sharra sent, Serves you right. You got your comeuppance real quick, didn't you?

Mista looked into her eyes. "That's right, partially. You can be bad if you want to, and you can't be sent away. However, I believe you are taking sword lessons from Charly?"

"Yes. You can't make her not give me lessons, either." She had the hint of a smirk in her smile, and her eyes were dancing.

"True. But I raised Charly, and she probably remembers some of my lessons. The sword is an excellent weapon, but it is also an excellent spanking tool. She can make it hurt really bad."

Janice glanced at Charly. She nodded. "Yep. I know how to use it."

Janice looked back at Mista. "I don't really want to be bad. I was just teasing."

Mista smiled. "I thought so. But this time I was not. If you do something bad, we will have to arrange an appropriate punishment. It will not be sending you away. That's final. But I do have other options. You girls have been very good, and I don't expect to ever have to think of punishment. And I hope not. But don't test me, okay?"

Janice squeezed his neck and said, "Okay."

Robin said, "Remember, I couldn't stand it when I thought you were mad at me. I don't ever want you to get mad at me."

"I can't promise that. I hope that it never happens, but only time will tell." He gave each of the girls a ten-dollar bill. "Your first week's allowance. Now, go change and -- pack your things. We will head south again real soon, now, since this court thing is over. Monday, Misch?"

"Leave tomorrow if you want to," Mischal said. "That would get us there before the end of the month, and we could go ahead and move onto the new property. Save you a month's rent. It's supposed to be ready, road graded, electricity, water and septic tank."

"Suits me. Everybody else ready?"

He got nods all round. "Okay, tomorrow, then."

Chapter 37

They loaded the vehicles out that evening, so that they would be ready to leave first thing in the morning. Mista had found another used trailer to be used for a staging area, and Mischal had modified it by building two rooms in the back. He had also built a back door. Jasmine made another modification. She put her medical supplies in one of the rooms and planned to sleep in the main bedroom. Shawnah took the room with the back door.

Em and Sheila had been with Mista on his shopping trip for the trailer. As they watched, Em said, "You know, we don't have a home while we are traveling. I'm tired of bumming a sleeping space, aren't you?"

"Yes, but I don't know what else to do."

"See that little truck over there? That's what they call a Class B camper. We could put two beds in the back, and have enough space for just us. What do you think?"

Sheila's eyes lit up. "Let's go look."

They had decided that it was perfect. It already had two single beds in the back, plus a small table where most campers that size had a bench seat.

Sheila had asked Mista about it, and he had agreed immediately. "If you want it, Sis, it's yours. Nothing is too good for you. And I understand your need for some privacy."

Em said, "And it's not so big that we can't drive it. We can take turns."

It only took a few minutes for the girls to load their things, and then Janice got on line one last time. Robin watched over her shoulder. Campbell contacted her almost immediately. Since Jeremy was getting their motor home ready to travel, and Molly was not in that evening, no one was monitoring Campbell mentally.

After a few exchanges by way of greeting, he asked her if she were really eleven.

"Yeppers. I'm really eleven. Why?"

"I just wondered if you had had sex yet."

"Oh, no. Don't you think I'm a little too young for that?"

"Not at all. I think eleven is the perfect age to start. Are you interested?"

"Well, yeah. I guess. No one ever asked me before. The boys I know don't even seem interested."

"Well, boys your age wouldn't be. I think the onset of puberty is the perfect time. You do know about puberty, don't you?"

"Of course I do. Mine started about a year ago."

"Yes, that's normal. Boys start a little later. I'd be more than willing to show you how wonderful it can be."

"Won't it hurt? I'm not very big yet. You've seen my picture."

"Where do you live? I could come over if it is in my area."

"Near Clearwater, but I'm not allowed to give out my address on the Internet."

"Well, what your parents don't know won't hurt them. I live in Clearwater, so it would not take me long to get there."

"Not tonight. My dad is in and out and he always looks at the screen and asks who I'm chatting with. You couldn't come over anyway while they are home."

"They? Who is they?"

"My parents, silly. It would have to be one afternoon after school, and before they get home."

"One day next week, then?"

"That will work. I'll let you know when is a good time. I know I'll be busy Monday and Tuesday, but after that, maybe."

"No maybe. I have to make an excuse to get off work. You can't chicken out on me. How about some internet sex so you'll know what to expect?"

"Not with my dad coming in and out. He'd ground me."

Janice said, "Robin, go get Jeremy. He needs to be in on this." Then she continued chatting with Campbell for another fifteen minutes before he got bored and signed off. Jeremy came in a few minutes before the conversation died. He reached out and contacted Campbell and listened. After a minute, he said, "He's hot tonight. He's ready to come over right now. I don't know if he wants to rape you or kill you. I don't think *he* does, either."

"I don't know if I want him to come over at all," Janice said. "You're scaring me."

"Don't be scared. We're better prepared this time. You won't have to see him."

"I'm not afraid of him. If he tries anything, I'll show him my knife."

"Whatever, Janice. Don't tell him your address tonight. Just play him along. We don't want him to know that we are up here still. Anyway, I don't know the street address. We'll have to get that when we get there. We'll need a few days anyway to set all the trailers up and out of sight from the road. We only want him to see one trailer."

Campbell sat and stared at his screen for a long time after he signed off. He didn't know whether he wanted to have sex with her – he did not consider it a rape – or whether he wanted to kill her and rid the world of one more prostitute. Finally, he decided to have it both ways. He also decided to double his pleasure. He would call Sam and trade the information on this girl for the name and address of another girl. Then he could have both.

Jeremy still had no clue to the whereabouts of this Sam, or even who he really was. He might or might not be the same person who had abducted Sheila so long ago. However, if he got the name and address of another of Sam's girls ... Maybe something was finally coming out of all the effort they had been putting in.

The land had been prepared exactly as Mischal had specified. The road that wound through the woods from the highway to the river was gravel. He had ordered a 24-foot swath to be cut through the trees with a 12-foot road in the center. It had to be wide enough to handle trucks and trailers and motor homes, but he did not want it to look like an industrial park. He and Njondac had agreed that they did not want the natural look of the land to be disturbed any more than was necessary.

The first parking spot was for the girls' trailer. The water and electric meters were located here, at the edge of the road. Power lines to the trailer from the meter were intentionally obvious. Underground lines from the meter to the other camping sites were not at all obvious, but water lines and electric lines were run to each of the sites.

The first site was wide and deep, and covered with a layer of gravel. It had room to park several vehicles. Mischal had not expected to have Em's motor home, but there was room in the first site to park it.

From here the road turned sharply to the left. Trailers could use some of the first site for an extra turning radius. It curved to the right after a hundred yards. The road was graded and packed after all the trees had been removed, and then seeded with grass seed. After the grass had grown, several thin layers of gravel had been added. The idea was to have enough gravel to make the road solid, but to look like a little used road.

The curve continued to make a 180 degree turn, ran straight to the property line, and then made another turn, doubling back on itself again, but not the full 180 degrees. From this point, the road curved slowly down to the river. Mischal had put a large clearing just past the first curve, on the river side. He shared this site with Charly and left room to build a playground in the area between the two motor homes. Mista's site was in the bow of the second curve. That made it directly behind the girls' trailer, but completely out of sight. He had cut a trail though the woods between the two trailers with several curves in it so that it was not a straight visual link.

Njondac's site was halfway to the river. He still valued his seclusion.

Em made the only objection. "I don't like being stuck out on the road with nobody nearby."

"Hmmm," Mischal said. "Why don't we have a site built for you across the road from Mista? Meanwhile, since the playground hasn't been built yet, you can park between Charly and me. Then the workers can finish the playground after they build your site. You know, I didn't expect you to have your own camper."

"I know. Yes, that will work fine."

It took all week to finish the construction. The land had quite a few small pin oak trees, and these they cut and split for their campfires. The three girls rode up and down the road from the main highway to the riverbank. Janice spent some time every evening online, but none in the afternoons. Campbell came on one evening, but made no reference to their sex talk of the previous week.

Thursday evening they all took a break and went to a local Maumday Thursday service. Janice was fascinated with the things she had been learning in Sunday School, Em's teaching and her own reading. She had always known that there were churches and Christians, of course, but had never had any contact with them except for the occasional benevolent meals provided. Robin had been to some church services from time to time, but there had been no consistency for her. She also was interested. The ceremonies and preaching at the Maundy Thursday service was entirely new to both of them, and they had many questions after they got home. Mista and Jasmine talked to them for an hour about what it meant to be a Christian, who Jesus really was and many other questions.

The last thing that Mischal and Njondac did was to watch the workers run a heavy roller over the new parking site to pack in several layers of gravel. Since the camper here was more of a truck than a motor home – although it was a Class B motor home -- it did not have built in levelers. Therefore, the lot had to be perfectly level. When they finished, Mischal would drive the camper onto the lot and park it at Em's direction. He would then check the levels inside the camper to make sure that it was completely level. He knew that he could always get after-market levelers, but preferred to have a level lot.

Chapter 38

The girls watched for a while, and then rode down to the river. Three rough looking men were sitting near the water, smoking.

"Ain't it interesting how people build roads to nowhere?" one of the asked. "This here road don't go nowhere."

"I think it's much more interesting what's coming down that road," another said.

"Well, looka there. Two pretty little girls and a boy. Where'd y'all come from?"

The three girls stopped their bikes. Janice said, "Up the road." She was surprised at being called a boy, but then she remembered that her hair was pulled up under her ball cap.

"You live around here?"

"Yeah, not too far." Janice was the only one that was not afraid. They did not look any worse that some of the men she had been around when living on the streets of Atlanta.

The men got up and sauntered over toward the girls. Robin whispered, "Let's go."

One of the men was close enough to hear and said, "Well, now, little girl, we're fun loving boys. We wouldn't want to be hurting a pretty little girl."

He stepped forward quickly and grabbed her arm. "You're a sweet one, I'll bet." He rubbed a finger across her chest. "Beginning to show a little buds, too?"

Robin tried to jerk away, but he held her. Another man moved toward Shawnah, while the one who seemed to be the leader stood in the center of the road, watching. Shawnah spun her bike and raced back toward the campers, looking over her shoulder to see if she was getting away. She was leaving the man behind, but unfortunately, she was not looking where she was going. Her bike hit the sand at the edge of the road and began to slide. She jerked the wheel and tried to right it, but the wheel turned completely sideways, and the bike flipped her over the handlebars. She landed up against a tree and blacked out.

Janice said, "Hey, you leave my sister alone!"

The leader leered and said, "What are you going to do, little boy? Fight for her? Come on. Let's see you fight." He stepped forward with his fists raised.

Janice leaped from her bike, letting it fall wherever it wanted. She drew her knife at the same time and flipped it open. She had no intention of pitting her small strength directly against a large man. She could hear Charly talking to her in her lessons. *Wish I had a sword right now, but this will do. He won't expect it.* Charly kept saying to always do the unexpected. Never be where your opponent thinks you're going to be. He has strength and reach. You have sure feet and fast responses. Use your advantages against him. This is not a contest of strength. "Run! Rob – Run! Get help."

But Robin could not run. The man held her with one hand and began to pull her shirt down with the other. "Come on, little girl show me your bumps."

Robin jerked back and tried again to run. The man slapped her. Not too hard, but enough to hurt and to get her attention. "You can't run, so don't make this hard on yourself."

Janice hit the ground running. She ducked under his fists and drove her knife into the closest part of him. She had hoped for his groin, but did not take time to aim. The knife sank up to it handle in his left arm. She twisted and pulled it free, running on to get behind him. She moved so fast that he did not realize that he had been cut until she was already circling behind him.

"Where'd you go, you little imp? You can't run away." He turned to his left to look behind him, but by this time Janice was already circling to his right. Now she remembered Charly saying, "Never be hasty. Take your time and aim for the spot you want. Anything else just wastes your strength and energy and doesn't hurt him at all."

All right. Forgot to aim. Got his arm, though, and it's bleeding good. Now if I take his left shoulder from behind ... She ran in, and starting high, she sliced his back from the left shoulder down to his waist. He felt that one.

"God! What did you do, kid? Hey! You've got a knife! So, you want to play rough? Okay, I have a knife, too."

Charly had said, "Stand ready. Always ready. Look at his eyes, not his hand. See EVERYTHING, but *Look* at his eyes. Where is he going to strike? Let him strike, and then you will not be there. Don't run! Just don't be where he expects you to be."

Janice stood loose. She could see the other man messing with Robin, and she knew she had to finish this quick, or it would be too late. She repressed the urge to turn and look. Rather she stood loose, like she was out of breath.

"You cut my back, didn't you? All right. Time for fun is over. You'll pay for that." He lunged at her, holding his knife high.

He's going to try to slice me. Got to time it just right, move after he starts his cut, so he can't stop it. She waited, breathing fast. It gave her extra oxygen, as Charly had taught her. To him, it looked like she was out of breath. She watched his eyes. Just before he started his downward cut, she leaped to one side, swung around and cut across his right leg. Then she was behind him; she spun and kicked out, hitting him in the seat. He went sprawling and landed on his own knife.

The third man now went into action. He had expected his friend to disable the boy in a few seconds, but now he was down and not moving. "Hey! Let's see you take me on! I know how to fight!" He pulled a knife and began a slow circle. Janice knew that he knew what he was doing. She turned in place, using minimum effort, but keeping her face toward him.

The man holding Robin grabbed her shirt front and ripped it open, exposing her training bra. Again, he rubbed his hand on her small breasts.

He began to fondle her. Robin screamed, "Leave me alone!" She made another lunge and this time succeeded in pulling away. Before she could run, though, he reached out and grabbed a leg, pulling it out from under her. Robin fell on her face in the gravel.

He pulled her sneaker off by brute force, wrenching her ankle. Then he held her upside down by one leg. "You're a feisty one, aren't you? Well, that's okay. The fight is half the fun. Let's cool you down some, though."

He waded out into the river until he was knee deep, and dropped her head into the water. He held her there for a few seconds and then raised her up. "Ready to play some, now?"

In reply, she spat a mouthful of water into his face. "Gaaah! Let's try that again." He ducked her under again, and then unfastened her belt with his free hand. Then he caught her other foot and lifted her up again. He was ready for another mouthful of water, but instead, she kicked at his face with her free foot.

"You little devil!" He pulled her other sneaker off and then grabbed both legs, one in each hand. One hand at the time, he changed his grip so that he was holding her by the hem of her jeans. He began to bounce her up and down. "I bet with just a little effort you'll slip right out of them jeans. You ain't got no hips."

She felt herself sliding out of her jeans, and knew that there was nothing she could do to stop it. He held her just above the water, and she felt her head going under as she slid out of her jeans. Just before she fell free, she thought fiercely, *I'd throw you in if I could!* She visualized him spinning head over heels into the river. Suddenly, she felt his grip loosen and she tumbled down into the water. She came up sputtering, not realizing at first that he no longer held her. He was nowhere to be seen. Then she spotted him, well out in the river, flailing frantically as the slow current carried him away. *Maybe he'll drown.*

She stood up and pulled her wet jeans back up and splashed out of the river. Janice was still fighting, but was having a hard time. She had blood all over her, and her left arm was hanging limp. Robin thought, I've got to help! She ran and grabbed her torn blouse, dipped into the river to get the mud off and put it back on. She saw her shoe lying on the ground and remembered that she had moved things before. She willed it to fly into his face. He threw it off and backed away.

Janice just stood there. This man was much better than the first one. Or perhaps, she thought, the first one was just not ready, and this one is. She had nicked him twice, but he had cut her badly. Her left arm was useless and she had a cut across her chest. He stepped back then and said, "Hey, you're a girl."

Her right leg hurt bad and did not want to move any more. She felt blood dripping into her sneakers, but could not stop to look. She stood and waited for him to attack again.

The man said, "Still got some fight in you? Well, this won't take long." He started toward her, waving the knife back and forth. Just before he reached her, a strong hand picked her up and set her to one side. "You haven't tried me, yet," Mista said. "Maybe you should pick on someone your own size."

Sharra had set a danger link to Robin and Janice. At the first sign of trouble she had been alerted. She was asleep at the time, and took a few seconds to realize what had happened. She sent a query to both girls. Robin thought that the man holding her was messing with her mind, and unconsciously closed her mind to the link. Janice was too busy fighting to acknowledge it.

Sharra jumped up, slipped her shoes on and ran out to find Mista. She found him sitting in a chair out in front of the trailer, watching Mischal park Em's van. "Mista! Robin's in trouble."

"What? Where?"

"I don't know. I just know she's in trouble."

Charly came up then, carrying two practice swords. "Where's Janice? We were going to drill some this afternoon."

Sheila said, "I think they rode down toward the river."

Mista leaped up and ran down the road, pulling his staff out as he ran. Charly was right behind him. She had always known that she could outrun Mista, but this day she could not keep up. Mista came to the end of the road just as Robin threw her shoe at the attacker.

After setting Janice aside, he took a fighting stance and waited. The man snarled, "A stick? You think you can fight with a stick?" He charged. Mista waited until he was almost there, and then stepped aside, slapping the knife hard as he did so. The blow numbed the attacker's hand and he spun around to renew his attack, switching to his left hand.

Charly came up a few seconds later. She saw Janice and ran to her immediately. She knelt down and put her arms around her. "You poor dear. Are you all right?"

"Yes! Let me go. I have to finish this. Quitters don't win."

She wriggled free and went back to the fight. She stayed clear of Mista, and circled around behind the other man. He saw her come and turned to keep her in sight, while at the same time pressing his attack on Mista.

Mischal ran up, and started to grab Janice. Charly said, "No, leave her. She wants to fight."

Mista moved in cautiously. Just as the man attempted another cut, Mista spun his staff. The leading end caught his hand and forced it down, while the other end came up and slapped him on the side of his face.

"Sneaky, aren't you?" He stepped back and shifted the knife to his right hand. Mista reversed the spin, slapping his right wrist, and then reversed it again, hitting the wrist again on the up spin.

The man stepped back and began to circle. He knew that the girl was back there somewhere. He had seen that she was not a boy when he cut through her shirt. He thought that he would be able to outmaneuver her, and attack her, catching this new man off guard. Mista did not allow that to happen, but pressed his attack. The man stepped back, and Janice dropped to her hands and knees behind him.

He fell over her onto his back, but she did not have the strength left to move. He was up again and moving toward her before she could move. Mista said, "No you don't!" He threw his staff straight at the man, the weighted end hitting him in his left eye. He fell back with a roar and turned toward Mista again.

"Hah! Stupid. Now you got no weapon." He charged Mista again. Janice made one last effort, and grabbed at one foot as he went by her. It was enough, and sent him sprawling. Mista retrieved his staff and then struck the man on the back of the head, putting him out.

When Mischal saw that the man was down, he ran and scooped up Janice. "Honey, we need to get you to Jasmine. You've won your fight."

"Okay." She relaxed and let him carry her.

Charly said, "Just call Jasmine."

"No, it'll be faster to take her up there." He ran, carrying Janice in his arms.

Mista stood breathing heavily for a second, and then Robin ran and threw her arms around him. "Daddy! I was scared."

He stooped down and took her in his arms. "I'll bet you were, Sugar.

"Your feet are all muddy and dirty, too. Where are your shoes?"

"I don't know. He pulled them off of me. Tried to pull my jeans off, too."

"Who? The man I was fighting?"

"No, the other one."

"What other one, Robin? I don't see anyone else. And where's Shawnah?"

"I don't know where he went. Maybe he drowned. Shawnah rode home."

"She didn't get there. You sure?"

Charly said, "Here she is. Oh, good God. She's hurt too. I'll take her up to Jasmine. You bringing Robin?"

"Yes. Here's one shoe. Where is the other one?"

"I don't know. Maybe he dropped it in the river."

"Well, we'll worry about it later. I'll carry you up." He stood up and picked her up. Robin put her arms around his neck and her legs around his waist and hung on.

"Hey, Little Bird. You're all wet. You should wear your swim suit if you want to go swimming."

She giggled. "I know. Didn't have time." Then the reaction set in and she started crying. "I was so scared, and I couldn't do anything."

"That's all right, Honey. You did good. We'll talk about it later. Right now I'm just glad you're all right."

They met Njondac coming down the road. "Whut's happening?"

"There are a couple of men down there that might need assistance."

"They attacked my girls?"

"Tried."

"Huh! I'll assist 'em. I'll assist 'em straight into Hell." He ran on down the road.

Robin said, "I didn't know he could run."

"He can probably move faster than you can. He's a fighter."

"But he looks so mean."

"Just his outside. Inside is a warm heart. If he'd have been there? That man would have been dead instead of just down."

Next they met Sharra coming to see about them. "What happened?" she asked.

"They're okay. Could you get her a shirt? This one's messed up. I'm going to take her up to Jasmine's new infirmary. The girls' trailer."

"Oh. Sure." She ran ahead and got a shirt out of the trailer.

"What happened?"

"Someone attacked them."

"Oh. Are you all right, Honey?"

"Yes," Robin said. "I'm okay. Just scared."

Janice looked up when Mista entered the trailer and tried to pull a sheet up over herself. Jasmine said, "Here, here. Be still. We're not through yet."

"But …"

"Here." She draped a paper towel over Janice's chest. "Now lie still. I have to check your leg out. Jasmine moved her hands up and down Janice's leg. Janice felt the warmth of energy flowing as Jasmine prayed for healing. Finally, she said, "It's not broken, but it's cut clear to the bone. That's going to hurt for a while. You take it easy until it's fully healed, okay?" Next she put a huge bandage over the leg cut and the chest cut, even though they were healed. "If the sheriff comes or an EMS worker, they will want to see you. I'll show them the bandages. They would never believe that God healed you like he does."

"Okay. Can I cover up now?"

"Yes." Jasmine pulled the sheet up over her. "You'll need some clothes. What do you want?"

"I don't care. Jeans."

"I'll get them for you," Sheila said.

Mista said, "Where's Shawnah?"

"I'm over here," she said. "My head hurts."

"Okay," Jasmine said. She ran her hands all around Shawnah's head. "You have a big bump and a bruise, and a little cut. You'll be all right." She gave her an aspirin for her headache.

"Okay, Robin, let's take a look at you." Sharra handed her a clean shirt when she got up.

Jasmine checked her out and said, "Well, the only thing I see is wet jeans. Do wet jeans hurt?"

Robin smiled and giggled in spite of herself. "No."

Njondac came in and said, "I called the sheriff. He'll be here in a few."

"Good," Mista said. "Now would somebody tell us what happened?"

Janice said, "We rode down the road, and these three men were there. They tried to pull Robin's shirt off, so I jumped down and attacked them back. Shawnah rode back to try to get help. The first man was easy, but the second was beating me. I'm glad you came when you did."

"Robin?" Mista said.

"He tried to pull my shirt off and tore it up. Then he held me upside down and dunked me in the river. He pulled my shoes off and tried to pull my jeans off. Then I got mad and wished he would go flying out into the river. And he did."

"Where is he now?"

"I don't know and I don't care."

Mista looked at Sharra. She sent, *That sounds familiar.*

Yep. Looks like we have a developing ESP user.

A man banged on the door. "Sheriff Gray."

Mista said, "Come on in, Sheriff. We're a little crowded."

"So I see. Who called me?"

"I did," Njondac said. "I found a couple of dead men down by the river."

"Found them dead, or just found them?"

"Found 'em dead. I'd of helped them die if necessary. They attacked my gulls."

Mista said, "I didn't know that he was dead."

Njondac just shrugged.

"Attacked them? Hurt them?"

"Yes," Jasmine said. Janice was cut up pretty bad. I put bandages on the worst ones. The one on her leg was cut clear to the bone. Shawnah ran to get help, but hit a tree on the way. Robin was not hurt, but they did try to drown her."

"Well, trouble seems to follow you people around."

Mista said, "Sheriff, we have the right to live peaceably on our own land, don't we?"

"Yes, but this is not peace."

"We did not attack anyone. They were trespassing and they attacked my daughters. I defended them. What am I supposed to do, let them kill someone first and then hold them at gunpoint while we call you?"

The sheriff gave him a wry grin. "That's what we have to do. At least it seems that way. Can't fight back until one of us is dead."

"Well, I'm not a police officer. I fight back."

"If it is as you say, you are within your rights to fight back. Show me the bodies."

Later that night Janice and Robin were both especially quiet when they came to say good night. Mista gathered them up in his arms and leaned back in his chair. "You girls are going to have to stop growing. You're getting too big for my chair."

"Get a new chair," Janice said.

"I might have to. Do you know that you've both grown about ten inches since you have been with us?"

"Uh, uh," Robin said. "Not ten inches."

"Would you believe seven and a half?"

"No," Janice said.

"How about two inches and two hairs?"

"Maybe," Janice said.

They were quiet for a minute and then Robin asked, "Daddy, why was I so scared today?"

"Why wouldn't you be if three grown men attacked you?"

"Janice wasn't scared."

"Hah! I was, too."

"Well, you fought and I didn't."

"What did you do? Did you just hang there upside down and say, Howdy-do?"

Robin giggled. "No. I tried to get away, I spit in his face and ... and I don't know. I wished him out in the river, and then he was. How did I do that?"

"You'll have to ask Jeremy that. But I suspect that you have a budding talent. Ask your new mother about that, too. Something like that happened to her when she was about your age."

"What?"

"You'll have to ask her. Now, Janice, why did you light into that man?"

"Cause. He was hurting Robin. I couldn't let him get after my sister. I told you last time, I should have been there. I need to practice with Charly some more. I wasn't fast enough."

"And you were afraid?"

"Yes. But I had to fight him."

"Hear that, Robin? Courage is not the absence of fear. It's doing what you have to do even when you are afraid. Only very foolish people are never afraid."

"Were you afraid?" Robin asked.

"No, not this time. But there have been fights I've been in when I was very afraid."

"But you fought anyway?" asked Janice.

"Yes. You do what you have to do."

Janice said, "Well, I wasn't going to quit, but I'm sure glad you showed up when you did."

"Well, girls, we are heading for a fight that does scare me. I don't know what we are getting into with these Internet guys, but I think it is going to be very dangerous. I always used to give a speech when we headed out on a quest. I wanted to remind everyone that some of might not come back. Some of us might not come back from this quest, too."

"Are you trying to scare us?" Robin asked.

"No, sweetheart. Just facing facts. Go to sleep now."

Robin reached up and kissed him, and then snuggled deeper into his arm. She was asleep in minutes. Janice did not go right to sleep, but lay quietly, thinking.

After a while, Mista asked, "What's on your mind, Hon?"

"I was just thinking. We're so different, Robin and me. But you love us both."

"I do. I don't love you because you're a certain way. I love you because you *are*. Love is something you do. You love Robin, and she loves you. Yes, you are different, but then everyone is different. You have learned to fight in order to survive. Robin is going to have to learn to fight, too, but she will fight with her mind. If the two of you learn to fight together, you will be an awesome pair. Your physical strength and skill will complement her mental powers. I'm glad I found you. And I don't want to lose you in the fight coming up, so please be very careful."

"I will. We will. Good night, Daddy." She kissed him and went on to her bed. She did not sleep for a long time, though. It all still seemed to be too good to be true.

Chapter 39

The next morning Mista took the girls to town and bought a cell phone for each of them. He made sure that they had the push-to-talk option – he did not want them to have to wait for a dial tone to connect in case they were in trouble. "Be sure that you always have them with you. If you had had them yesterday, you could have called for help."

Janice said, "I didn't have time."

"Me neither," said Robin.

"I guess that's true, but when it was over, you might have been in a world of hurt, and then you could have called us and told us where you were."

"Well, I've been wanting one, anyway."

"I would have done it before now if I'd thought about it. But then you weren't mine until last week. Which reminds me, if you'd been wearing your badges you wouldn't have gotten into trouble."

"Why is that?" Robin asked.

"Because they clearly say that you belong to me, and you should be returned to me for the $5.00 reward. And that implies that if they mess with my property, they would be in trouble."

Robin snickered. "They got in trouble anyway. And besides, we're not property! You said."

Mista smiled and tousled her hair. "Well, that's true. Probably would have ignored them anyway."

When they returned, the girls grabbed Mischal and Njondac. "Our bikes are still down by the river. Come with us to get them."

"Well," Mischal said. "Could be you learned a lesson yesterday?"

Janice gave him an impish smile. "Only thing I learned is that I need more practice. And a real sword."

"You did very well against two men," Mischal said. "And when you think you're getting good, Charly will ask me to help. We'll both attack you at once, not wait like your man yesterday did."

"Two at once? That's not fair!"

"You want fair? Try reading fairy tales. The bad guys don't fight fair, and don't you ever forget it. You don't have to fight dirty, but you do have to know how they fight and how to combat it."

"Oh, okay. Whenever you're ready."

"No, whenever *you* are ready."

When they got to the river, the site was still taped off with crime scene tape. "Well, no bikes for a while," Mischal said. "We don't cross that. There is somebody's shoe, too."

"Mine," said Robin. "The other one must be in the river."

"Why in the river?"

"He held me upside down and pulled them off. Didn't even untie them. My ankle still hurts. He was dunking me in the river when he pulled off the right one, and probably dropped it right there."

"Well, you can hope it's still there and not ruined. Time you get it back, it might be ruined by the water and mud. If you sweet-talk your daddy he might buy you a new pair."

Janice called Mista later that afternoon. "Daddy, that man is on again, and he wants our address."

"Who is there with you?"

"Nobody, right now."

"I'll be there in a minute. I don't want you girls on line if no one is there with you. Anything could happen, and help might be too late."

"Okay. I forgot."

"Well, don't forget again. Stall him for a minute – send a BRB or something. He might be real close by and be able to get here before I do. Then send him the address, but tell him not to come over today."

"Okay. Sorry, Daddy. I won't forget again."

Campbell scratched his head and thought about the situation for a few minutes after Janice signed off. So, I can't go over while her parents are there. Maybe I should, anyway. Might solve a few other problems. No. No point killing people just because I can. Well, okay, one day next week. Her pictures don't look like much, but who knows? Maybe there is more than meets the eye. Maybe she'll be a natural at sex. And nobody cares in the dark. Hmmm. Call Sam, first and trade names, then have her and the next one.

By this time, Mista had alerted Jeremy and he was listening. Campbell sent an IM to one of his names. He was not too surprised when he got no answer, since it was Saturday afternoon. He sat and waited for a few minutes, debating. He wanted to call him on a land-line. He had been told not to call except in extreme cases – but it was time to strike while the iron was hot. He called. Jeremy could not follow the call, but he did pick the number out of Campbell's mind.

A man answered after three rings. Jeremy knew that that was long enough for caller ID to identify the call, and assumed that the delay was on purpose. A man said, without preamble or identification, "I told you not to call."

"Got a hot one, Sam, and wanted you to know right away. I don't think she has a permanent address, so she might not be there next week."

Silence. "Hey, man I'll send you her pic. I think she's hot. Eleven."

"All right, but you better be right. Shoot."

Campbell gave him her screen name and address. "I'll send her pic on e-mail. What do you have for me?"

"Here is the only new one I have at the moment. She's a little past 12, but a looker. I have more business for her, so be sure nothing happens to her."

"How would I do that?"

"Just make sure that you don't do anything to her." He disconnected. Campbell went back to his computer and e-mailed the picture to an address. Jeremy made a note of the address to go with the telephone number. It would take a court order to get the physical address and client's name, but he believed that they could get that. He felt sure that they could get the address for the telephone number, anyway. It might even be an open listing.

Mista was still in the trailer with them, so he told him all that he had. "Good," Mista said. "We'll start tracing it first thing Monday."

Chapter 40

Robin looked up from her computer and said, "Can we go down to the beach, Daddy? Can we?"

"Well, it's a little chilly for swimming, still."

"I don't mean swimming. I just want to go to the beach. I like to watch the waves and the minnows swimming around."

"Okay. It'll be a good break. Let me put on some shorts and get your mother."

"Can we go to Crystal Beach?" asked Janice. "That's where you used to live, isn't it?"

"Yes, but it's changed over the years. I haven't been back in a long time. Sure, why not?"

After he left to get Sharra, Robin said, "Put on a skirt, Janice. If it's not too cold, we can wade some."

"Okay. I thought you didn't want to go in."

"No. It's too cold for swimming, but not for wading."

Mista found a street that ended with a barricade at the beach. He left his shoes in the car, but Sharra did not like barefoot walking. The girls were already at the water by the time Mista was ready to leave the car. He walked slowly, trying to visualize the beach as it was when he was a boy, but there had been too many changes. He pointed out the spoil islands about four miles out. "The large one on the left was called Honeymoon Island. I don't think the others have names. As you can see, they break the large swells coming in from the Gulf, and the waves on the beach here are quite gentle."

He glanced over at Robin and Janice. They had stopped at the water's edge and were looking into the water intently. "What do you want to bet that they go in?"

"No bets. I think Robin likes getting wet. We'll have to see about Janice. But if Robin goes in, she won't be far behind."

"I'll keep an eye on them, but I don't want them to know, so I'll pretend to be looking anywhere but there, and just catch them out of the corner of my eye."

"Unless something happens."

"Right. Unless something happens. But if it does, I'll see it."

Robin stopped just short of the water, watching the waves come in and fall away. She followed the next wave as it went back out, and then backed up when the next one came in. She could not see any minnows. She dodged several small waves, but then missed one and it washed over her feet.

Got my shoes wet. Oh well. Well, since they're wet, I can wade on out some. Maybe I can see some minnows.

She looked around. Mista was looking at something out at sea. She waded out knee deep and stood still, waiting for the minnows to come to her. Mista said, "Don't look, but that didn't take long."

Robin looked back at Janice. "Coming?"

"I don't know. Is it cold?"

"No. Not cold at all."

"What does the bottom feel like? Any crabs or seaweed or anything?"

"I don't know. Still have my shoes on. They got wet, so ... Look. Stand right at the edge of the water. If you happen to be looking up at me, a wave might catch you by surprise and get your feet wet. Then, since you will already be wet, you might as well come on out here. The minnows are fun to watch."

Janice walked out carefully on the wet sand. However, since she knew what she had planned, she couldn't pretend not to notice the waves coming in. She shrugged, and just waded out. Robin had gone a little deeper, pulling her dress up when the waves rose on her legs.

The minnows finally came and began to nibble at her legs. When Janice came up, they all scurried away. "You scared them! Stand still, and they'll come back." While talking to Janice, she failed to pull her dress up in time, and got it wet up to her thighs. "Oh, well. Saves some trouble."

"You'll get in trouble for getting all wet."

"No I won't. Daddy said the wet won't hurt clothes. After all, we do wash them. He's not watching, anyway."

"He's not?" Mista said.

"Oh!" Robin said. "You scared me."

"It's just me. As long as you're in this far, you might as well go all the way. He gave each one a quick push in her back so that they lost their balance and went under the waves.

They came up sputtering. Robin said, "You got me all wet!"

"I just helped you along. You were doing pretty well by yourself, but it was just taking too long for you to get completely wet."

"Hah!" Janice said. "You just wanted to get us wet. Let's get him wet, Rob!" She jumped up and grabbed Mista around the neck, throwing her legs around his waist so that her wet clothes pressed against him. "Get on his back, Robin, and let's drag him under."

Robin climbed up onto his back so that she was riding just below his shoulders. Mista said, "Ahhh! That's one idea that didn't work out so well. Say, your mother hasn't gotten wet on this trip. Why don't you go talk to her?"

"Okay," Janice said. They hopped down, getting thoroughly wet again, and then ran to Sharra. Since Sharra was no taller than Janice, they did not have to climb on her, so Janice hugged her from the front and Robin from the back.

"Thanks, Mista. I'll remember this," Sharra said.

That night when Robin came in for her good-night loving, Mista picked her up said, "I'm thinking about spanking you." He tapped her bottom lightly.

"What for?" Robin asked, instantly apprehensive. She knew what she had done, but had not thought that Mista had figured it out.

"How did you get so wet this afternoon?"

"You pushed me in."

"No, before I came out there. You were already waist deep."

"Oh. It was an accident."

Mista did not say anything.

Janice was ready for bed and about to come into the room, but when she heard that exchange, she stopped and waited to see what would happen.

"Sort of."

"So, tell me. What happened?"

"Well. I was standing down by the edge of the water, trying to see the minnows. I kept backing up when waves came in, but then I forgot to back out on one big one."

"And the wave knew that you weren't looking, so it jumped up on your feet."

"No, Daddy. But it did get my feet wet because I wasn't looking."

"Oh, I see. And since your feet were already wet, you decided to wade out a little further."

"Yes! I kept pulling my skirt up when big waves came in, but then I looked back to see if Janice was coming, and a wave caught me by surprise."

"Ah, I see. And all of this was completely unexpected, right?"

"Well." She looked up at him from under her lashes. She sighed. "Not completely."

"Not completely."

"Well." She blew out air and her eyes misted. "I knew you'd figure it out. No. I knew that if I played around the water long enough that I'd get wet. Do I get spanked, now, for getting wet?"

"No, Sweetheart. Just remember, I want you to always be honest with me."

"I was! I told you everything."

"Yes, after just a little bit of prompting."

"But, I didn't lie to you."

"No, that's true. But you were playing around on the edge of the truth, and that's always dangerous. Just be straight with me, okay?"

"Okay. But do I get spanked?"

"No, dear. YOU CAN COME OUT, NOW, JANICE."

Janice clapped a hand to her mouth and stepped through the door. "How did you know?"

"I probably would have done the same thing. It's okay. Come on in."

Robin said, "I was afraid you'd be mad because I went in the water."

"No, Sweetheart. I don't mind if you get wet. Water won't hurt you or the clothes. You might want to be careful what shoes you wear into the water, though. Or you could leave them behind."

"Oh. I didn't think about that."

"I'll even help you get wet if that's what you like. I'll turn the hose on you any time you want."

"That wouldn't be any fun!"

"It could be. Or you can wash the car and get yourself wet as well. It might even wash some dirt off of you. Unlike Sharra, I believe dirt sticks to you."

"Of course it does. Dirt sticks to anybody."

"Not your mother. Dirt doesn't stick to her."

"Nuh-uh. How can it not stick to her?"

"You could ask. Or you could test it by throwing some dirt on her."

"Can I?"

"Don't ask me. It's your own bottom you'd be risking."

"Oh. I'll ask."

"Good plan. By the way, I see you took a shower tonight."

"How did you know?"

"Because the salt is off. Whenever you go in the ocean the water leaves salt on you when you dry. That's why you felt all sticky."

"Oh. I wondered about that."

After another minute, she asked, "You really don't care about me getting wet?"

"Not at all. I only care that you learn what is right and wrong and that you do what is right. Getting wet is neither right nor wrong. It just is."

"Oh. I'm glad you're my daddy."

"So am I," Mista said. "Now, you girls need to get to sleep early. We have to get up early in the morning."

"Good night, Daddy. Good night, Mom."

Sharra looked at Mista after the girls left and raised an eyebrow. "Well?"

"I don't know. I can only hope. Right now they're walking on eggshells. When the new wears off, and they begin to really feel at home – I can only hope that the lessons I'm teaching now with stick with them."

Chapter 41

They held their own sunrise service that Easter morning down at the river. They had long ago declared themselves to be a local church, since they were often traveling and their assignments took some strange turns. Jasmine acted as pastor, and had agreed to hold the service that morning. She also provided grape juice and crackers so that they could observe communion.

When they got back to the trailer, Janice said, "I have some questions."

"Go ahead," Mista said.

"I don't understand what that was all about. Who died, and what really happened. When you die, you die. That's the end."

"Well, you've been reading about Jesus." He explained the basics of Christian beliefs. "So, you turn to God like a father. It's like being adopted into the family of God.

"Like you adopted us. Okay. I want to do that."

"Okay, then you go down to a church and ask to be baptized."

"They dunk you in the water," Robin said."

"Okay. Can I wear my white dress?"

"Wear whatever you want."

"I want to be baptized, too," Robin said, "but I don't have a white dress."

"You don't have to wear a white dress. Wear whatever you want. If you want to wait a week, we will buy you a white dress this week."

Robin thought a minute. "No. I want to do it now."

"Well," Mista said, "we could take you down to the river and baptize you right now. Jasmine does have a license, and we do consider ourselves to be a church."

"In that dirty river? No way. I got dunked in it once."

By this time Mischal and Sheila had breakfast ready. The girls ran out to eat. Sharra looked at Mista and said, "You think it's real?"

Mista shrugged. "Time will tell."

"They don't really know what they are doing."

"No, not really. They know that they are committing to be Christian, whatever that means. I heard a preacher explain it this way once, 'A child gives as much as he understands of himself to as much as he understands about God. As he grows he learns more about himself and more about God, and continues to give as much as he understands.' I kind of like that."

Tuesday afternoon Janice and Robin signed onto the Internet after school. One after the other, they saw Campbell's screen name. He made no attempt to contact them, and a few minutes later he signed off.

About 20 minutes later they heard a car drive into the lot. Robin got up and looked out. "Oh, my God! It's him!"

Janice pulled out her cell and punched up Mista. "Daddy, that man just showed up. He didn't call or anything. He's just here."

"Okay, who's there with you?"

"Uh ... nobody."

"I'll be right there. I'll wait outside until he starts something. I want to give him some room. You okay with that?"

"Yes. I'm not afraid of him."

Mista called Jeremy. "Trouble. We have a visitor. Meet me on the trail behind the girls' trailer."

"Gotcha."

Jeremy ran. While he was on the way up to the front of their land, he made mental contact with each girl. *Jeremy. I'm here. I'll monitor your conversation and be ready to act if you need help. You can start the camera recording, can't you?*

Yes. Already did, Janice sent.

The girls were back at their computers when Campbell walked in. He did not knock, just opened the door and walked in. "Well, good afternoon, girls. You must have been expecting me. The door's not even locked."

Janice whirled around and said, "We don't usually lock it. You think we should?"

"Most people do. Especially girls living alone."

"We don't live alone. Our father should be home in a little while."

"Yes, but he's not here now, right?"

"No, he's not here now."

"Then," Campbell said, "it's a good time to have a lesson in sex. That is what you wanted, right?"

"You suggested it," Janice said.

"That's technically true, but you did want it. All girls want it. Let's start with you." He turned to Robin. "You look like someone I've seen before. But that's all right. You only sent me a face picture. Let's see what the rest of you looks like."

"No. Daddy said, ..."

"Daddy said you shouldn't send good pictures? Daddy said you shouldn't take your shirt off? Yeah, but Daddy's not here, is he? So you can do whatever you want to."

"I could, but I don't want to."

"Well, why not? You can't learn about sex with your clothes on." He pulled his golf shirt over his head. *"See? I've got mine off already. Now it's your turn."*

"No. I can't do that. We're too young for sex, anyway."

"Never too young. You're just the right age, puberty just starting. Let's see what you've got." He walked across the room and reached for her.

Mista opened the door and stepped in. "Well, what's going on here, girls?"

Campbell jerked around. "Good afternoon. You must be the famous daddy. Don't I know you from somewhere?"

Mista said, "I don't think so. How can I help you?" Then he sent to Sharra, *Call the sheriff. Let's get this guy off the street.*

Consider it done, dear. You need help?

Might.

"Well, it's not you I came to see. I've been talking to these girls on line for some time now, and they asked me to come over and give them a lesson in sex."

"I find that hard to believe. Is that true, Janice?"

"No, Daddy. I never asked him to come."

"Me neither," Robin said.

"Oh, isn't that interesting. Who do you believe, sir? A respected mature business man or young girls who would never admit to such a thing to their own father. You didn't expect truth from them, did you?"

"As a matter of fact I did. Robin, are you sure you didn't ask him?"

"No! Yo —"

Jeremy sent, Don't say that! Let Mista tell him about the log when he's ready. Just continue to deny it.

"You know you can trust me. I never asked him."

"Yeah, right. I suppose you never sent me those pictures, either. Including the one in the shower in your nightie. Tsk, tsk. You shouldn't have sent the pictures if you didn't want to see me."

Robin turned red and started to cry. "Daddy, I didn't! I swear to God I never did!"

Mista said, "Well, I would like to believe you. You understand how important it is that you always be honest with me, don't you?"

"Yes, Daddy. I'm not lying."

Mista said, "Okay, I believe you. Sir, you must be the one who is lying."

"Hah. Believe her if you wish. They also told me that they were 16, and that it was perfectly legal for me to come over here. Since they obviously are not 16, I'll just be leaving. I don't think I need to stay any longer."

The sheriff stepped inside the trailer. "I'll decide who's leaving. Who called me?"

Mista said, "I believe my wife called you, sheriff."

"Where is she, then?"

"Not here at the moment, but this place is getting pretty crowded. This man solicited sex with my underage daughters."

"Is that true, sir? May I have your name, please."

"My name is Greg Adams. They asked me to come over and have sex with them. I had no idea that they were so young, or I never would have come."

"Mr. Mictackic?"

Mista said, "It is not just my word, sheriff. I log every chat that my daughters have on line. I'll make you copies of the logs. I also have a video recording of this room when I am not here, for my daughters' safety. Would you like to see what has just happened?"

"I certainly would."

Mista sat down at Janice's computer and logged into his network. Then he called up the video of the afternoon events and displayed them on her screen. "The recorder is still running. It records and plays back at the same time."

Mista made comments as the video played. He also sent a message to Sharra, *Be ready for anything. Better tell Jeremy to get to the door, also. He looks ready for violence, and I'm about to give him the lie.*

We're ready.

"You see here, sheriff," Mista said, "he says that they did not invite him, but that he only assumed that they would want sex. ... and here he says that eleven is the perfect age to learn about sex. That proves that he knows that they are not sixteen. ... And here. 'Only a face picture.' Need anything else? I'll make you a copy of the video and the logs."

Campbell realized that he was trapped. He pulled his knife and started for the door. "I'm leaving. Don't anyone try to stop me."

The sheriff was no fool. He had expected something to happen, and his gun appeared in his hand. "Stop right there. Stop, or I'll shoot."

"Hah. Your bullets can't hurt me." He kept walking, and the sheriff shot. The bullet bounced off and went through a side wall. He was afraid to shoot again, not knowing where a bullet might ricochet.

Janice took action. She pulled her own knife and charged Campbell. He laughed. "You can't hurt me, either, little girl. I'll even stand still and let you find out for yourself." He stood with hands raised while Janice charged across the room, striking him in the side. Her knife also bounced off his armor. Campbell, however, struck down at Janice while she was off guard. Mista saw it coming, and brought his staff up. He was unable to hurt the man, but he did knock his arm up and deflected the blow aimed at Janice.

Mista shouted, "Get out! Janice. Get out, now! You can't hurt him and he can hurt you."

"He's right, little girl. Better leave. Now, who's going to try to stop me?"

Jeremy stepped in through the back door, and shooed the girls out. "I'll stop you," he said. He formed his wall of air around Campbell. They could hear him growling and clawing at the air, but he could not break through.

Mista said, "Jeremy, call Jasmine. I believe we might have a demon trapped there. If so, that wall won't hold him."

"Right." *Jasmine! We need you in here right now. We think we're facing a demon.*

Coming.

The sheriff said, "You people don't really believe in demons, do you?"

Mista said, "We only know that there are spiritual things and beings that we know nothing about. They might be demons, angels or something else entirely. I'm taking no chances."

Mista turned to Jeremy. "Can air pass through your wall?"

"Obviously. You can hear him. I could seal it, though."

"Do it. We might have to extract the oxygen so he can't breathe."

Jeremy made a mental adjustment, and sounds from the circle ceased. The Jasmine came in. "What do you have?"

Mista pointed. "Do your thing. Jeremy, better let sound in."

When she heard the man, Jasmine said, "Enough. GET YOU HENCE, IN THE NAME OF JESUS CHRIST I COMMAND YOU TO LEAVE US. YOU HAVE NO PLACE HERE."

"Oh, little girl, this is my place." That was all he said, and nothing else happened. Campbell was still trying to claw his way through the wall of air.

Mista said, "Well, Jeremy. I guess you better extract the oxygen."

Jeremy sealed the circle again and then pulled all the air out. Campbell began to gasp like a fish out of water, and then he collapsed. Jeremy said, "I'm going to release him, sheriff. I suggest that you have cuffs ready, hand and foot."

"I hear that. Go ahead, before he dies."

Jeremy released him and the sheriff immediately put a plastic tie around his wrists, behind his back, and then his ankles. Then he called for backup, "Danny! Get over here. Got a prisoner to transport." He gave him the address.

Then the sheriff asked Mista, "What made you think you had a demon here? I didn't see anything happen when you commanded him to leave."

Mista said, "We are not people who see demons in everything, Sheriff. But we know that they exist. If this was one, when he was commanded to leave, he would have had no choice. We would not necessarily have seen anything. If it were not, then no harm was done. However, we have met this man before. He is the same one who attacked Robin and me a few months ago. We did not press charges then, but I do wish to do so now. I expect that when he comes to, he will have no memory of how or why he is here, or even where he is, just like the last time."

"Yeah, right. They all say that."

"Well, it might be a lie, of course. But I suspect that he will actually have no memory that he can recall. A psychiatrist or perhaps a hypnotist could dig it out of him, but he will have no conscious memory."

"Well, that's as may be. And if he does not, then what?"

"He's in your hands. Whether or not he remembers, he did come here, and he did solicit sex with a minor."

"Okay. Gather your evidence for me, please, while we take care of the prisoner. You will be required to support the evidence in court, if we bring him to trial."

"I understand. No problem."

At bedtime, Robin came hesitantly up to Mista. "Daddy, you do believe me, don't you?"

"Come up here, Honey. Do you remember what I said a few months ago? Once you break trust, it is ten times harder to regain it?"

"Yes. But I've tried awful hard, and I've proved it."

"Well, let's check your logs and see."

"Daddy, you have to believe me."

Mista made no comment, but went over to the computer and called up her chat logs. Robin sat on his lap and watched. "You'll see," she said.

Mista did expect to find that she had been telling the truth. He read her body language well enough that he had no real doubt. The log reading exercise was primarily to drive the lesson home. She wanted to be trusted, and she was not.

Afterwards, Mista cuddled her and said, "It is important to you to be trusted, isn't it?"

"Yes. Terribly important. Will you trust me now, Daddy?"

"I will, Honey. But you must maintain my faith. Even if you do something that you know you will be punished for, you must be honest."

"I will, Daddy. I will."

"Now, that doesn't mean that you have to go out and do something just so you can prove it."

Robin hit his arm. "I won't do that!"

"Okay, Sweetie. You can come in, now, Janice. You didn't have to wait."

Janice walked in with her hands on her hips. "How do you always know?"

"Ah, my secret. You were very brave in there, Janice. But you were fighting something that you could not hurt."

"Why did you say it was a demon?"

"I don't know that it was. But I have met good and bad spiritual beings, and neutral ones, too, in my travels. Some things you would not believe. I am very much afraid that we are fighting something like that here, and if we do – well, the fight won't be easy."

"Okay. Good night, Daddy."

Robin was already asleep, so Mista put her to bed at the same time Janice went to bed.

Chapter 42

The next morning Mista looked up Chandri. "I have a problem for you. How can we put a tracer on the three girls so we can find them if they get kidnapped?"

"Well, you could always put a microchip under their skin, like people do their pets."

"Yes, but that's kind of invasive. Any other ideas?"

"I'll think about it."

After lunch, Chandri showed Mista what she had found.

"This is your microchip. Basically to identify lost pets; we used these to positively identify stolen cars last summer."

"Right. Inject it under the skin. It's an RFID chip. But I already know who my daughters are, and I'm pretty sure I'll know Shawnah if I see her, too."

"Yeah. Not much help. These phones have GPS locaters in them."

"Yes, but if they're kidnapped, they'll probably take the phone first thing. But, however … You remember when Mischal put a blade in your sandals?"

Chandri laughed. "Of course. I thought he was just cutting them up."

"These phones I bought for the girls are so slim, they could be put in a shoe, like under the heel. Keeping the batteries charged could be a problem. Tell the girls, 'be sure to keep your shoes plugged in when you're not wearing them.' That'd be wonderful."

"Yes. But the batteries would probably last long enough that you would know where they took them. Not Robin, though. She'd go wading in her phone-shoes."

"Yes. Charly liked to get wet, but not as bad as Robin."

"If I'd had my phone with me when I was kidnapped, you could have found me right away. But, I didn't. Now, look at these phones. I didn't buy these – they're $500 apiece." She showed him a picture. "It's a watch with a built in GPS finder. You can monitor their location real time on the Internet, or with available software on your computer. But it looks just like a kid's watch. The strap locks on, so the kid can't take it off. Or in our case, the kid-napper."

"Perfect. Thanks, Chandri. We're going shopping."

Mista went back up to his trailer and called the girls in. "Who wants a watch? One with an atomic connection so you will know that your watch is always exactly right?"

"I do! I do!" they all said at once.

"Well, I have an idea. Janice let me see your favorite shoe."

"I have them on." She took off one sandal.

"Now your phone."

"Okay."

"If I cut the heel off, an…"

"Whoa! What are you doing?"

"Well, this phone is so thin that I thought I could put it under the heel of your shoe. Then when your foot vibrates, you know you have a call, and you just take your shoe off to answer it."

"No way. That's stupid."

Mista laughed. "Well, there was a TV show a long time ago called 'Get Smart'. It was about a secret agent named Maxwell Smart. He had a phone in his shoe. That was a long time before cell phones were invented. Now, Robin, you can't have one."

"Not that I want one, but why not?"

"You'd be sure to go wading in your shoe phone."

"Daddy! I would not!"

"You sure? I bet you'd forget. Anyway, I have a better idea. I want to get you all watches. We'll go get them in a minute. They are special. They really are watches, and look like watches. But they lock on so you can't lose them. They're waterproof, so you can swim or shower with them on."

"I wouldn't lose mine," Janice said. "It doesn't need to lock."

"Well, they do lock. Here's why. They also have a special feature built in. You've seen the GPS tracker in our cars? These watches have one built in. It doesn't show you where you are, but I can track you on the Internet, wherever you go. I'd know exactly where you are. Even if you sneak down to the beach."

"I told you I wouldn't do that any more, Daddy," Robin said.

"I know, Honey. I'm just teasing you. But I am afraid that you might get kidnapped. You are all pretty girls, and as you already know, you are eleven years old. We know that Mr. Campbell contacted someone who appears to manage some young girls as prostitutes. Just like what was done to my sister Sheila when she was eleven."

"Does he know about us?" asked Robin.

"I think he does. Mr. Campbell gave him your address and this man, named Sam, gave him the name of another girl to take for his pleasure. So I think that you are in danger. This way we will know where you are, and can come and get you."

"Okay. Can you unlock it later if I have a date when I get older?" Janice asked.

Sharra burst out laughing. "Trust a girl to ask that question."

Mista said with a straight face, "No. In fact, it has a hidden camera so we will not only know where you are, but what you are doing."

"I don't think I want one."

Mista smiled and tousled her hair. "No, Honey, I was just teasing. It can be unlocked. I trust you all not to run off and I am not going to follow you around on your dates. You will have proved your trustworthiness by then, and I'll take your word for anything. Of course, if you aren't trustworthy … I could attach a camera to it …"

Sharra said, "Mista, stop teasing those girls."

The girls were happy with the watches. They had been afraid that they would look like something geeky. Mista showed them a recessed button. "I need to put my number in the watch databank. Then, if you do get into trouble somewhere push this button. It will call me and alert me. We'll test it when we get home.

Janice held out her arm as soon as then entered the trailer. "Program mine and let's see what happens." She pushed her button when Mista handed it back to her. Nothing happened. Then Mista's phone rang. A computerized voice said, "ALERT! ALERT! ALERT! THIS IS AN EMERGENCY CALL. ALERT!"

"It doesn't say what is happening or who is calling,: Janice said.

"It doesn't know who is calling or what is happening. But if I get a call like that then I will know that one of you is in trouble. And if I know you, that probably will mean that all of you are in trouble. If something does happen, alert me. And try not to let them see you push that button. They might not know what it is for, but they will be alert for something like that. Notice, nothing happened that you could hear."

Robin held her arm out. "Do mine."

Mista programmed her watch and then Shawnah's. "Now, I'm going to lock these on you. There won't be time to lock them after you get into trouble, and I don't want your captors to be able to take them off. As long as they are on you, I can trace you, and get there to rescue you."

Chapter 43

Thursday afternoon Jeremy sent Robin out to play after only a short lesson. Then he took his list of screen names to Mista. "I've tried to get these names identified, but they tell me I have to have a court order. I know how to ask for one, but I don't think that a judge will give me one without some kind of hearing. And that means time."

"A judge would need to see some kind of evidence that our suspicions were justified. Right now, he would only see suspicions. However, we could take these to the sheriff in the morning and ask him to pursue it. Since he has Campbell in custody – maybe he will take the list seriously. Of course, you might have to explain how you got the list."

Jeremy grinned. "I could explain it. He might not believe it."

Mista shrugged. "Let's try. What have we got to lose?"

They heard a car drive down the gravel road, but no one paid any attention except Sheila. She looked out the window and gave a little cry. "Oh!"

"What is it, dear," Mista asked.

"Nothing. I thought I saw a familiar car, but it's silly. Just didn't get a good look."

"Who was it?"

"I don't know. They went down the road. Since it ends at the river, they'll have to come back in a minute."

"Unless they are going fishing," Mista said.

The car came back a few minutes later. Sheila was watching and called Mista. "See? Remember I told you that a black limousine picked me up? It looked just like that. The windows were darkened like that. But that was 25 years ago. It can't be the same one."

"Well, most black limousines look pretty much alike. It isn't new, is it? Wonder what he wanted. Maybe just cruising. Maybe he took the wrong road. Well, if he comes back, we'll stop him and ask if he needs help."

Half an hour later, Mista looked up from his reading and asked, "Where are the girls? I haven't heard them for a while."

Jeremy said, "Out riding their bikes, I think. I sent Robin out when I came up here."

"Hmmm. Let's go look for them," Mista said.

He and Jeremy walked down to the river. They found three bikes beside the road, but no sign of the girls. Jeremy said, "Are those watches waterproof?"

"Yes, but they wouldn't go in the river. Not even Robin would go in the Hillsborough, as dirty as it is."

Just then, his cell phone beeped. He answered, and immediately put it on speaker. It was saying, "ALERT! THIS IS AN EMERGENCY CALL. ALERT!"

They looked at each other. "Let's go!" Mista said. He ran up the road to his trailer with Jeremy a few steps behind him.

Chapter 44

The girls rode up and down the road for a while. It was not a race – Janice was faster than the other two. Then they dropped their bikes beside the road at the river and walked down to the water. Robin said, "I wonder if there are fish in there?"

The water was black and murky, covered with hyacinths for the first 15 or 20 feet on each side of the river. Janice said, "There are fish everywhere. I bet there are some in there. We could try to catch some if we had fishing poles."

"Yeah. Let's ask for some." She walked out to the edge of the water and sank several inches in mud. She pushed some of the hyacinths aside and peered into the water. "I think I can see minnows."

She started to wade into the river, but could not pull her foot up. "Oh! I'm stuck. Janice come help me get out of the mud."

Robin pulled one foot out and then the other, while Janice held her hand to help her keep her balance. "Whew. Good thing I'm wearing sandals. I would have lost my shoes in the mud. Hey! There's my other sneaker on the bottom there. I wonder if I can get it?"

"Don't try," Janice said. "It's probably ruined by now, anyway."

"Yeah. Probably." She sat on the gravel at the end of the road and swished her feet in the water to get the mud off. "I wish it weren't so muddy."

"It's also dirty," Janice said. "If you want to go wading, lets go down to the beach."

"Okay. Let's go ask." She was not about to go again without asking.

Just then, they heard a car crunching on the gravel. "Maybe that's them. Let's ask."

What they saw was a black limousine. The back door opened and a man stepped out who looked even older than Mista. His hair was white and his face lined. He said, "Hi, girls. Having fun?"

They looked at each other before answering. They were not supposed to talk to strangers. Finally Janice said, "Yes. Who are you?"

"Oh, you don't know me. I've known your father for a long time. Knew him when he was growing up over in Crystal Beach. I'm sure he's told you not to talk to strangers, but after all, I'm not a stranger."

"Well, we didn't know who you were. What's you name?" Janice asked.

"Oh. Sam Smith. Say, I wonder if you'd do me a favor. I'm just in town for a few days, and since my old friend Mista is here, I'd like to buy him a birthday present. You knew that his birthday was next week?"

They looked at each other. "Nooo," Janice said.

"Oh, well, with your being adopted, I don't suppose he mentioned it. I told him that I was going to visit with you for a few minutes. I wonder if you'd go with me to help me pick out something for him. You would know what he likes, and I haven't seen him in some time."

"Well," Janice said, "we'd have to tell him we were leaving."

"Ah, but that would ruin the surprise. It won't take but a few minutes."

Robin said, "He knows Daddy. It would be all right."

"I don't think so. We better ask."

"But it would ruin the surprise."

"Yeah. Well, okay."

When they got in the car, they saw another man sitting on the rear-facing seat. Sam said, "This is Carl, my very good friend and helper. You know, when you get old, you can't do so many things any more without some help."

Once the door was closed, they could no longer see outside. They had seen the darkened windows, but assumed that they would be able to look out. They also found that the car was so well insulated that they could hear nothing outside. They didn't even hear the gravel crunching under the tires as they drove out.

"This sure is a nice car," Robin said.

"Yes," Sam said. "I like my quiet."

Janice glanced at her watch after they had been on the road for half an hour. This was taking more than a few minutes. Sam saw her looking at it and said, "Nice watch. May I see it?"

"Oh, no. I can't take it off. Daddy was afraid we'd lose them."

"Oh, I see."

Janice cupped her right hand around the watch and felt the depressed switch. Should I call? He'll be mad that we went off. And if this man is nice like he seems, and we are just buying him a present… but if he's not, then we are definitely in trouble. I'll wait a minute. As long as I hold my finger here, I can push the button real quick.

They stopped a minute later and the driver called on the intercom, "Airport, sir."

"Airport?" Robin said. Janice pushed her button. "But you said—"

"I decided to go a little further," Sam said.

The man across from them reached over and jabbed each of them in the leg with a small needle. They were asleep almost instantly.

Chapter 45

Mista slammed the door open and ran to his computer. He activated the Internet search immediately and waited minutes for the map to form and a dot to appear on it. The dot did not seem to be on a road, and was moving north at a high rate of speed. "They're flying! Sharra can you reach them?"

"No. They are asleep or unconscious."

Sheila said, "It *was* the same car."

Mista said, "Probably not. But probably the same man. Watch the screen, Jeremy. I'm going to charter a plane. Sharra, call Mischal and Charly. We're going after them."

Mista reached a charter service in Tampa. "I need to fly immediately. As soon as you can get a plane ready, and as soon as I can get there from Clearwater."

"I don't have a destination, yet. North. … I'll give you a cash bond, any amount you need. I suspect that I need to go to Louisville, Kentucky, but I don't know that yet. Can we file for Louisville and then change the flight plan in the air?"

"Jet, preferably, eight passengers."

"Five thousand? No problem. I'll be there as soon as I can get there."

"Jeremy, you need to go, and I assume Sharra will. Mischal and Charly – good, you're here. Armed? Of course. Pack your weapons in a box. We'll have to put them in the cargo compartment, probably, even though we do have licenses. Chandri, too? Okay. Let's roll."

Chandri said, "I got Njondac, too. He'd never have forgiven you."

"I can believe that. They've got his girls. Sheila, you're coming, too, aren't you?" Mista asked.

"I don't know if I want to."

"I don't think you want to miss this. If it is the man who took you, you will want to face him in person. If not, nothing is lost."

"You're right. Can I kill him myself?"

Mischal said, "If that's what you want, I'll hold him down and you can use my sword to cut off his head."

"I don't want to kill anyone. I might spit in his face, though."

They were at the charter desk in twenty-seven minutes. Mischal parked the Range Rover while Mista drew cash on his American Express card and signed for the charter. He asked for an Internet connection for his laptop for one last check before they left. As he had guessed, the dot was not quite halfway to Louisville. "We'll have to assume that Louisville is their goal, unless you can access the Internet while flying. Wait. We'll try this software on the laptop. I don't think it needs an Internet connection. Hope not."

By the time they had landed in Louisville, Mista had traced the girls to an address on Fourth Street, not far from the University of Louisville. His software worked fine. They rented two cars and drove up Fourth Street to locate the house and sight it. It was one of several nineteenth century brick houses that had been converted to businesses. Then they drove on downtown to find the closest hotel or motel. They could not very well sit in cars on the street until something happened.

Chapter 46

Sharra tried again to contact the girls, but they were still out. They took supper in the hotel dining room, and then all gathered in Mista's room to await developments.

About 8:30, Sharra said, "Hah! Robin!" *Robin, Honey, it's me.*

Mom! I was so scared.

Be brave. We know exactly where you are, and are working on a plan to rescue you.

Good. I don't know where we are.

You are in Louisville, Kentucky. We went by the house this afternoon, so we know exactly where they have you. Let me contact Janice, now.

She's awake, too, and worried.

Janice! It's me.

Mom! Where are you?

We are in Louisville, Kentucky, and that's where you are, too. Don't say anything about us. When the time is right, we'll rescue you. Now, I need to contact Shawnah. She doesn't know that I can do this ... Don't forget – don't say anything.

Shawnah! It's me, Sharra. This is called mind-speaking. We are nearby, and will rescue you in a little while.

How? How can you do that? And how can you rescue us. We don't even know where we are.

We do. Remember the watches? We know exactly where you are.

Oh. Okay.

Do not say anything to each other about this contact. We don't want them to know.

Okay.

Sharra reported to the others that the girls were all awake and that they knew that the group was in Louisville. "Now how do we get them out?"

Mischal said, "We know where they are. Just walk in and take them out."

"Not that easy," Mista said. "We want him arrested for kidnapping and soliciting sex with minors. We also want to nab as many of his clients as possible. If we just barge in, we will get the girls all right, but lose the perps."

"Then what do you suggest," Mischal asked.

"I think we need to get the FBI involved. He did kidnap our girls and transport them across state lines. They might also have an interest in their Internet activities, and the whole sex thing."

"I agree with that," Jeremy said. "I'll call the FBI field office and get them involved."

Meanwhile, Sharra spoke to Janice again. Honey, how are you all doing? What's happening there?

They took all our clothes and tried to take the watches, but they wouldn't come off. I told them that you were afraid that we'd lose them.

Good girl. Anything else happening?

Not yet. We woke up in a room with four beds. They took our clothes and gave us robes to wear. Then they made us take a hot shower. They did bring us some supper. They have treated us very nice, but it's no fun being a prisoner.

That sounds like what happened to Sheila. If they continue the pattern, they'll give you a medical exam in the morning.

Yes, I remember.

Look, I can't keep this contact up very long. I'm going to set a link in your mind, though. If anything happens, you just think MOM! And I'll answer.

That's cool.

I will also set one with Robin. I'm worried that my danger sense didn't alert me when you were taken.

Oh. How does that work?

Anytime you are in danger I should get a message. Just that, that you are in danger.

Well, we never were in danger, that we knew of. He said he was taking us shopping to buy a birthday present for Daddy. But I knew something was wrong when he took too long. Then when we stopped we were at the airport.

I pushed my call button right away. I just had time to push it when he stuck us with a needle and we all went to sleep.

Well, that explains that, then. You call me if anything happens. They might move you or one of you. If they do, be sure to call me.

Okay. Robin is dying to talk to you.

Okay. ROBIN! How are you doing?

Scared. Are they going to make us, you know, like Aunt Sheila?

I think that is what they want to do. We do not intend to let that happen, of course.

How can you stop them?

We're going to rescue you. We are also going to arrest all the people doing this and put them in jail.

Well, hurry up. They made us take a shower, and then they took pictures of us, naked.

The man did?

No a woman took the pictures. She also checked to make sure that we got clean.

Okay, Honey, I'm going to set a link to your mind. All you have to do is think or say MOM! And I'll hear and answer you. You know by now, that I can't keep this contact going for very long.

Yeah, Jeremy has talked about how much energy it takes.

Good, then you understand about the link. If anything happens, if they move you or one of the others, call me.

Okay. I love you, Mom.

Love you, too, Honey.

Janice called Sharra. MOM!

Yes, dear.

If you unlock Shawnah's bracelet, I can drop it in that man's pocket. Then if he gets away, you can follow him. I guarantee that he won't know it's there.

Good idea. We'll unlock it. Can you put it someplace where they won't know it is there until you need to use it?

I think so. I love you, Mom.

Love you too. Good night.

Jeremy reported, "They want us to come into the field office at 8:30 tomorrow morning. I guess they want to examine our evidence and see if we really did discover a den of thieves."

"Well, we can show them. Maybe. I'll take my laptop, but we can't get a position while they are inside the house. Just telling them that we traced them to the front door might not be enough. I'd like you and Sharra with me, Jeremy. The rest of you might want to lurk somewhere near the house. Drive around the block or something, if you think you're being too obvious."

Sheila said, "I'd like to go with you, George. It might help if they hear my story."

"Sure, Sis. The three of us will be armed, but I don't expect a fight. Not there, anyway."

"How will you be armed," Mischal asked.

"After all these years? My staff, of course, and Sharra and Jeremy always travel with their weapons – their minds."

"Hah! I should have known what you meant."

Chapter 47

They had an early breakfast the next morning, and then the two groups went their separate ways. Mista parked and waited in the car until just before 8:30. He wanted to arrive at the office exactly on time.

The man who met them introduced himself as the special agent in charge, Paul Ross. Two other men were in the room with them, whom he did not introduce.

"Who called us last night? I only expected one person."

Jeremy said, "I placed the call, sir. But, you understand, this is a family affair."

"Would someone introduce me, then?"

Mista said, "I am George Mictackic, this is my wife, Sharra, my sister, Sheila, and my son-in-law, Jeremy. Two of my daughters have been kidnapped and brought to Louisville. We have come to rescue them, and thought you might be interested."

"We are more than interested, Mr. Mictackic. But, we do not barge into a private home without convincing evidence. First, where were they kidnapped, and how do you know who kidnapped them?"

"They were kidnapped near our home near Tampa, Florida. We followed them here. I don't know for sure who kidnapped them, since I have not seen him. I only have my daughters' mental picture of the man."

"I see. And how did you follow them here?"

"I took the precaution of putting a GPS tracking bracelet on each of the girls. I always knew exactly where they were, once they had called me and alerted me. Unfortunately, I can't show you now, because the GPS system cannot work under a roof."

"Then, how can you know that they are still there, Mr. Mictackic?"

"I know that they have not left the house. Therefore, they must still be there."

"Maybe they took those bracelets off?"

"No, they lock on and cannot be removed."

Mr. Ross studied his desk for a minute and then said, "Tell me, Mr. Mictackic, why did you decide to put such a device on your daughters? Did you trust them that little?"

"Not a matter of trust, Mr. Ross." He told them of their investigation and what they had found so far. Then he asked Sheila to tell her story. "Now, we cannot be sure that this is the same man, but whoever he is, he is still a criminal."

"Well, we will need to do our own investigation before we can make any move. Have you shared this information with anyone else?"

"Yes. We have worked with the sheriff of Pinellas County in Florida. He has made a couple of arrests already. But this just happened, and we wanted to strike while the iron was hot."

"Well, Mr. Mictackic, that has a nice ring to it, but we cannot always strike immediately. It will take us at least several days, perhaps longer. Now, if you had pictures or other hard evidence that your girls were inside that house, and that they were engaged in some kind of illegal action, then we could move immediately. Absent that, we must develop our own."

Mista's eyes narrowed. *"Are you telling me, Mr. Ross, that you cannot act until they have used the girls as sex objects for someone?"*

"That would constitute proof."

Mista's eyes turned steel blue and took on a glint. *Sharra, we are about to leave here. I suspect he will not want that to happen. See if you can lock their guns in their holsters.*

Gotcha. She heated the metal of the guns hot enough to melt the plastic parts of the holsters and fuse them in place. The men felt their guns getting hot, but assumed that it must be just their imagination.

Mista sat quietly, rubbing his chin until Sharra sent him a message, *Done!* Then he said, "Well, Mr. Ross, I don't think I'm going to wait. I have no desire to spend the next several months trying to heal my eleven-year-old daughters after they have been raped, while I did nothing. I am going after my daughters."

Ross said, "Mr. Mictackic, I don't mean to be antagonistic. Let me explain our position here. You are a stranger and come into our office telling us that your daughters have been kidnapped, and you know where they are, but you show us no corroborating evidence. I would like to believe you, but I have responsibilities to other people besides yourself. If it turns out that you are wrong, them we will have broken into an innocent person's house without justification. You understand?"

"Yes, but I am not wrong."

"I cannot question the loss of your daughters, and I understand your pain and your desire to protect them and to get them back. However, I need some hard evidence before we can act."

Sharra sent, He's right, you know. We cannot prove what we know.

Yeah. Same old story. Well, we'll have to get him some proof.

Mista relaxed perceptibly. "I understand your position, Mr. Ross. I can show you the internet site that describes the GPS trackers …"

"I don't doubt that you bought trackers, Mr. Mictackic. We are familiar with such devices. Yours depends on satellite signals, right? Which means that you cannot see her when she is under roof. We have devices that can work indoors. Unfortunately, the battery life is very short on these devices, but usually we can find out what we need to know while the battery is still active. Now, if you had a way to put one of these on your daughters …"

Mista said, "Jeremy?"

"Yes, of course. She is my student. I have another idea. Why don't we put one on the big bad man, also?"

Ross said, "Who is this big bad man, sir?"

"That is part of the problem. We don't know who he is, we just know where he is. He will probably turn the girls over to his local organization and then disappear. If we had a tracker on him, we could follow him, or you could."

"I can provide you with two tracking devices if you have a way to deliver them."

"I do."

Ross signaled to one of his associates, and the man left the room. "I don't suppose you want to tell me how you intend to get them there?"

"You wouldn't believe me if I told you," Mista said.

"Try me, Mr. Mictackic."

Mista shrugged. "All right. My wife and my son-in-law both have strong ESP powers. They can contact the girls, and move small objects from one place to another."

"You're right, I don't believe that. I am aware that there are people who claim to have demonstrated that power, but I have never seen it." His man came back in the room and handed him two small electronic devices. "These are commonly known as 'bugs,' which is somewhat of a misnomer. We can track them."

Jeremy held out his hand, took the bugs and closed his eyes. *Robin, dear?*

Yes, Jeremy.

I'm going to send you two tracking bugs, like the ones inside your watches. I want you to put one in your pocket or something, so we can track you, and put the other one in your captor's pocket. You remember how to move an object, right?

Sure. He just walked in to check on us. There's a nurse here, also, doing a medical check – just like you said.

Okay. Cup your hands, and I will put them there.

Jeremy closed his fist on the bugs and concentrated on her hands in space. Robin sent, *I have them. ... one is now in the monster's pocket. Janice also put one or our watches in his pocket. I didn't know she could do that without his knowing it. And the other is in my pocket. They gave us little white robes to wear, like the robes angels wear in Christmas plays.*

Good. Now we will know where he is if he leaves there. Be brave, honeypot.

"They are in place, Mr. Ross."

"Well, let's see." He turned to a computer on his desk and activated a program. After a minute, he said, "Well! They are both in the house where you said they would be. I am more inclined to believe you now, Mr. Mictackic. Still, we need to be careful. I would like to discuss the possibilities with you."

Chapter 48

When the girls woke up, they were in a strange room, with four beds and no other furniture. A woman in nurse's uniform was sitting on one of the beds, waiting. As soon as they were awake, she said, "Take off all your clothes and give them to me."

She collected the clothing in a pile and then said, "Shoes and watches, too."

Janice said, "We can't take off the watches. Daddy locked them on so we couldn't lose them."

The woman tried to remove Janice's watch, but gave up after several minutes.

She handed them each a white robe and told them to follow her to the showers. She watched to make sure that they washed thoroughly, and then took them back to their room. Then she produced a camera and took pictures of each girl from several angles. "Here is underwear and a nightshirt for sleeping. I'll see you in the morning." She left the room, taking all their clothing with her.

"Now what?" asked Janice.

"I don't know." Robin said. "I'm scared."

"I knew we shouldn't have gone with that man," Janice said.

"He seemed so nice, though. And he said he knew Daddy."

"Yeah, well, I guess he didn't really know him. Hope my call went to his phone like he showed us."

Sharra contacted them a few minutes later and set their minds a little at ease. They couldn't be sure that they would be rescued until it actually happened, but at least their parents knew where they were, and were in the same city.

The light went off at 9:00. They could find no way to turn it back on, so Janice said, "We might as well go on to bed. We'll find out tomorrow what is going to happen to us. Not much we can do about it, anyway."

The woman came back at 8:00 the next morning, pushing a cart with three breakfast trays on it. She watched while they ate, and then collected the plastic forks. "You will take another shower, now. Wash your hair with this shampoo and then apply this conditioner."

Again, she walked with them to the shower room, watched them bathe, and gave them clean underwear. "Back to your room."

"But …" Janice said.

"No one will see you."

"Are we the only ones here?" Janice asked.

"No."

Back in the room, she checked each girl's eyes, ears, throat, teeth and privates, starting with Shawnah. She handed her a robe to wear when she finished. She checked Janice next, and then Robin. Janice took Shawnah's watch and put it in her robe pocket while the woman was checking Robin.

The man known as Sam Smith opened the door and entered the room just as she handed Robin's robe to her. Robin clutched it in front of her, but the man hardly noticed. He asked the woman, "How are they?"

"No signs of disease and no scars. They seem healthy."

"Good. Give them a thorough exam later. We want you girls to be happy here. I have visitors scheduled for two of them immediately. Have them ready."

"I want to go home," Robin said.

"I will give you much more than your father – your foster father – could ever give you. You will want for nothing."

Janice walked up to him, face-to-face, and said, "I want my father." She dropped the watch into his coat pocket at the same time.

"Well, that I cannot give you. You may think of me as your big daddy, if that helps."

"Nope. That doesn't help."

At that same time, Jeremy contacted Robin and sent her the FBI tracking bugs. She moved one to the man's pocket, and dropped the other into her robe pocket.

"You girls will be happy here if you do not fight the program. If you do fight – then you will never be happy." He turned and left the room.

Chapter 49

After an hour of discussions with the FBI, Mista had made no progress. He was convinced that the girls were to be used that very day, and he was determined not to let that happen. The FBI people were sure that they had time to plan their action. As they were talking, Mista glanced at the screen showing two dots from time to time. Suddenly, he noticed that one of them was moving toward the front of the building.

"I believe your man is about to leave."

"He is not our man, yet, Mr. Mictackic. We have no legal reason to hold him. If he does leave, he has our bug, and we will know where he goes."

"But if he leaves that building, you will have no probable cause to arrest him later. His leaving will sever any connection he has with those girls."

"That is not our problem."

Mista's eyes turned a steely blue. His voice was deadly calm. Jeremy and Sharra recognized danger there, but the FBI men assumed that he was still relaxed, since he had not raised his voice. "It is my problem, then, since you disown it. I will not allow my girls to be harmed." *He sent to Sharra,* Call in the troops. He must not leave.

Done.

She sent to Mischal, The man we want is about to leave that house. He must not leave.

You got it.

Mischal said, "Let's go, Stubbs. Our man is about to escape. We do not let that happen."

"You betcha!" He put the car in gear and pulled around the corner, stopping in front of the house that they had marked the night before. A black limousine was already waiting there.

As they rounded the corner they saw Sam Smith leaving his front door, walking down his walk to the limousine waiting there with the motor running. Njondac pulled up in front of the house just as the man reached the car. Mischal and Charly opened their doors and stepped out. Mischal shouted, "Stop where you are! You are not going anywhere." He had his sidearm out and aimed generally in the direction of the limousine.

Suddenly, two men leaned out of windows on opposite sides of the limousine with assault rifles in hand. Mischal and Charly dived back into their rental car, and Mischal yelled, "DOWN!" Both men opened fire in full auto mode. The engine died and a cloud of steam rose. All the windows of the car were broken out, or crazed in the case of the windshield safety glass. The limo sped off.

Chandri opened her door and followed the fleeing car with her rifle. She fired one shot and saw a rear tire blow. The car never slowed, but screeched around the corner. Chandri raised her rifle. "Too risky to shoot again," she said.

Mischal pounded his fist on the back of the front seat. "Failed again! Mista won't be happy."

The limousine raced on for several blocks, turning two other corners. When it was apparent that they were not being followed, the driver stopped to change the blown tire. One of the guards pulled the spare out of the trunk while the other was loosening lug bolts. The driver jacked the car up at the same time. They had the tire changed in a little over a minute.

Chapter 50

Meanwhile, on the second floor, the woman took Janice to another room and told her to wait. She left and locked the door behind her. She then led Robin to another room and locked her in.

Janice looked around. The room had one bed and a straight chair. *I can break that chair and use a leg for a weapon.*

A man opened the door and stepped inside. "Ahah. Just right." Then Janice called Sharra. *MOM!*

Yes, dear?

It's happening. They put me in a room and just now a man walked in, with one thing on his mind.

Can you fight him off? We're on the way.

I'll fight. He's big.

Do you know where you are?

No. I have no idea.

Okay. Charly's downstairs in the house. I'll send her to find you.

Thanks, Mom.

Sharra sent to Charly, *CHARLY!*

Here!

They just put a man in a room with Janice. Don't know where she is. Can you find her?

Tell her to scream if she hears me outside.

Right.

Janice – Charly's coming. If you hear her, scream.

Thanks, Mom.

Another man walked into Robin's room. She gasped. *MOM! They sent a man in to me! What do I do?*

Fight him.

How?

Use your mind. What has Jeremy taught you?

I don't know.

Well, think of something. Move something. Break something of his. Form hard air and punch him where it hurts.

Robin grinned. Okay. But I might need help.

We're on the way.

Sharra said, "It's happening. They have sent two men in to the girls. Jeremy, talk to Robin. She doesn't know what to do."

"Got it."

He contacted Robin and sent, Be brave, Little Bird. I'm with you.

Mista said, "You heard her. We're out of here. I will not let my girls be harmed."

Ross said, "I cannot allow you to do this. Stop him, men."

Mista said, "You cannot hold me. I have committed no crime, and you have no reason to hold me. You are protecting a criminal and attempting to prevent me from stopping another crime."

"I have no evidence of a crime in commission. I can hold you because of your threat of violence."

"I have offered no violence. I will rescue my girls." He walked to the door. The two men in the room attempted to pull their weapons, but they found that they could not. In their confusion, Mista opened the door and walked out, followed by the other three. One of them had presence of mind to forget his weapon and grabbed Sheila. Mista whirled, staff in hand. "Unhand her at once!"

"Don't," Jeremy said. "They want an attack." He formed a band of air around the man's hand and squeezed until he let go of Sheila.

The man screamed. "What are you doing to me?"

"I'm not touching you, but we are leaving. Come on, Sheila."

As they walked out and started down the stairs, not waiting for an elevator, Ross called the front desk. "Ross. Four prisoners are attempting to escape. Stop them."

The guard on the front desk had his pistol raised when Mista stepped into the reception area. "Stop, or I will fire."

Sharra sent an illusion of a snarling dog running in the front door and leaping at his throat. He turned and empted his automatic into the illusion, harming nothing except his telephone, his desk, two windows and a lamp. Mista and family walked out.

Ross next called the Louisville police department and told them that he had reason to suspect an assault on a certain house. "I don't think this is a false alarm, but if no one shows up, then I will apologize later."

Mista got to the house before the police arrived. When they did arrive, they found Chandri and Njondac sitting on the front steps of the house, looking at their ruined car. Mischal had not moved from the back seat.

Two officers jumped out with weapons drawn. "What is happening here?" one of them asked.

"Couple of men just shot up our car," Chandri said.

"Were you shooting at them?" the officer asked suspiciously. After all, he had been sent to stop an illegal entry. He also saw a second car behind the first, apparently unharmed.

"No, sir. They were leaving just as we arrived. We asked them to wait, but they must have been in a hurry. I guess they thought we would chase them, so they disabled our car."

"Yeah, you can say that again. What'd they use, assault rifles?"

"Yes. Looked like AK-47s."

"You can tell that quickly?"

"Yes, sir. I have some training." She showed him her ID card and badge. They were not on active call, so the badge had no meaning at the time, but it did serve to relieve the officer's suspicions.

"Georgia? What are you doing here?"

"We are not on active duty at the present time, but to answer your question, we are here to apprehend the criminal who just escaped."

"Do you have his license number?"

"Yes." She gave it to him. "Probably a rental car, though."

Chapter 51

Janice stood ready. When the man moved toward her, she picked up the chair and smashed it against the floor. Then she took one of the legs and said, "Leave me alone."

"A fighter, eh? I like that." He reached for the chair leg to pull it away, but Janice snatched it back just as his hand closed where hers had been, and swung the chair leg around to hit him on the head.

Then she backed off. "Leave me alone."

"Hey, little girl. Fighting is one thing. You don't have to try to kill me."

"I'm only defending myself."

"Well, I paid good money for first go at you, and I'm going to get my money's worth."

She fought for another five minutes, but he was twice as big as she was, and eventually he grabbed the chair leg and disarmed her.

Janice heard Charly running down the hall, shouting for Janice, and screamed, "In here!"

Charly stopped and kicked the door. It bulged in, but did not give. The man inside said, "What's going on?"

She kicked it again, and then slammed it with her sword. On the third kick, the lock gave and the door flew open. Charly stood in the doorway with her sword raised.

"Oh, my god," the man said. "What is this?"

"This is the rescue squad, bud, and you better make tracks." He did.

Robin had a harder time. She was not a trained fighter, and had no weapon. She did not realize that she knew enough to use her mind as a weapon. She backed into a corner and waited.

The man said, "Come on, girlie. Let's see what you look like."

"No. Go away."

"Not likely." He unzipped his pants. That gave Robin an idea, and she reached out with her mind and zipped them back up.

"Hey! He said. "How did you do that? Never mind."

He unbuckled his belt and dropped his pants. "Let's have that dress off, honey."

Robin reached out and pulled his pants up again, and ran across the room for the door. It was locked. He ran after her, and she turned and dropped his pants. He stepped on one leg, trapping the other foot, and stumbled, falling on his face. He raised himself up on his elbows, nose dripping blood, and said, "I'll get you, you little imp!"

He jumped up and ran at her. All Robin could think of was to kick him as hard as she could. She was barefoot, but her aim was good, and she hit hard enough to put him down, screaming.

The door was still locked. Then she remembered she could move things. She reached out with her mind and pushed the latch back, and opened the door. She ran. She had no idea where to run, but she just ran. She ran down the stairs and headed for the front door, just as Mista and Sharra came in.

"Daddy! Daddy! Daddy!" She ran into his arms, and he picked her up. She wrapped her arms around his neck and hung on.

"It's all right, Little Bird. I've got you." Mista turned and walked back out the front door. He called the police sergeant who had just arrived and was talking with Chandri. "If you search this house, you will find at least two men who were attempting to have paid sex with my daughters. You won't find the owner who arranged the sex act after he kidnapped my daughters. He had his guards shoot up one of our cars, and then he left in a hurry. You might find a few other interesting things, though."

Mista turned to Sharra. "What about Janice? I haven't seen her."

Charly came down the stairs with her arm around Janice. She had stopped to get another robe for her. "Your newest little fighter is fine," Charly said.

The sergeant said, "Would one of the men be that man who just ran out?"

Charly said, "Yeppers. I don't think he likes me."

The sergeant called out, "Don't go anywhere, sir."

Njondac said, "He ain't goin' nowhere." He looked at the man and raised his ax. "Was ya tryin' ta have sex wit my gull?"

"Well, I paid. I didn't know it was your girl."

"Don't matter whose she was, she was a gull! Mebbe I'll jes hack it offen ya, and then ya won't be tempted ta do that again."

Sheila was waiting in the front room of the house. She had found a locked file cabinet in a small closet behind the desk in the front room.

She called Mista. "Better have a look in here. Bet you'll find records."

Chapter 52

The sergeant called his station house. "You better send out a detective squad. We got a major mess out here." The police searched the house. They found the other man groaning on the floor. They found Shawnah, still locked in her room. They found the 'nurse', and found four other girls; two were twelve and two were thirteen.

They also found a safe in the same room as the file cabinet, with contracts from men wishing sex with pre-teen girls. Among them they found contracts with the two current. They found Internet records of screen names of other contacts.

The detective lieutenant introduced himself as Joe Brown. The first thing he did was get ID from everyone involved. Then he said to Mista, "You put us onto quite a little operation, here, sir. How did you happen to be here and find out about it?"

"Well, they kidnapped my daughters, you know. They were inside screaming for help. What was I supposed to do, stand outside and say, 'wait a minute while I call the police'?"

Brown laughed. "No. Not hardly. Just wondered how you happened to be here."

"You have to have reason to believe that there was a crime going on, right? We gave my daughters some of those GPS kid finders, so if they did get kidnapped or something, we would know exactly where they were. It has a built-in phone that sends its position, and it can also be used to call one number. I put my number in, of course. We knew what was going on in there."

"Your home address is Toccoa, Georgia, sir? But you came here from Florida?"

"That's correct. We were on vacation near Tampa when it happened."

"The girls were kidnapped in Florida?"

"Yes, that's correct."

"That's a matter for the FBI, then."

"Yes, I thought so. In fact, we contacted them first, but they were not interested."

"Oh, they were interested. I had a call from an agent named Ross. They wanted me to arrest you for breaking and entering."

"Yes. Well, they didn't believe that we had a case."

"Humph. I'd say you had a case. Looks like this has been going on for a long time."

"At least 25 years. They kidnapped my sister 25 years ago. We didn't have the tools we have now, and found her years later, only by accident. So, we were already on their trail. They made it easy when they kidnapped my daughters."

"You will be available for testimony, won't you?"

"You better believe it. So will my sister. That's her over there."

"Whew! She's a looker! Married, I suppose?"

"No. Hasn't found a man, yet."

"Well, you are free to go, so long as you remain in contact."

"Here is my cell phone. I always have that with me. And if you can't find me, for some reason, you can call Commander Karl Spicewood of the Georgia State Police. He will always know where I am. Meanwhile, I'll send you logs of Internet chats, and a list of screen names. There is an extensive network of people involved. I was working on getting a court order to find out who owns these names, but after this, you should be able to get it much easier than I could."

"Yes, that is correct. I'll be waiting for that information. Why didn't you give that to the FBI? They should be investigating that ring. It's probably an interstate ring."

"Probably. I couldn't seem to get their interest. You can pass it on to them."

Mischal was standing with his head down, waiting for Mista to finish. When he turned from the lieutenant, Mischal said, "I resign. I messed up again."

"You can't run out on me, now. How do you figure you messed up?"

"I was the perfect Marine in service. Never failed a mission. We fought magic users and bandits together for twelve years, and we never lost. But three times you have asked me to protect a girl, and I failed every time. If I can't protect a girl, I'm not much use to you."

"Three times?" asked Mista.

"When Chandri was acting as bait for the white slave traders in Brunswick, when we were fighting the terrorist in Jacksonville, Chandri was stolen right out from under my nose, and now your girls."

Mista clapped Mischal on the arm. "Misch, you did not fail, here. You did exactly what you were supposed to do. You waited out of sight, and were ready as soon as we called. The man must have suspected something or he would not have shot up your car like that. You're lucky you weren't killed."

"Be better if I had been."

"Nonsense! You haven't failed. We're still in action. The girls are safe and back with us, and now we need to track down this Sam Smith, or whatever his name is."

"How? He's gone."

"He has two tracking devices on him. Janice put one of the watches in a pocket without his knowing it, and the FBI sent one of theirs. We'll know wherever he goes, and then we go get him."

"Right. He will not escape again." He started to walk to his car. "Oh. I have no car."

Mista already had his cell out. He called a wrecker and then called the rental company. "We need a replacement car. Ours failed to survive a hail of bullets."

Ross came up before the wrecker arrived. He had a squad of six men with him. He stopped short when he saw that the local police had two men in custody, and Mista was standing free. He also noticed the damaged car. "What is happening here?" he asked.

Detective Brown said, "Nothing to see here, sir. Please be on your way."

Ross showed his badge and introduced himself. "I have an interest in this case."

The sergeant said, "Oh, yeah, Lou, he's the one that called it in the first time. That's how we happened to be on the scene. Good thing this man was here, Mr. Ross. He heard his daughters inside screaming for help, and went in to rescue them. Caught these two men in the act of trying to have sex with eleven-year-old girls! That's good enough to send them away for life."

"Oh," Ross said. "You have enough evidence?"

"Yeah, don't worry about that. Caught them in the act. Talk to Mr. Mictackic, here. He has more information about an interstate prostitution ring, using under-age girls. Found four more girls inside the house. He's undercover for the Georgia State Police, too."

Ross turned to Mista. "You didn't tell me that. All I had was the claim of a stranger. We cannot operate on hunches."

Mista said, "I didn't tell you, because we are not currently on duty. This was not an official investigation. But it was not a hunch. I knew exactly what was going on here, and I knew what kind of man we had. That car is evidence of his disdain for the law."

The lieutenant said, "Just got a make on the plates of that car. It's registered to a David Brumley."

Sharra went white. "That's my stepfather," she whispered. "Taking our girls was no random find. He knew exactly where we were and that we had the girls."

"You don't know that," Mista said.

"Yes, I do!" she blazed. "It's payback for running away from him. Well, I wanted to know what had happened to him. I guess now we'll find out."

Lt. Brown said, "Mr. Brumley is a millionaire. He owns Darkling Freight Lines. Trucks, airplanes and I believe some ships. Are you sure that this is the man that you want?"

"I'm sure," Mista said.

Chapter 53

Sharra leaned against Mista's chest and closed her eyes. "I wanted to know what happened to him, but ... It was hard the first time I went through this. This will be even harder."

Mista put his arms around her and looked around the room. They had all gathered in the front room of the old house. The three girls stood in one corner, still wearing their white robes. Ross was looking through the records on the desk, and Lt. Brown had just closed his cell phone.

Mista said, "My three girls were brought here yesterday and their clothes were taken from them. Would it be possible for them to go try to find them, if they are still here? I'll ask my sister to go with them."

"Sure," said Lt. Brown.

The sergeant said, "We found a big bag of clothes in a little room behind the kitchen. They might be in there."

"Sheila, would ..."

"Of course," Sheila said. "Come on, girls."

Robin did not want to leave Mista's side, but since Janice followed Sheila willingly, she also tagged along.

When the girls had gone, Mista asked, "Well, do you want to go find him?"

Sharra shuddered, and then stepped back. Her black eyes flashed like twin obsidians. "Yes. Let's get it over with."

"All right. Let me go out and get my computer. Remember, he has two bugs on him. Ours and the FBI."

At the mention of the bugs, Ross looked up. "Jones, go get my laptop. Let's see where the perp is."

Mista opened and started his laptop at the car, and they brought it inside while it was booting. He started the tracing software, but got only a blank screen. He rubbed his chin as he looked at it. "I hope it is still working. But seems like … oh. He must be inside a building. GPS can't see him there."

Ross said, "Wait one. I'll tell you where he is." After another minute, he had a dot on the Louisville map, near the corner of Mohammed Ali Blvd and Fourth Street. "He's not on the street, looks like that is the Seelbach Hotel."

"Well, let's go get him," Mista said.

"*We* will get him," Ross said. "Well, you can come along, if you wish."

Mista said, "We only have one car. Who wants to come with me?"

Mischal and Njondac both responded at once. "We'll be there."

Charly said, "I'll wait here with the others. You should have asked for a van since we have the girls, now."

Sharra said, "I want to go. Jeremy should go, also."

At the hotel, Ross identified himself and asked if Mr. Brumley was in.

The clerk looked at his register and said, "We do not have a guest by that name, sir."

"Call the manager, please."

When he came to the desk, Ross said, "Special Agent Paul Ross, FBI. We have traced a man to this hotel. He has a tracer on his person, and we know he is here somewhere. Go with us while I ascertain his current room."

"Well – this is a little irregular. Do you have a warrant?"

"No. He has just fled the scene of a crime. Since he was involved in that crime, we do not need a warrant to follow him."

"Okay. That computer tells you where he is?"

"It gives me direction and distance. It doesn't know about up and down. We can go up until we get the shortest distance, and then assume that we are on the correct floor. Then we go down the halls until we find him."

They eventually came to a room door where the computer said the bug was seven feet away. The manager knocked and called, "Hotel Manager. Open, please."

Getting no response, he knocked louder and called again. Ross said, "Open it." He had his weapon in hand. One of his men stood on the other side of the door, weapon ready. He waved Mista and his group back.

The manager opened the door. No one was inside. He went to the room phone and called the desk. "Wilson here. Who has this room?"

"It's registered to a man named Sam Smith, sir."

"Thank you." He turned to Ross. "This room is not Mr. Brumley's. It is registered to a Sam Smith."

Ross asked Mista, "Does the name Sam Smith register with you?"

"Yes. It is the name he gave the girls when he kidnapped them."

"None of you have seen him, right?"

"That is correct," Mista said. "Maybe his coat is still here. You can see that your bug is here somewhere. Jeremy, ask Janice what he was wearing."

Jeremy called Janice, Janice. What was Sam Smith wearing this morning?
I don't remember. A coat.
Picture him.

She called to mind her memory of him when he came into their room. Jeremy said, "He was wearing a brown corduroy jacket and dark pants."

Ross opened the closet door. It had one brown jacket in it. He searched the pockets and produced one watch and a small bug. "Is this your watch, Mr. Mictackic?"

"Yes."

"Mr. Wilson, please seal this room. We will obtain a search warrant and return to search it. Looks like it was not used much."

"I wouldn't know, sir. We have too many guests to track individual usage. I will seal the room for one day."

Chapter 54

When they left the room, Ross said, "Mr. Mictackic, I apologize for any hardship I may have caused you. I was doing just as I thought best, given the information that I had in hand. I do not apologize for my actions."

"I understand," Mista said. "But I know that many houses have been broken into on less evidence than I had."

"That is true, and it has caused us much embarrassment. I do not intend to add to that series of legends. We will pursue this case. Please send us any information that you have on him."

"You already have a name."

"At this point, all we have for sure is a name that could be an alias. You have no proof that Mr. Brumley is in fact Sam Smith."

"The getaway car was registered to him."

"True, but you do not know that Brumley was in that car. Sam Smith, who might or might not be Brumley, came here in that car, left his coat, and disappeared. We do not even have a good description of him."

"You could ask his employees."

"We will do that. Employee. The woman is the only person that we knew worked for him. I am sure that there must be others, but that is what we must find out. Please leave this to us."

"I will send it as soon as I get back to Florida." They did not speak again on the way back to the cars.

Mista went back to the house to join the rest of his group, and Ross and his men returned to their office to pursue their investigation.

Sharra said, "I hate to admit it, but he was doing what seemed right to him."

"Yes, I know. I could have been a neighbor with a personal grudge for all he knew. Seems like when we put his bug inside that house, though … oh well. Let's go home for now and plan our next moves."

Mista looked around at his group at the airport. "Eleven tickets. Probably be cheaper to charter a flight."

"It cost you $5000 to come up here," Sharra said.

"That was an emergency, and most of that was deposit, which I will get back."

It cost about as much to charter a flight, but they would have had to wait until the next day to get eleven tickets on the same commercial flight. Mista called Jasmine and gave her the arrival time and the gate number. "We need for somebody to bring a couple of cars and meet us. I left the Range Rover there, but it was a little crowded with eight people in it. Now we have eleven, and even though the additions are all small, I don't think we will fit."

Mista said to the girls, "If you learned anything at all from this, be careful who you accept rides from."

Chapter 55

After breakfast the next morning, they all gathered around a bonfire Mischal had built on the edge of the playground. Mista sat quietly with a sad look on his face while everyone gathered and chatted. Sharra pulled a chair up beside him and asked, "What's wrong, darling? You worried about me?"

"No," he said, laying a hand on her arm. "Not worried about you. But very unhappy about this whole thing."

Sheila pulled a chair up on his other side, and said "Don't worry about me, George. Mista. I can't get used to that name."

"I'm not worried about you. You'll be fine. But I am extremely unhappy. I am not a vengeful man, but this man has completely ruined my sister's life. I cannot let that go by."

"It's all right. It's all past, and now you have found me and given me a wonderful home, and I have a future again. Let it go."

"No. I cannot. Not just you, but he tried to ruin Sharra's life before she was out of his house. Who knows how many others he has ruined."

"That is past, dear," Sharra said. "We should put it past us, too."

"I wish I could. But he will not let that happen. Now he has come after my girls. If he had done what he did sometime in the past and then gotten on with his life, I could forgive it, since you are able to. But he keeps on. No telling how many girls he has turned into prostitution before they were even in their teens. And how many more when they were older."

Mischal said, "There are always prostitutes."

"Yes, but this is different. It's one thing when a woman chooses that path. It is not good, but it happens. That is often a tragedy, but at least it is an adult choice. You remember what we went through with the so-called temple system that raised Jania and so many others. They were brainwashed into believing that what they were doing was right."

"Don't you think that it's back in full operation now that we are gone?" asked Jeremy.

"Probably. But I don't have to like it. But this is worse. This man has taken countless girls from their homes and made them slaves against their will. Their lives ruined, their families traumatized, and all for one man's gain."

"But men seek that kind of thing," Jeremy said. "Even if we shut him down, someone will supply their wants."

"That is true," Mista said. "The world seems to have a surplus of evil. But that is not reason to ignore the evil in our face. I want to eliminate this one evil blot. Personal revenge has some effect on my desire, I admit. But more than that, I have seen his evil first hand. If I ignore it, then I am actually condoning it. Even though someone else will take his place, he will go. Someone has said, 'to see an evil act and do nothing is to participate in the evil.'"

"What do you intend to do?" Charly asked. "Mind, I'm not complaining. You know that I hate evil, and I saw what he tried to do to our girls. Whatever you want to do, we'll back you 100%."

"You got that right," Mischal said. "I have a mistake to make up for."

Mista sighed and leaned back. "Thanks, folks. It's good to have you at my back. I haven't decided how, but I intend to take him down. Once I can prove that he kidnapped my daughters, I intend to sue him for the maximum the courts will allow. And if there is no statute of limitations on kidnapping, then I intend to sue him on your behalf, too, Sis. And if I can prove that he has taken other girls, then I'll sue on their behalves."

"Why are you so intent on suing him," asked Jeremy.

"This man lives for one purpose – to sate his pleasure. And money is his means to do whatever he wants to do. He has found ways to make tons of money and does not care that it ruins lives in the process. I would like to take every penny he has, and then let him rot in jail."

"That makes sense to me," Jeremy said. "Do you have any idea how much he has?"

"No, and I don't care. If it's a hundred million dollars, I want it. Not that I need more money, I just want to deprive him of it. I will give it all away – maybe to the Mayo Clinic. I just want to take it away from him."

Everyone was quiet for a minute, and then Robin came and jumped into Mista's lap. "Hey. That's my daddy."

"Well, we are talking busine – you're wet! How'd you get wet so early?"

Robin giggled. "I was hot. And I got sand all over me, so I washed off my legs in the shower outside."

"Well, run along and play, now. We're talking business."

"Can I listen?"

"You can, but you'll get bored. Don't ask questions, okay?"

"Okay." She leaned back against him.

Mista said, "There is another thing he has done, or probably did, that we have not mentioned. And I know that there is no statute of limitations on murder."

"Murder?" asked Robin. "The man that kidnapped us killed somebody? Then you ought to run him down and kill him."

"That is exactly what we are talking about, Sweetheart. Now be quiet."

"But…"

Mist put his hand over her mouth. "Let us talk."

Sharra said, "She can hear."

"I'm not trying to hide it from her. What happened to your father, Sharra? How much do you remember?"

"Not much. I was only six when he disappeared. And now I have the false memories – plus what we did – in that other world mixing in with the real history."

"We can open your memories and find out," Mista said.

"I couldn't have known much. I don't think you'll learn much. And I'm not sure that I want to know." She took Mista's hand and squeezed it. "You have helped me forget all that. It would only hurt to bring it back, and might not solve anything. I'm with Sheila there. Not sure I want to know."

"I understand. This man married your mother shortly after, though, and took over the business. If he murdered your father to get the business and your mother – or maybe just the business, and the mother was necessary baggage – don't you want him punished for that?"

"Yes. Definitely. However, I doubt that I knew anything substantial. I'll have to think about that one."

"Daddy, if…" Mista put his hand over her mouth.

She pulled it away. "But Daddy, if she remembers, we would have proof and could send him to jail."

"I wish it were that easy. It will take more that enhanced memories to send a man to jail. Memories can be falsified, can be manipulated, and are not always complete. However, it might help us find out some real evidence."

"I could help," Robin said.

Mista said, "Charly have you been coaching this child?"

Charly laughed. "No, but I'll take her on. She's a girl after my own heart. Don't let him intimidate you, hon. He's just a big teddy bear."

"You mean, don't be afraid of him? I'm not afraid of Daddy. He can't even spank me."

"Maybe not, but I bet he'd be willing to assign the spanking to me, and I can do that *good*. I remember how it hurt."

"Enough. Why don't you go play. Better yet, go put some dry clothes on. And bring me two or three towels."

Robin kissed him and jumped up and ran off. "She'll probably run through the shower on the way to get dry clothes. Might even forget about the dry ones," Mista said. "I think we need to go back to Georgia for now and begin a campaign to find facts and bring this man down."

"Sounds good to me," Mischal said.

"I think we'll be back here soon enough. This seems to be a base of operations. I like the idea of this campground, Njondac, but for long term stay, I'm thinking house. I looked on the internet, and there are some houses for sale in Crystal Beach. Some of them are really big old houses. Room enough for all of us. I think I'll buy one."

"Whut shud I do wit tha land?"

"Keep it, or sell it as you wish. It would be a good place to park the campers, even if we live on the beach."

"Works fer me. I mght jes stay here anyways. Be security fer tha campers and all."

"Then we might as well pack up and head home. Take us a day or so to clear up everything, won't it?"

"Probably," Mischal said.

Robin came back on that question, dry, and holding towels. "We can't leave."

"Why not? Thanks for the towels."

"Because. We haven't been to the beach in warm weather. You have to teach us to swim."

"In your clothes?"

"No, in our bathing suits."

"But, you don't have any of them."

"I know. You have to take us and buy some."

"Right away, I suppose?"

"Yep. Right now."

"Well, okay. We'll have to get your mother in on this, too, so she can say what's good. I might let you buy something no bigger than band-aids. What do I know about bathing suits for girls?"

"I don't think you would do that," Sharra said. "But I'll go."

They were able to find suits that the girls liked and that Sharra approved, and then headed home to change and go down to the beach. The girls were in the water before Mista had the car parked. He got blankets and beach chairs out of the back of the Range Rover and headed down.

The girls came back up and claimed him when he came down to the sand. "You have to teach us to swim," Janice said.

"Yes, come on," Robin echoed.

"You asked for it," Sharra said.

Mista let them lead him into the water and then spent half an hour holding first one and then the other up by placing a hand under her stomach while they leaned to paddle and kick. Then Mista went back and rested while the girls played..

A little later, the girls came and got him again. Janice said, "We can't quite get it. Come help us some more."

Mista spent another half-hour helping them get their confidence up. At the end, they swam away from him without realizing that he was no longer holding them up. Then he left them again.

When they came up the next time, Mista was writing in the sand. "What are you doing, Daddy?" asked Robin.

"Oh, just a little exercise in math. It just occurred to me that I bought bathing suits back in December, when you first came."

Janice said, "Well, those are old. And we've grown up since then, anyway."

"Yes, you have grown. Up and out. Now, let's see. I've spent about $4000 for clothes, $2000 for toys, $1000 for watches and phones, and about $5000 for air fair to Louisville and back, to say nothing of rental for trailers and gas. Plus lawyer's fees to adopt you girls. All in four months.

That's about $50,000 a year for you. I'm not sure you're worth that much. I wonder how much it would cost to send you back and undo the adoption."

"Daddy! You said you can't do that!" Janice said.

Robin put her hand in her mouth and her eyes got big. "We could take the bathing suits back."

"Besides, this afternoon I did more work than I've done in a month."

Sharra said, "Mista you better stop teasing those girls."

Mista grinned. "You need to learn when I'm teasing and when I'm not. Because if I'm not teasing, then what I say to you might just save your life. And by the way, the adoption is safe. I don't even know if it can be reversed, and I'm not going to try to find out. I don't want to lose you, even if you do cost me a fortune. You're worth every penny. And I'm not teasing about that. You remember, when I made those $5.00 reward buttons, I told you I would pay a lot more than that if something did happen. Well, it did, and I paid it without even a quibble. You are worth more to me than any amount of money."

"Can we bury you now?" asked Robin.

"We don't have to ask that. We just do it," Janice said.

"Get your fun while you can," Mista said, "because sometime this summer we are going to war. It will not be easy, and someone might get hurt, but it is something we have to do."

"Okay."

They pulled him out of his chair and buried him up to the chin, and then went back to the water. Mista raised his head and watched them go.

"It's going to be a long hard summer," he said. "And I just hope the girls don't get hurt."

"Nor one of us, dear," Sharra said. "I'm glad we are doing this, but it gives me shivers to even think about facing him again."

"Well, this time you are not a 13-year-old. But, I'll tell you one thing. If he lays a hand on my girls, he's a dead man."

THE END

Author's Notes

This book is a work of fiction. No characters are based on real people. And names and places used fictionally.

It addresses a problem that exists in many countries today, using underage girls for commercial sex. It goes by many names, sex tourism, white slave trade and others. Recent arrests of prominent people involved in this activity shines a light on the problem. "Men love darkness rather than light because their deeds are evil." Mista and his group will continue to shine the light on deeds of darkness. This is an issue which needs to be brought into public awareness.

There is a large KOA campground in Palm Springs, Florida.

The spoil islands were created when the Intercoastal Waterway was created in the 1930's by dumping the dredge spoil outside the channel.

Many large brick nineteenth century mansions on Fourth Street, Louisville, Kentucky have been converted into businesses.

The GPS watches are commercially available.

List of Characters

Chief Characters

1. Mista — Magic user and Sage
   AKA George Mictackic
2. Sharra Darkling — Magic user and Psi user
   Mista's wife
3. Samantha — year and half old daughter
4. Mischal Yoeder — Paladin for God. Also known as Cato momCato — Barbarian Fighter
5. Chandri LaFreet — Ranger
   Married to Mischal
6. Cato — Son of Mischal and Chandri
7. Chantilly — Daughter of Mischal and Chandri
8. Njondac — Dwarf Fighter
9. Josie Mithraldiver — Njondac's wife. Dwarf.
10. Brut Njondac — Njondac's son
11. Charly — orphan found when 10 years old
    Public name: Deisa, a paladin for God
    Charlotte Talljohn -- full name
12. Jeremy Bates — Psi Instructor
    Married to Charly
13. Jasmine Taalong — Christian minister
    Nurse Practitioner
14. Jania Mistletoe — Med Student, assumed to be

Mista's niece	Adopted by Mista
15. Sheila Demallis	Mista's long lost sister
16. Gary Demallis	Her oldest son --24
17. Molly Greene	Former Student
	Joined group as free agent
18. Susan Jones	Molly's daughter
19. Janice Stormes	11-year-old girl
20. Robin Smith	11-year-old girl
21. Shawnah Kingsberry	11-year old girl
22. Candy Muttons	11-year-old girl
23. Em Evockovic	Nurse caring for Sam, teacher
	Emaroud Evockovic, full name

Supporting Characters

Karl Spicewood	Commander of Ga. State Police
Special investigation unit.	
Joseph Aramson	Mista's Lawyer
Jeffrey Felder	Mista's banker
Catherine Golightly	Mista's broker
Don Miguel Ridrigos y Manteno	Coffee plantation owner in Puerto Rico
Paul Ross	FBI Agent

Antagonists

Sam Smith	AKA David Brumley

www.ingramcontent.com/pod-product-compliance
Lightning Source LLC
LaVergne TN
LVHW040137080526
838202LV00042B/2943